YOU NEVER KNOW

ALSO BY ISABEL HUGGAN
THE ELIZABETH STORIES

ISABEL HUGGAN

You Never Know

ALFRED A. KNOPF CANADA

PUBLISHED BY ALFRED A. KNOPF CANADA

Copyright © 1993 by Isabel Huggan

All rights reserved under International and Pan-American copyright
conventions. Published in Canada in 1993 by Alfred A. Knopf Canada, Toronto
and simultaneously in the United States by Viking Penguin, a subsidiary of
Penguin USA. Distributed by Random House of Canada Limited, Toronto.

Canadian Cataloguing in Publication Data

Huggan, Isabel, 1943–
You never know

ISBN 0-394-22733-6

I. Title.

PS8565.U44Y6   1993   C813'.54   C93-093241-2
PR9199.3.H84Y6   1993

The author wishes to thank the Canada Council and the Ontario Arts Council
for their financial assistance.

First Canadian Edition

Printed and bound in the United States of America

Toronto, New York, London, Sydney, Auckland

For Bob,
last and best

TABLE OF CONTENTS

YOU NEVER KNOW

END OF THE
EMPIRE

Long ago, when I was young, I was in love with King George the Sixth. It was, as you might imagine, a rather lopsided relationship, but within its limitations so real that his death, in 1952, diminished for some time my expectations for happiness on this earth. Even now I sometimes suffer from a vague and aching sadness, a sorrow wandering in the halls of memory, as if in some hidden part of myself I am still mourning the day he died.

In King George, I recognized a soul very like my own— someone who had, inadvertently, without having any say about it, landed in the wrong life. In him I recognized such a gentle and bewildered dignity my heart was quite pierced through with arrows of devotion. Neither his daughter's well-meaning and anxious stiffness nor his grandson's self-deprecating wit can duplicate the winsome charm of his stammer, his long-faced sincerity and sweetness. Nothing can bring him back, he is forever gone; and without him, both the world and I have changed.

The day he died I was so stricken with grief I had to be kept home from school that afternoon, my face swollen and purple from crying. We received the news of his death on the CBC at noon, from the small brown radio on top of the refrigerator. My father was on evening shift at the foundry that week so he was home and we were all sitting at the kitchen table eating lunch, our usual Campbell's chicken noodle soup and soda crackers and carrot sticks. As the announcer's deep rolling voice and the tolling British bells brought the truth home to us and the rest of Canada, I fell from my chair in a swoon, and with a terrible gasp of "Oh no, my King!" toppled to the floor at my mother's feet. My father, never one for emotional display, told me to straighten round immediately if I didn't want the belt, and my mother said, "Now, now, there's no need for that," but it was not clear whether it was to me or to my father that she spoke.

I gathered myself up and ran sobbing from the kitchen to the bedroom I shared with my older sister, whose jeering laughter I still heard as I slammed the door—cold, older-sister laughter. I flung myself across the white chenille bedspread, lay there face down and felt the fuzzy ridges of its pattern pressing against my cheek as I wept out my despair. My hope for rescue was gone, gone to the grave.

My love for King George had been, until that moment in the kitchen, a private thing, a passion too rare to be shared with a family such as mine. I'd always known that: it was part of what made my royal life a necessary secret. My mother said she had no notion of what made me tick and whenever she said that, my father would mutter she had better be careful, because bombs tick too and then go off. It was meant as a joke, suggesting I was a tricky bit of business he didn't understand, and although it seemed rather a mean thing to say about his child—a bomb, indeed!—he was essentially correct.

Offsetting them, in fortuitous counterbalance, King George understood me absolutely. He and I were united at a deep and invisible level, as if connected by a silent underground river running beneath our lives. This became apparent the first time he saw me, the lids of his blue eyes fluttering momentarily and then opening with something like astonishment or delight. He saw me for the first time many times, as I refined the pleasurable details of the scene. But always the heart of it remained the same: we belonged together, the King and I. Because of his age, and mine, the way in which we would fit would be father and daughter, but that was merely a matter of convenience and fate. Our destiny was interwoven, of that I was sure.

The events leading up to King George's happy discovery of me, Hannah Louise Clement, were always the same. I would have been found in a large green park by his younger daughter, Princess Margaret Rose, who would take me home to the Palace. Although I knew her to be a dozen years older, on this occasion she always appeared to be nearer my age, looking rather as she did in the photograph of herself and her older sister that hung on the dining room wall at my grandmother's house. She and Elizabeth were seated at a grand piano, wearing matching dresses of pink lace and tulle tied round with satin ribbon; they were smiling, and there were two small brown Corgi dogs at their feet.

Even in the park where it was rainy and chilly, dusk coming on, mist rising from the lawns, Margaret Rose appeared to be perfectly turned out, as if royal radiance kept her dry. The park in my mind's eye bore a fairly strong resemblance to

Victoria Park, a few blocks from where I lived in London, Ontario. A small and very ordinary city park crisscrossed with asphalt paths, it extended in my imagination far past its normal boundaries, became larger and greener, full of rose beds and glass-globe lamps shining dimly in the fog. The weather was always English and wet in this sequence: there was never sunshine, never snow, as if I knew instinctively the climatic demands of my private mythology.

Although Princess Margaret Rose seemed above ordinary physical discomfort, it distressed her royal heart to see me, Hannah Louise, huddled on a park bench . . . hungry, outcast, alone. She would scrutinize me by bringing her dimpled face in its nest of curls very close to mine and then she would stand back, and pronounce her sentence very clearly: she would take me home to her father, the King.

Exactly how I knew that King George would want to adopt me as soon as he set eyes on me, I am not to this day sure. I saw *him* only infrequently in black-and-white newsreels at the movie house on Saturdays, and in a few colour photographs in magazines or in the corridors at school. But I knew, with the intuition of the truly blessed, that he and I were cut from the same cloth. That is not to say that I had delusions of grandeur or believed myself to be of royal blood, my lineage lost and muddled over the years because of some Dickensian nursemaid. Rather, it was from the fine and innocent certainty that station in life meant nothing, a kind of childish notion of pure equality. Nobody gets to choose who her parents are, nobody gets to choose the time and place of his birth—we all start out the same, having no say in anything at all. I felt sure that King George was not any different from, and longed to be attached to, the real world of common people. Like me. And I sensed that he was, like me, a little scared. And I knew that he knew that I knew.

I was a thin, unadventurous child who preferred fantasy because less than a decade in this world had convinced me that reality was a punishing and difficult affair. Sometime shortly after kindergarten, perhaps as a result of a determined teacher insisting I use my right hand instead of my left, I developed a slight stutter, which had a way of coming and going so that I never knew exactly when I was going to stumble and fall over a syllable. The very random nature of this thing meant no one could find a way to cure it, and the family doctor simply assured my mother that I would, eventually, grow out of it. Which, of course, I did, except for occasional lapses when I am angry or afraid.

As a child, I found a lot to be afraid of. My mother used to say she thought I looked for trouble and she was probably right. In those years after the war, it was hard for a child to differentiate between the horrors one saw in magazines and newsreels and the horrors one imagined. It was impossible to grasp the levels of hate and fear in the world and translate it all properly so that none of it applied to you.

There were, for example, in our end of the city, several "foreign" families known as the DPs, who'd come out of central Europe after 1945. Tough, hardened survivors ready to make a new life in the new land, these *displaced persons* did not fit into the already established patterns of London, Ontario, and they were discriminated against at every turn, especially in working-class neighborhoods such as mine where their presence was a continuing reminder of the ups and downs of fate.

Their children who went to my school were known as the Dumb DPs, and were mocked and scorned and treated with disdain. In my fearful heart, I knew how these kids felt, in their moth-eaten, hand-me-down cardigans, with their funny accents and garlicky breath and knobby knees. I felt like that when I was teased for my stutter or for being a beanpole or a smartypants. It was all the same, and it wasn't fair. And pity swelled within me for their awful plight.

It did not make me open my heart to them, you understand. I befriended not one solitary DP child. I turned instead for companionship and solace to the King of England.

Margaret Rose, on the other hand, had a heart of gold, and I feel for her still a grateful fondness. She did not hesitate to rescue a wet little waif from the park and to share, with angelic generosity, her father and her life. Elizabeth generally I found a touch surly, a bit sulky in a selfish way—much like my older sister. I could see *she* wanted to remain the apple of her Daddy's eye, unthwarted by any snotty-nosed stranger; and I always had the shaky feeling that if Elizabeth had her way she'd whisk me out of Buckingham Palace quick as a wink, no matter what her silly sister said.

I would be led to the throne room by Margaret Rose, who'd take my hand in a bossy but kindly way. As a rule the Queen was never present but her absence was easily explainable—a Queen was meant to be out and about, hovering by veterans' wheelchairs, offering sticks of candy to poor children, cutting ribbons, pouring tea, the impersonal, dutiful charities of *noblesse oblige,* requiring little of her but large hats and powdery smiles. I was not cynical but I knew the Queen did not matter.

The King, however, preferred sticking closer to home and that was as it should be, a king on his throne, ruling. He didn't wear a crown, but he usually had on a peacock-blue smoking jacket, made of shiny, patterned brocade. It must have been handed down by his brother, I think. It made a nice, if surprising, change from the military gear he so often wore, and the informality of the costume made him appear relaxed, nearly jolly. He would be sitting with his hands folded in his lap, as if he'd been waiting for me to appear, and when I did, he would say to Margaret Rose, "What's this, then?"

I would walk carefully up the long purple carpet to where he sat, and make a deep curtsey, and he would rise from his throne and touch my hair with his hand and say, "There, there, child. Enough." And I would look up at his face—the long, sad cheeks, the remarkable expanse from nose to lip, the thin lip itself—and see in his lovely eyes the perfect understanding of which I spoke earlier, and the flicker of paternal joy.

Bashfully, for neither of us were any good at making conversation, we would talk to each other about our lives. This episode would usually serve as a review of what I was doing in school at the time, and I would tell the King everything I knew. The routes of the explorers, the toughest multiplication tables, all the verses of the poems I had memorized by Walter de la Mare and Christina Rossetti—all these things and more, without hesitation or stutter. And he too spoke clearly and calmly, in a voice rich and warm and even, in the voice a king should have. In the voice I gave him. And he would say, in this wonderful voice, that he was amazed at the depth and breadth of my knowledge.

"Why, I think you know more than either of my girls do," he would say. And then: "What would you think about coming to live here at the Palace? You are just the sort of girl I like to talk to."

It was the kind of swift decision-making one might expect from a king. For although the invitation was phrased as a question, there was no doubt that it was a royal command, and that I would now live there forever, with him.

Conveniently, I was only recently orphaned, my insensitive family having perished in a car accident or a tragic fire or from food poisoning at a picnic, and thus there were no obstacles to surmount. I would shyly nod my assent, and the court stenographer would be called to draw up immediately the adoption papers. I'd sign my name, Hannah Louise, with a flourish, and King George would raise his eyebrows in appreciation of my fine hand, and then apply himself to his own signature. This would be followed by a hot wax seal, red and dripping, as the parchment would be lifted up, and the announcement made: "Hannah Louise Clement is now of the House of Windsor."

Generally speaking, I never progressed beyond this point. The ceremony in itself was the culmination of all my hopes and dreams, and there was no need for dénouement. And it was only the King's death that brought me back to the suburban street and two-storey frame house in which I dwelled with a father and mother who couldn't figure me out, and a sister who thought, if she ever gave me a thought, that I was weird.

Her name was Phyllis Anne, and in the weeks following my downfall in the kitchen she needled and teased me and made me miserable at every turn. Three years older than I, she was exactly the right age to take the approaching Coronation seriously, and she began a scrapbook, starting with newspaper clippings which told how Princess Elizabeth had been given the news she'd be Queen while she was at Treetops in faraway Africa. Then she added to her collection the countless magazine articles and pamphlets flourishing in those days leading up to the event, full of Windsor family photographs, charts of royal succession, historical essays on the meaning of the Coronation, the symbolism of the orb and crown and etcetera, etcetera.

All very cheery and positive, this business of putting that Elizabeth on the throne. Phyllis Anne purposely left stuff out on the bureau, knowing I would see it and read it, knowing it would make me suffer. Well, perhaps she didn't do it on purpose; but the bitterness of my grief must have been apparent to her, she must have seen how I mourned.

I had longed for that name change with my whole being —I had heard in the King's last name the *win* and *wind* and *soar* of Windsor—and it made me feel strong and free, an eagle, a lark, lifted high above the ground where my unimaginative family congealed around me, dull and hard as cement. Clement, cement, stuck in my name forever. I felt so weighted with sadness I could not bear to think of it, and tried to avoid facing the dreadful truth. Spurred by some self-preserving impulse I trudged off to the public library where I took books off shelves and flipped over pages, searching for something, anything to take me away from my life.

And by a chance as serendipitous as being discovered by Margaret Rose, one day I took from the top of a return cart an old novel by Zane Grey, and within a few paragraphs found what I'd been looking for. The words seemed to blaze from the page, so vivid and real I could feel the heat from the small campfire against my face and the dark prairie night cold at my back. I knew, as deeply as anything I had ever experienced, what it was to ride for hours across sand blowing with tumbleweed, through the cactus and the sagebrush and up into the purple hills, riding and riding and riding. And I turned to the Wild West with a passion.

It was only a small step from those novels to the cowboy comic books and movies suddenly surrounding me—how had I never noticed them before? Waiting for me, as if they'd known I'd be coming just at that moment, were Roy Rogers and Dale Evans, King and Queen of the Cowboys. They welcomed me into their movies—I spent every cent of my allowance on the Saturday matinees, often the only girl for rows around—and met me once a week on the little brown radio, which I was allowed to take upstairs for the precious half hour of the Roy Rogers Show. I would lie on the bed looking up at the ceiling where my imagination brought me the unfolding adventures of Roy and Dale. And I always took the radio back down to the kitchen feeling calm and contented, prepared to ride along my own happy trails until, next week, I would meet them again.

The universe expanded, allowing me to accompany Roy's sidekick Pat Brady in his jeep Nellybelle, but in no time I found myself riding my own palomino, Golden Girl, just a little behind Roy and Trigger. Often he would turn toward me rather than to Dale or Pat when things got tough and he needed a hand. Almost overnight I became a rip-snorting cowgirl who never rode sissy sidesaddle, who could blast the eyes out of a rattlesnake with her six-shooter, who was vigilant in her defence of justice out there on the lone prairee. Roy and Dale said they didn't know how they'd ever managed before I came along, and I wondered myself as well.

My mutable soul transformed itself in all that sunshine and fresh air and my allegiance transferred itself—effortlessly, painlessly—from one king to another. The hot dry winds of the desert swept away the park bench where Margaret Rose had found me; even Buckingham Palace receded into the distant fog. It had been easier to believe that things were all of a piece when King George was on the throne—England, Canada, Canada, England, hardly any difference, really—but now with Elizabeth up there, well, things weren't the same any more.

I didn't care. Once I discovered riding the range I was no longer waiting to be adopted in order to make life happen. I was becoming tough, brave, independent, and prickly as a cactus. Maybe even a little dangerous. I was growing up. The Palace, if it ever did come to mind, seemed an awfully dull and confining place compared to sleeping out under the stars and listening to the coyotes howl.

One day, as I was riding on ahead of Roy and the sheriff's posse to show them the way, the entire Royal Family slipped into the cold grey ocean separating their little island from the land of the free. They vanished from my thoughts as completely as if they had drowned, they dissolved into the mists of time with the ghost of King George. I kept on riding into the wind and left all my old dreams behind—I had to git along, I couldn't look back.

Only now, all these years later, do I wish I'd turned to say good-bye.

THE VIOLATION

It had been one of those January whiteouts, the kind of storm that obliterates landscape and leaves you with no sense of place. When we looked out at dawn the wind had died and the snow was smooth as far as we could see, marred only by the tops of fence posts sticking out like cigarette butts here and there. Ray said right away that he'd snowshoe into town, and would I call the vice-principal at eight and arrange for someone to take his first period French in case he was late. And would I also call Garnet to come around and do the lane since it looked as if the worst was over.

Once Ray was out the door I made the calls and settled into the woodstove warmth of the kitchen, comfortable in the padded rocker by the window. I was five months pregnant, barely showing but conscious of every kick and flutter inside my rounding belly. It was all happening so slowly, far too slowly, and I felt dragged down, as if the new weight in my body were pulling me under. Some days I felt I could hardly move, and spent hour after hour wrapped in a shawl, dreaming and discontent. I like changes to be immediate and definite, and it seemed then as if all the changes in my life were subtle and organic.

The move from Toronto had been definite enough, and I had relished that, had known exactly where and what I was. Ray and I together were changing the pattern of our orderly lives, trading our carefree existence in a rented apartment for something else—hard physical work and the compensating pleasure of seeing our labour turn place into *home*. But since late summer when we'd taken over this small rundown farm in the Valley, I had felt myself slipping and spinning, the nausea of those first few months of pregnancy like motion sickness. Dizzy and disoriented, I could not believe that this confusion was the beginning of putting down roots. I longed for time to collapse so that we would not have to endure the process, could instead suddenly *be* what we wished to become—real country people, whose lives would be one with the land.

We knew that up and down the concession roads there was talk about how long we'd last, and probably the placing of small wagers as to the actual date we'd give up and vacate, hightail it back to some highrise. We had doubts, too, but we'd persevered through a difficult fall and had gained confidence from that. Ray was still teaching to bring in a salary, but we had plans for him to quit within a year or two. I felt good thinking of all the work we'd already accomplished and the new skills we were acquiring. We were trying to become as self-sufficient as possible—but of course, there were all kinds of problems. Like the long lane in winter. We couldn't manage to clear it ourselves, so we did what most of our neighbors did and called Garnet, who'd dig you out for a price. He was the kind of crafty farmer who survives best in the Valley, the kind who even profits from bad weather.

Garnet had ploughed us out to the road five times so far that winter, and twice he'd come in for coffee when his rounds had brought him to our house late after supper. Ray and I had been eagerly hospitable, anxious to make a good impression on someone who obviously carried gossip from kitchen to kitchen. I served fruitcake and refrained from commenting on his rural and right-wing opinions about the growing ranks of the unemployed or the problem of Quebec or the increasing cost of medical insurance. In part I was being polite and politic, taking on what I believed to be the expected role of a farm wife. But my silence also sprang from the fact that Garnet acted like a magnet, gathering up all my particles of dissent, leaving me empty-handed. I was mesmerized by his forceful down-home logic. And by his eyes.

Garnet was well into his fifties, a squat man whose large head sat squarely on broad shoulders, whose feet planted themselves as if each step meant business. His solid body and coarse features were a startling contrast to large soft brown eyes, the kind of eyes you would call sexy in another face.

The noise of the plough woke me from my dozing in the chair after lunch and I looked out to see Garnet's pumpkin-coloured rig pitting itself against the heavy drifts. Something dinosaur-like about the machine gave the scene an animal dimension so that Garnet seemed like a prehistoric cowboy, riding against the herds of snow. As if he had caught my thoughts, at that moment he looked toward the house and waved his cap in the air above his head. An old bronco buster at the edge of the ice age.

I moved away from the window then, over to the stove where what was left of the chicken soup I'd had for lunch sat cooling. I poured it into an enamel dish and was fastening on a waxed-paper cover when Garnet knocked at the door. I could see him through the frosted glass, standing on the porch, his breath rising in clouds around him. I unlatched the door and he stepped forward onto the rope mat inside.

"Hello," I said. "Trouble?"

"Nope, just thought I'd leave her sit for a moment, she's been going full-tilt all morning. Thought maybe I'd warm myself up if I could get a cup of coffee," he said, pulling the door shut behind him. "Saw you there at the window, figured you weren't too busy to give a fellow some."

"Well, sure," I said, a little taken aback by his assumption. He was right of course, I hadn't been doing anything, I'd only been sitting there, staring at all that white. But still, his presumption bothered me, as if somehow he thought I was waiting there to serve him. "Cream and sugar, isn't it?"

"Yup," he said. "And say, look now, could you make me a sandwich to go with that? I don't know when I'm going to get done the route today, the way this here snow's packed in. I could be real late getting home."

That said, he removed his cap, parka, and boots, then began to strip off the heavy overalls he wore on top of his everyday clothes. I stood by the sink, immobile, but moved inwardly by a flood of feelings I find difficult to name even now. Part of my nature was responding with pleasure and pride to think that Garnet, one of the local farmers, would choose *my* kitchen for his lunch, believing that he'd get a good meal. Surely this was a sign that Ray and I were accepted now in the community. The image of myself as bountiful earth mother rose up glimmering in the winter sunlight.

But there was something else, a kind of instinctive suspicion. A quivering in the air. I was a doe in the forest, nostrils dilated to sniff the wind, catching the scent of the hunter. All my cultural conditioning to set forth food to fill men's bellies was being thwarted by another more powerful womanly urge to run, hide, take cover. This is male, this is dangerous. The sudden terror was a mindless thing, starting at the base of my abdomen and spreading up my spine and out my limbs, as if my body was determined to be frightened, as if it knew more than common sense would admit.

It was the way he took off his clothes. So casual, so cocksure, confidently taking over my kitchen. His eyes glowed in his ruddy face and he smiled expectantly, waiting for me to move, to walk across the scrubbed pine floor to the breadbox, to begin waiting on him. Hand and foot—wasn't that what my mother always cried in her fits of anger at being treated like a servant by my father? "I've spent my life waiting on you hand and foot!" Not for me, that role. Ray and I were equal partners, we'd drawn up an agreement right at the start. But no sooner had my heart welled up in indignation than embarrassment brought me down with a thump. In the breadbox, only stale, store-bought bread. Humiliation above all else for a real country woman to be caught short. I was snared by the pull of wanting to please, and the push of wordless voices in my blood, warning me of danger. My head spun. I looked over my shoulder at Garnet who sat there in that stolid, silent way farmers have, waiting. I was about to offer him the leftover chicken soup instead, when the voices found words.

Warning me: You know, if you go to a lot of trouble and

fuss over this lunch, Garnet's going to get the idea you like him dropping by like this. He'll think you're lonely and he'll make a point of stopping by during the day every time he's out. Why, look at him, even today, he's watching you with those big brown eyes of his, and don't think for a moment he's not having ideas. He's just waiting to see how interested you are.

And the voices multiplied, got angrier and louder and finally led me to a courtroom, where I shrank before the defence lawyer's cross-examination.

"So. You *say* he forced his attentions upon you. But haven't you already admitted to the court you made it abundantly clear to the accused that he was welcome? In fact, *more* than welcome? Do you deny that you offered him homemade chicken soup? And grilled cheese sandwiches with your very own chili sauce on the side?"

The knowing leer, playing now to the jury. "I ask you, ladies and gentlemen: Would a woman trying to discourage a man's attentions serve him a lunch like that? Everyone knows the time-honored adage that the way to a man's heart is through his stomach. And indeed, is it any wonder that this normal man, with normal male appetites, thought he was being offered a little more than *lunch?* This was not rape, my friends, this was the result of culinary invitation!"

And I imagine the courtroom in shambles as the case is reversed, as I am accused and found guilty of seducing poor Garnet with country cooking.

No, I decided, I won't take the chance of leading him on with my good chicken soup. Stale bread is all the old devil will get from me.

Unnerved by the clarity of my imaginings, I let the bread-knife slip from my hand and it clattered to the floor, taking with it a dollop of the Kraft sandwich spread I was slathering on the dry bread. I bent down to retrieve the knife and, as I was wiping the pale glop off the floor, looked over at Garnet. He was sitting sideways in his chair, smiling cheerfully at my clumsiness, as if I had done it to amuse him. He had finished rolling three cigarettes and had begun to smoke one.

"Listen," I said, in a falsely apologetic tone, "this isn't going to be much of a lunch, I'm afraid. With the storm and all, we haven't got a lot of food on hand. We're out of fresh milk, too, do you mind if I use powdered for your coffee?"

With that, I plopped in a spoonful of milk powder, turning the instant coffee a sickening grey-brown, with little lumpy white bits floating on the surface. I set the cup and plate in front of Garnet, and sat down at the table across from him. I noticed then that he'd been tapping the ashes from his cigarette into his leathery hand, and I got up and brought him an ashtray from the cupboard. I felt his eyes upon me as I moved across the room.

When he reached for the ashtray he seemed to contrive to touch my hand, I was sure of it, and I flinched from that contact like someone burned. My face felt as if there were small flames licking around my cheekbones, ignited by fear —the fear that he could reach out and with one swipe of his enormous flat hands draw me up against the tobaccoey stench of his red-and-black plaid shirt. And in this place, in this snowbound and desolate house so far from the main road, what could I do?

There was the irony. Back in the city, where dreadful things were always happening to women, I had been safer than here. In Toronto I was accustomed to being wary of men, and I would have been loath to allow even a repairman into the apartment if I were alone, let alone serve him lunch. Safety in numbers, safety in cynicism—urban precautions no good to me now.

I looked over at Garnet and could see by the way he set his teeth into the second bite of his sandwich that it was just as awful as I'd thought it would be. But he kept his country courtesy intact and munched the horrible thing slowly and carefully, as if he were savouring it. He took my sitting down again as a signal to talk, and started, as one would expect, with the weather; he remembered winters here in the Valley that made this year's snowfall look like a summer's day. This led him to a theme for which I felt some sympathy, that most people today expect life to be easy and aren't prepared to cope with hardships. Worse than that, he went on, they have a diminished sense of foresight.

"Just no horse sense at all," Garnet said, stopping to take a small sip of his coffee. "Take that new young couple on the fifth, the Ealings? They build a house and they build it facing square northwest. So what do they have this winter? They've got drifts half covering their front picture window and a heat bill that's sky high. I happen to know that on account of Franklin at the Co-op, he told me he had to fill their oil tank again last week. If they'd taken the time to ask a few people around here for a little advice, they'd have had that bungalow as cozy and snug. . . ." He stopped, to finish the last corner of the sandwich; I rose, prepared to offer to make him another but hoping he would take it as a signal that lunch was over.

"Now you and Ray, for example," he said then, his broad face spread further by a smile. "You seem to be doing fine your first winter up here, near as I can tell. But I bet the two of you still have lots to learn from us old-timers who've spent our lives in the Valley. Yup, some of us old dogs know a few more tricks than you young pups do, if you know what I mean." And he winked and laughed and lit his second cigarette.

I was filled with an unclean horror, a knowledge I didn't want, the way I feel when someone tells a dirty joke and says "Get it?" and I get it and wish with all my heart I didn't. An old dog, yes, of course that's what Garnet was. Under those few layers of clothes he was as much an animal as any ram or bull or stallion, the same energy runs through them all.

Even Ray, I thought, feeling strangely disloyal.

I stood by the counter and, with the knife in my hand, gestured toward the breadbox but Garnet shook his head no. "I suppose that's true, we do have a lot to learn yet," I said, thinking maybe not the knife, maybe the scalding water from the kettle. No, that might burn *me* as well.

And I imagined myself standing over the prone body of poor Garnet, the knife in my hand, dripping his blood. Having killed a man to save myself from what? A few searching kisses from a man testing out the limits of his age? A pat or two, a nuzzle, chatty old Garnet simply wanting a little warmth, needing only the touch of my skin in order to reacquaint himself with youth. Would I really stab living flesh to save myself from so little peril?

Not for myself, I thought, but for the baby. To protect that small curled-up being inside me I knew I would do anything.

Again the voices echo in the courtroom of my mind, and again I am in the witness box, head lowered. This time the lawyer is my own, striding up and down in my defence.

"You see before you an example of severe hormonal de-rangement, a normally mild and virtuous woman in the throes of temporary prepartum madness. Members of the jury will believe me when I say that such an upright person would never ordinarily make such a violent. . . ."

"Sorry," I said. "Pardon?"

"I said, you don't have any family, do you?" Garnet was leaning forward. He had a sly look around the eyes.

Oh god, I thought, he's checking to see there's no one in the house with me, he wants to make sure he has me all alone. I must act as if I'm not aware of what he's up to. As if everything were normal.

"Well, not yet," I replied, smoothing my loose-fitting shirt over my stomach, "but we will come the spring." I smiled significantly, and at that moment was filled with a tremendous surge of power as if, miraculously, there were adrenalin flowing from my womb.

"For the luvva mike," said Garnet, and sat back in his chair as if he'd been pushed. "That's a real surprise, that is!"

"We're just starting to tell people," I began to explain. "But we haven't told any of the neighbors yet. The only person around here who knows is Joe Warrington—he sold Ray some nice white pine for the cradle he's making. And oh, his wife Annie, she knows, she's teaching me to knit and crochet so I can make my own things for the baby."

I was on safe ground now, inside the holy porch of motherhood. The ambiguous menace in the air evaporated like mist in sunlight. The fetus kicked inside me. I was sacred, a repository for another human being. I could no longer be a sexual object for Garnet's fantasies. He would not touch me now, I felt sure. A farmer, he would have too much reverence for the life force, too much respect for maternity. I was no longer threatened, I would not be harmed.

Garnet's face clouded as I went on about the plans we had for making the front room a nursery, and how glad we were we'd be raising our family in the country instead of the city. As I kept talking happily he gathered up his last cigarette, his tobacco pouch and yellow packet of papers, put them in his breast pocket and stood up. I was so startled by his sudden rising that I involuntarily gasped, and my hands flew to my chest like those of a timid maiden. Garnet looked at me, his liquid eyes full and deep.

"Can't be sitting here all day, there's work to do out there," he said, and reached for his heavy overalls. He drew them on, and then his parka, and sat down again to pull on his flappy-tongued boots. The room was silent except for the sound of laces through leather and the shift of burning logs in the stove. Flustered and uneasy, I felt I should make some kindly gesture, try to find out why he was leaving so abruptly. Had I been wrong all along? Was he shy of baby talk the way some men are? Or had he really hoped to seduce me, and was his ardour cooled by the notion of my occupied belly?

"Do you have a family?" I asked impulsively. It seemed, once spoken, far too personal a question.

"Well now, I'll tell you," he said, arranging his cap on his head. "I didn't want to get into this, but on second thought I might as well. The wife and I don't have any children, and not because we intended it that way. Oh, we're used to it now, but we started out all fired up like you two, and it took us a long while to get used to our life the way it had to be. She had two miscarriages to start with, and then there was a stillborn boy and well, more trouble after that, so the doctor told us to put a stop to it, just stop trying to have a family. He said we should settle. And we did, we settled down okay and accepted what was what. I'm not complaining, mind you, I'm just explaining it's the way things are."

I felt tears coming in my eyes and a warm saltiness at the back of my throat. But Garnet had an air of composure, as he leaned on the back of the wooden chair and spoke in that direct, hypnotic way.

"And I guess I should say what I think, which is don't go getting yourself all tied up in this here coming baby. Because it might work out and it might not. And if it doesn't, there has to be more to your life than all these plans. Don't plan too much on anything, that's the thing to keep in mind. You never know from one season to the next how things are going to go. You'll find that out, farming."

He put on his fur-lined mitts and opened the door.

"I didn't mean to come over all gloomy," he said, "so that's why I thought I better get on my way. Thanks for the lunch, it was just fine."

He stepped out into the bright winter light, smiling.

"Thank you," I said, not knowing what in the world I was thanking him for. I didn't feel grateful, I felt wounded and angry. He had violated my happiness with that sad story. Like a malevolent angel he had brought a message of destruction and despair, all the more alarming for being disguised as sensible words of caution. What right had he to barge in here and tell me what to hope or not to hope?

Garnet boarded his machine, and I closed the door after him, leaning against it and locking it. I felt stricken and cheapened by my panic and fear, caught in my own trap of superstition and uncertainty. I put my hands on my abdomen, feeling for a reassuring jitter of life. Nothing. Nothing. Was Garnet some prophet of doom, sent to forewarn me of disaster?

What could I be sure of, after all? Outside, the snow stretched flawlessly across the fields, blotting out familiar landmarks as far as I could see. White, only white. And here inside there were no signposts either, for the journey I had just begun.

ON FIRE

They open the first bottles of beer in the early afternoon, sitting by the water where two small children are paddling. The children (as well as a baby asleep in the cottage behind the cedar hedge) belong to Alex and Casey, who have invited David and Lily up to the lake to spend the last weekend of summer. Casey sits under a large navy-blue umbrella, while Lily lies near her on a towel, trying to brown her body with a mixture of tanning oils and lotions. But the late August sun hasn't much power and although she's been on the beach since morning her skin appears unchanged. Lily likes to go into the winter with a little additional colour, she says, or else she looks washed out by the new year (she and David have not yet begun their annual Christmas trips to Cozumel).

Casey, on the other hand, guards her paleness like a virtue and is the same shade of ivory all year round. A decade before skin cancer becomes a fashionable concern, Casey is making pronouncements about the sun being her enemy, about dangerous rays and who-knows-what-all; Lily is really getting fed up with these exaggerated claims and phobias.

Casey never used to be like this when they lived together—there was a casual ease to her then, a daring. But now she is so careful, measuring out time and food and experience in precise bits, everything weighed and measured. Lily thinks having three babies in less than six years has affected Casey's brain as well as her body for she has changed in some terrible and irrevocable way. She'd expected Casey to be a wonderful mother, possibly a little frazzled and disorganized but happy, definitely happy; instead, she has become tight-lipped and tidy. Even with all her attention to diet she has gained weight and she sits now in the blue shade of the big umbrella like an early Picasso, thickened and humourless. Worrying.

Lily finds herself annoyed by her old friend much of the time they are together (which is not often any more, maybe twice a year). She suspects that her irritation isn't only because of Casey's fretful ways, but probably has to do with her own deep frustration at being childless. She cannot prevent herself from believing that she'd be much better at motherhood than Casey is, that she'd be more relaxed, more joyfully maternal. Yes, and grateful. Casey seems not to have a shred of gratitude for these wonderful babies.

Lily turns over on her stomach and lets the sun do its business on her spine, the backs of her long legs, the soles of her feet. But what can you do, she thinks, trying to bend her thoughts in a more philosophical direction. This is just the way things are. Maybe it doesn't seem fair but who ever said life was fair?

David is further down the beach with Roger, the eldest

child, who has come out of the water blue-lipped, rubbing at himself with a beach towel in a sad, little-old-man way. David is kneeling, trying to distract the small boy from his shivering by building something in the sand. Hearing his voice, Lily raises her head and watches—it is only David who is making the fort, piling up pails of sand, laughing and talking as he works. He uses a small red shovel to smooth the sides, to fashion the turrets and towers with crenellated edges. He has sent three-year-old Vicki in search of sticks and feathers—fevvers, he calls them—to decorate the top when they are done.

Roger is sitting to one side, idly arranging piles of stones. He has clearly lost interest but David is happily humming to himself and starting to dig a small trench down to the water's edge. His idea of being a father, thinks Lily as she closes her eyes against the scene, is to become a child again himself. Perhaps it is not such a bad thing that they do not yet have children. Perhaps they will never have children and that will be for the best, the laws of nature working to prevent them from becoming the awful parents they'd no doubt be. She probably wouldn't be a better mother than Casey is, not really. She'd just end up being David's mother too.

With that, she feels the prickle of self-pitying tears and blinks rapidly, burying her head in the sandy towel. She has ended up crying about one thing or another the last few visits with Alex and Casey and she can't let it happen again.

The four of them have been friends for a long time, she and Casey since their first week at university when they met in a line signing up for Journalism. "How come *you're* taking this bird course?" Casey had asked her, and Lily had been astounded and offended. She wasn't going to study journalism because it was meant to be an *easy* option: she'd already decided it would be her major. She wanted to write for a newspaper, she loved writing more than anything in the world: she'd been cultivating a fantasy of herself as a hotshot reporter since she was fourteen. But this wasn't the answer she gave to the short rude girl next to her in line.

"Because I'm a bird," she'd said, drawing herself up to full height, one foot curled around her other leg, her thin arms wrenched up and out like spindly wings, and her large, rather beakish nose thrust out in what she hoped was the supercilious demeanour of a stork or flamingo.

"Oh, thank you," Casey had sighed, her grey eyes round with delight. "I've been really worried there wasn't going to be anybody to *like* around this place. What's your name?"

They had become inseparable after that, sharing rooms and flats for the next four years until, the summer of their graduation, Casey had married Alex and had gone off with him to Pasadena where he'd been given a large and prestigious fellowship. Alex was a graduate student in astronomy when they met him; he'd turned up auditing the same music appreciation course they were taking, given by a dotty old professor who'd known Stravinsky's daughter and who played all his music at top volume in a small basement room in the chemistry building.

Those Thursday evening music classes had had such an unlikely air about them it had heightened the romantic sense of destiny surrounding Casey's falling in love. Alex didn't much appeal to Lily—she found him too moody and remote. She much preferred the sociable, gregarious boys with whom she worked on the student paper, with whom she could talk easily and crack jokes and be herself. Alex always made her feel awkward and apprehensive. But she found herself spellbound by the dazzling intensity of Casey's passion, felt herself drawn into their ardour. It had happened so swiftly; one night, after the old man had played *Rites of Spring*, Alex had declared himself and instantly Casey was his. Their love was radiant, magical, as mysterious and overwhelming as Stravinsky's strange music. Even after Lily met and married David, she still felt a lingering nostalgia for that time, that place—the stuffy little room, the eccentric professor, that richly complex, dissonant music. A lingering envy.

With David, love had taken more time. There had been a lengthy engagement while she worked for a small newspaper in the town where he was establishing his law practice, since they both wanted to make sure they were compatible before committing themselves. For Lily, it had been a period of disillusionment, discovering that the career she'd dreamed of did not satisfy her at all; she knew she ought not be bored and restless, but she was.

She thought it might have been different if she'd started on a big city daily—there'd be excitement there, a core of energy—but as it was she found daily reporting a monotonous chore and began to think more and more about raising a family. She threw out her pills and waited for the signs which would mean she could ask for maternity leave, knowing in her heart she would never return to the paper.

They've stayed in that town, David and Lily, renovating a large, turn-of-the-century house, room by room. Nearly two years ago Lily quit her job hoping, as her mother had suggested, that staying home and leading a less stressful life would allow her to get pregnant. But although she and David have followed all the suggested procedures, nothing has happened. They are considering putting their name in at the Children's Aid Society, since everyone says adoption is a surefire way to suddenly find yourself expecting, and Lily thinks she wouldn't mind having two babies at once. But the only babies available seem to be ones with problems or mixed parentage, and neither she nor David are entirely sure about shouldering that kind of burden. Still, sometimes it seems to her that anything, anything would be better than this waiting for something to happen.

She has a standard answer now whenever friends inquire how she's getting along. "I'm just a lady in waiting," she says, and gives a small self-mocking and apologetic chuckle. One night at a party David overhears her saying this and adds, "Brooding about breeding is more like it!" She laughs as loudly as everyone else at the time, but when he repeats the same thing later she looks at him sharply to see whether he is trying to wound her with his wordplay. But no, his big handsome face is flushed with good humour, he is simply enjoying the sound of language, the taste of it in his mouth. It is what makes him such a fine litigation lawyer and is why his practice is flourishing, why they can afford to have Lily stay home. She has been thinking of doing some freelance writing for magazines, maybe trying her hand at some fiction, but the house seems to take so much of her time. She is stripping the varnish off all the woodwork, doing the jobs that might be difficult or dangerous once a baby comes.

Alex has left the beach. He has gone up to the cottage to check on the sleeping baby and to bring down more beer. Casey has said she won't have any more, one is enough, but Lily is already looking forward to the bitter liquid sliding ice-cold down her throat. She hopes Alex won't take too long, and with that passing thought suddenly realizes she misses Alex when he is absent. She is at a loss to know why, for in all the years they've known each other she and he have seldom talked alone: she has known him through Casey and with David, but never directly.

To some extent she still sees him as he was a decade ago, slouching in his chair at the back of the music class, thin and sullen and burning with desire for Casey. He wasn't talkative then and seems to speak even less as time passes. He only teaches one course now at the university and the rest of his time is spent doing calculations. His work is solitary, enormous, bright with portent and infinite possibility.

But he never speaks of it, maybe because none of them will understand what he's talking about. He barely talks at all, is even more self-absorbed than he was as a student. And yet as she thinks of him now, Lily sees him as the silent centre of their circle, the still pivot around whom the other three turn, talking, talking. Perhaps, she thinks, spending so much time on her own has brought her to a new appreciation of Alex, a feeling of unspoken affinity and connection—for she has found, working on the house day after day, a pocket of quiet within herself, a need for solitude she'd never known was there.

Sometimes when David comes home in the evening, spilling over with the news of his day in court, wanting to share everything word by word, she wishes he would stop. He is too overwhelming, too verbose. She will often pick up a book, or busy herself with something to avoid these conversations. "Could we chat later, Davey? I'm just in the middle of this right now." Always nice about it, or at least she means to be.

David is singing something silly and hearty from Gilbert and Sullivan as he cheerfully digs the moat deeper on Roger's instruction. The little boy is charmed by the way the sides cave in as the water rises and he urges David to go faster, faster. Soon the walls of the fort give way to the water and David is laughing along with Roger at the ruins, not minding that all his work has been for naught. He seems to have a child's easy understanding of pleasure as an end in itself.

Watching him place a small feather in Vicki's hair, Lily is moved by the exquisite gentleness of the gesture. Maybe he would be an excellent father after all, she thinks.

Alex reappears carrying three bottles of beer held against his chest and the baby slung on one shoulder. He calls out as he comes through the hedge, "Travis was awake, Case." Lily looks up from her towel to see a grimace pass across the other woman's face, but she can't tell whether it is from resignation or resentment.

"Oh Alex, you bugger, I'll bet you woke him. He should have been good for another hour."

Alex plumps the baby down on Casey's legs in a jolly way, as if his movements might forestall the anger he sees flashing from her eyes. In her pale face the round grey eyes have always been startling, but now they are quite haunting—she has a way of opening her lids very wide, as if to see through the endless dark tunnel of baby-bound fatigue, which makes them seem even rounder and more expressive.

There is a grim set to Casey's jaw as she turns her attention to Travis, a yellow-haired and pink-skinned baby rolling in fat. "Little pig," she says, but she says it fondly, tenderly, almost as if she were speaking to a lover. "Little pig," again, as she pulls up her shirt on one side to reveal a large, brownish-purple nipple which has begun to leak milk even before the baby attaches himself.

Lily is both attracted and slightly nauseated by the sight of the blue-veined and bruised-looking breast. She tries to imagine herself with that slurping infant pulling at her body, but she cannot. "God, Casey, you must feel so useful doing that," she says affectionately.

"That's what you always say, Lil," says Casey, tossing her head back and looking at her old friend as from a long distance. "You think I'm feeling utterly fulfilled, don't you? Well I'm here to tell you what I feel is *drained*. Don't sit there and create a fantasy about motherhood, I'm telling you."

Lily feels a surge of indignation at Casey's tone of maternal condescension—it seems to her this is increasingly Casey's manner—but all she says is: "Here then, drink some of my beer and replace your bodily fluids. I'm going to swim."

She walks to the water's edge where Vicki sits with her short chubby legs stretched out in front of her, whooping with glee every time a wave washes over her feet. Lying beside her is Alex, eyes closed, balancing a bottle of beer on his flat stomach. His dry skin is freckled and almost entirely hairless (unlike David's, whose entire body is covered in crisp, wiry dark hair). On his chest the nipples are small and bright pink, like two sugar rosebuds on a cake; looking down at him, Lily thinks what foolish and futile things men's nipples are, only for decoration. As she stands there, she is filled with a rushing desire to crouch down and taste their sweetness. Alex opens his eyes and looks up at her, one eyebrow arched quizzically. "Would you care to dance?" he says.

Lily has the unnerving idea that her forehead has opened up and Alex has seen the picture in her mind. She feels her face redden and so she scuffs the sand with her toe and does a comic turn.

"Can't dance. It's against my religion," she says, and runs into the lake. She is stricken by the intimacy that has passed between them—nothing remotely like this has ever happened before. Even little Vicki seems to be caught in the crackling web of electricity and has thrown herself upon her father's body, smothering him with kisses and upsetting his beer. Alex is smiling.

Lily runs out through the shallow water to where it is deep enough to swim. This late in the summer the bottom never really gets warm during the daylight hours and the coldness Lily feels around her ankles and knees is somehow thrilling. Her bones ache as she plunges down into the dark water, her racing pulse slowed by the murky silence around her. Swimming, she feels her long hair streaming out behind her, feels it falling like scarves around her shoulders as she rises to the surface. She has swum directly out into the lake and is unable to touch bottom; she does this every time she comes here. Being frightened and not succumbing to the fear always makes her feel powerful, in control of her life. Something left over from her childhood, she guesses, this moment of decision, this moment of knowing she *will not* drown. She never allows the welling panic in her chest to rise up and close her throat.

As she swims back to shore Lily squints to see more clearly but from this far away the people on the sand are only blurs and smudges. Like a Seurat painting, she thinks, small dots of colour, my universe broken into fragments of light. Casey, the children, Alex, even David no longer solid . . . just dots of colour, unconnected. Dots. (Her mother, sitting very close to her on the couch, both of them perspiring in the summer heat, that summer she had turned nine. Her mother, explaining the facts of life. "And the little egg from which you came is no bigger than the dot a pencil makes, like the period at the end of this page.") Dots. Tiny little dots within her body which somehow are not making themselves available to David's eager and dizzyheaded sperm. Her fault, her dots.

With a smooth crawl she slices through the water until her knees drag on the sand and then she rises and runs toward David, shaking her hair so that the spray flings out wildly and glistens all over his body and face.

"You should have come in," she says. "It was wonderful."

David wipes away the droplets of water from his eyes and looks up at her mildly. "But you were having such a nice time out there by yourself, Lil, I could see that. I didn't want to intrude."

She feels absurdly angry at his observing her so closely and knowing her so well. He's right, she would have felt encroached upon had he joined her—but this knowing of her is invasive, too. Is this how Casey feels about her baby sucking at her, she wonders. Is this part of marriage and motherhood inevitable, this sense of being known, being owned, being completely overtaken?

"Another beer," says Lily. "I need another beer. You want one?" He shakes his head and she walks up the beach without asking Alex and Casey who are sitting together, talking intently over Travis's head. There are four stone steps up through the hedge to the cottage which belongs to Alex's parents; they allow Alex and Casey to use it every August. It is at least sixty years old, a white clapboard structure with dark green trim around the windows and eaves and a wide screened-in porch which once looked out over the lake but now has its view blocked by the cedar windbreak. There is a sparse, dry lawn, and on either side of a flagstone path leading to the porch there is a round bed of straggly petunias made even more forlorn-looking by a rim of white-painted rocks. The yard is rich in aromas—cedar, and the honeysuckle and trumpetvine growing up over the porch, and the sweet grass which thrives in this sandy soil.

Inside the cottage there are strong, specific smells of mothballs and damp wood and years of spilt coffee on the old woodstove. The cottage has electricity (there is an ancient Kelvinator out of which Lily takes the beer) but this family of Alex's clings to old ways as much as possible when they are at the lake. As if going back in time can provide some kind of balance to their present lives, as if not flicking on a light switch can somehow transform them into people with "real" values.

Lily leans against the refrigerator to drink the first half of her beer, enjoying the coolness of the kitchen and the way its vine-covered windows convert sharp sunlight to dappled green shadows. There is something secretive and hidden about this little cottage she likes a lot; she feels as if she were still down in the cold dark water of the lake. Maybe Casey's right, she thinks. Maybe the sun *is* our enemy.

Later, in the early evening, the kitchen has become bright and warm. The four adults jostle each other within its confines, sharing the tasks of making supper and feeding the children. David is inventing a new spaghetti sauce concocted from various tins found in the cupboard; Casey is making salad and Alex is setting the table and supervising Roger and Vicki, who are eating hot dogs with ketchup. There is a steamy closeness which is not unpleasant, a grittiness which comes from sand underfoot and the sensation of still-damp bathing suits on the skin.

They will change into comfortable clothing once the children are down ("putting the children down" is Casey's phrase and strikes Lily as peculiarly sinister, suggestive of doing away with them). Lily has asked if she might give Travis his nightly bath in the sink and Casey has agreed, adding, "Just don't get moony, Lil."

It seems to Lily that with each visit the last year or so Casey has taken on more responsibility for her emotional well-being, monitoring her every shift and swell of feeling, constantly on the alert for any display of sentimentality or self-pity. As if she can't bear to see the reality of Lily's unrequited longing for babies. Lily keeps reminding herself that intervention is a kind of love, but she wishes Casey would simply let her be sad.

At this moment, she has pretended not to hear her, and has gone instead to open herself another beer—her fifth—while the tap is running for the baby's bath. She feels languid and happy, as if she were still in the lake. Travis is a remarkably placid baby, nearly nine months old and very bright-eyed. As she lathers his fat body with soap he squirms with pleasure and as she washes the folds along his thigh he squeals and splashes her. She is conscious of his small penis floating in the bubbles like a wrinkled little rosebud, and she is shy of touching it, afraid he will emit such a scream of delight the others will turn and say, "Lily, what are you up to with that child?"

Lily wonders if there is any difference between her enjoyment of Travis as she washes him and what a mother would feel. Are there levels of feeling which can be identified, labelled, and categorized? She lifts Travis out of the sink, amazed at the weight and heft of his shining body. "He's not a little pig, he's a Buddha," she says to the room at large. "A little pink Buddha."

Beside her, David is chopping onions for the sauce, and he slides his hip along the counter so that he is touching Lily as she is drying Travis. She feels surrounded by sensation—the baby's flesh, David's hip, the smell of onion, smoke, soap, beer—enveloped and enclosed. She looks at David, whose cheeks are streaming with tears, and at first she thinks that he is overcome by the sight of her holding the baby and then realizes it's the onions making him cry. Still, she feels interfered with, as if he is attempting to join her in whatever she is experiencing with small Travis. Why should she be so antagonistic, she wonders; it doesn't make sense. Yet both Casey and David set her teeth on edge with their caring.

The meal, when it is finally served after many lullabies to the children, is exactly like scores of others they have shared. The pasta is overcooked, David's sauce is highly original and almost inedible, and the salad is too sharp, tingling with lemon juice and garlic. There is a lot of bread and a lot of wine— two bottles of Hungarian red—and the local mild cheddar they always buy on the way up to the lake. Two oil lamps are burning on a shelf above the table and from outside night sounds drift in: a few final whippoorwills, crickets, frogs, and the occasional lap of a wave. Alex says that every seventh wave is larger than the previous six. He always says this and no one ever challenges him or asks if it is really true. Because he knows about the heavens, somehow they all assume he must know about the natural world as well. Even David, who loves to argue and ordinarily will not accept statements without question, gives Alex a kind of elevated station and never disputes the business of the waves.

Alex goes at the close of the meal to a cupboard and brings out a bottle of German dessert wine. "It should be cold, honey," says Casey, in a tight, careful way they all understand means that she wishes him not to open the bottle. Instead, he goes to the Kelvinator and takes out a metal tray of ice cubes, and as he drops a cube in each glass of white wine, he smiles at Casey. It is much the same way he plopped the baby on her lap earlier in the afternoon, deliberately merry, making a movement which in itself swerves around disaster.

Lily knows this oversweet wine will give her a headache but she is past caring. She wants to drink more, she feels reckless. Casey used to drink as much as the others, but the last few years she has been breastfeeding or pregnant much of the time and so there's always been a reason to avoid excess. Lily wonders if Alex drinks this much when he and

Casey are alone together or if it is only when she and David are around.

For now they are sitting around a table as they have so often, the wine slowing them down and bringing them into tight focus: they belong in the same frame. Alex is smoking Camel cigarettes steadily and David is lighting and relighting his pipe with his usual earnest, jaunty dignity.

Casey, who once went through a pack a day, has become an ardent nonsmoker, but even her show of being affected by the smoke—clearing her throat, wiping her eyes—does not deter the men. Alex shoves a pack across the table toward Lily and although she has never felt at ease with Casey's disapproval, she takes a cigarette out and smokes it. The gesture feels strangely defiant and adolescent.

Casey has become the centre of attention. She is animated, her grey eyes luminous, her round face glowing like a pearl in the light from the lamps. She is heated, having had just enough wine to fuel the rage she is now loosing upon them. "I'd damn well rather do it myself than have to have my husband's signature," she says.

She is telling about her latest conversation with her doctor, the obstetrician-gynecologist who has brought her three babies into the world, who knows her, she says, inside-out. She speaks of him with the fierceness women reserve for their fathers and doctors, those men with too much power. This man—she calls him Mac, they've been friends for years—is denying her the right to have a tubal ligation without Alex's consent.

"Consent!" she says, her voice harsh, and higher than usual in its force. "Consent! It's *my* bloody body and it's mine to do with as *I* bloody please!"

Lily looks at her friend and thinks how beautiful she is;

with the extra layer of milky fat covering her bones, her even features are still perfectly defined but riper, more sensual. The bright colour now in her cheeks and the way she holds her head high are somehow thrilling, make her seem nearly glamorous in her fury at Mac. Someone else entirely from that frowning blue woman on the beach. Lily has the wildly unsettling notion, all of a sudden, that neither of these Caseys bears any resemblance to the one she thinks of as her old friend. She doesn't really know who this woman is. Nor does Casey know Lily, neither of them are the same any more. They've changed beyond recall.

"Be fair," Alex says softly. "It isn't just Mac, you know, it's the hospital's policy. And he has to work there, he has to do the operation within their regulations."

"Oh Christ, Alex, don't stick up for him." Casey's voice cuts in like a scalpel before Alex is finished, scornful and dismissive. "Mac is part of the system, he's no better than that old fart whatsisname who runs the place. He goes along with it all, he's a pig at heart the same as the rest of them."

David sucks noisily on his pipe, leans back in his chair the way he likes to do before making some sort of legal pronouncement. Lily watches him and wonders what on earth he does in court without his pipe as a prop. He is very calm and his large body stretches out from the chair, his face ruddy from the wine and the earlier laughter. But she can tell from his tone that he is upset by Casey's agitation and is responding in the only way he knows—by dampening her vehemence with reason and composure.

"Now you see, Case," he is saying, "these fellas are in a real bind. They can get themselves in trouble if they go ahead with one of these sterilizations and then later the husband says he didn't know, or he only wants her if she's fertile, etcetera, etcetera. Believe me, this is fresh ground for the courts, and everyone's being careful, not just your Mac. There are lawsuits and nasty precedents in the offing if anybody makes a wrong move. They aren't asking for consent so much as your husband's acknowledgement."

"Bullshit, David," says Casey. "If Alex signs, then that's consent. Look, you only see it from your point of view, the law. See it from mine. I don't want any more babies. Me, the baby machine."

Alex, who has been hunching over his last glass of wine and smoking heavily, speaks directly to David now as if somehow he, in his legal role, has become the arbiter of this dispute. "Look, Dave, I told her I'd go and have it done, I don't care, it means nothing to me, I only want Case to be happy. It's easier for us anyway, snip-snip in the doctor's office and done. I've told her."

His face beneath his freckles is livid with emotion. When he drinks he never gets sweaty and red-faced the way David does, he seems to become even drier. How does he drink so much and stay so lean, Lily wonders. For that matter, how do I?

"Oh, Alex, can't you hear what I'm *saying?*" Casey speaks now in a tone of sorrowful exasperation, as if to a child. "I'm fighting this on the very issue you're talking about. You don't need my permission for your snip-snip, but I need *yours.* Can't you understand? It's about my subordinate role, it's about male domination, but it's not theoretical stuff, Alex, it's real. Goddamit, listen to me!"

Lily realizes she may be a little drunk because she feels as if she is in a play but she has forgotten her lines. She knows she is meant to be on Casey's side and yet her sympathies are shifting somewhere else. "Surely having babies is not subordinate," she says. "It's because it's the most important thing in the world that these men get so uptight about it.

Face it, Casey, you're only thirty years old. Couldn't Mac be concerned that in a few years you might want to have a baby again?"

Casey turns on Lily with quick, icy disdain. "You're such a romantic, Lil."

Lily is hurt but self-righteous—it makes perfect sense to her that a husband should know what's going on, after all, it takes two, doesn't it? She takes the rebuff with a thin smile, and gets up, goes to the bedroom and takes from David's overnight bag the bottle of French brandy he had stuck in at the last minute. He'd bought it last week after winning a particularly long and difficult case. "Didn't we bring this to celebrate with?" she says to David as she comes back to the table.

"What in heaven's name are we celebrating?" Casey asks, raising her eyebrows and making her eyes very round.

"The complexities of our existence," says David, in his pompous lawyer's voice, taking on a comic role to divert attention from the hostility in the air, anger so intense it is almost tangible. He loosens the heavy cork stopper and pours a little of the caramel-coloured liquid into four plastic tumblers. "You have some too, Casey," he says. "It'll do young Travis good to get some Courvoisier with his milk tonight. Here." He passes round the glasses and lifts his high above them. "To our complexities."

Lily drinks hers at one swallow while the others are still sipping. She feels an urgent need to act, to prevent the conversation from slipping back to that perilous place they've just been. She leans forward and takes the bottle by the neck, pouring herself another two fingers.

"I feel like a swim again," she says, inspired.

"You talkin' suit or you talkin' skinny?" David asks, in a mock accent he often affects to make people laugh. He has a good-ol'-boy aspect himself that makes the accent seem appropriate, even engaging.

"Skinny, honey," Lily says, flirting back in a way she never does if they are alone. "Have I evah been anythin' but skinny?"

They all laugh, for it is one of David's longstanding jokes that her knees, elbows, and hipbones are lethal weapons in bed, all of them sharp enough to draw blood. Lily *does* seem a ludicrous name for someone so angular and so unlike a flower, she thinks.

(She has had, over the past few months, a battery of fertility tests, one of which was meant to discover whether her hormonal development was retarded, but the results are inconclusive; her boyish body is no indication. There have been other tests of her inner workings as well, which have so assaulted her sense of privacy she is still, weeks later, injured in her spirit. She had lain, strapped down on a metal table under the eye of a camera, and watched on a small monitor her uterus, a white pear-shaped object glowing and fluttering on the dark screen; and then, not the neat bullshorns of medical diagram but two winding bits of thread, two tendrils of a climbing vine. Casey wants these same slender, slivery tubes of life cut, or cauterized, or plugged with plastic. Getting your tubes tied. A simple operation, nothing to it.)

"Listen, Lil, honestly, we can't go out on the beach naked. You know, we're not in the middle of nowhere." Casey is sober and sensible, and although she is laughing she is taking it upon herself to keep Lily and David in line.

"Goodness, chile," David says, "it's after midnight. There ain't gonna be no pryin' eyes down there this hour. Why don' you jest whip off them rags and come dippin' with me and my fren'?" He turns the full force of his charm upon her, a man who can disarm with his caution-to-the-wind lopsided smile—and Casey is suddenly and inexplicably taken with this jovial mood he offers. She abandons her stance and rises from the table, agreeing to swim skinny.

"But we'll take the oil lamps down with us," she says. "I don't want to leave them alight in the cottage with the kids asleep. And we have to be quiet, I mean it, David. No chortling!" She is going along with him but she is making rules—as always, Lily thinks. She always has to be the mother now.

Lily looks across the table at Alex, who is stubbing out a cigarette. His clear green eyes make her think of water, which is odd because his skin is so dry and patchy, his tangled blond hair like a small forest fire springing from his forehead. "You're coming too, aren't you?" she says, knowing his preference would be to stay quietly at the table alone. He responds by taking the lamps in his hands and holding them out as if he were leading a parade. Casey gathers the towels and they all enter the night, David and Lily giggling and shushing each other.

Out on the sand there are transparent layers of mist lying between them and the water, shreds and strands of gauze floating in the dark. Only the occasional star glitters, only a handful of distant cottage lights glimmer along the shore. The sole sounds are of crickets in the hedge, the small lapping of waves, and from down the lake someone's stereo playing music which is too urban for this setting—the sad, sophisticated undulations of a tenor sax. Alex places the lamps on the sand and Casey piles the towels beside them, glancing anxiously back at the dark cottage and her sleeping children.

Lily knows that by convention she must not look at the others while they undress but she is caught by the sight of her husband as he slips off his shorts and underwear, by the clownlike appearance of his penis hanging from its fur collar of black hair—like a false nose, like a fleshy handle. (David had done his tests first, since after all his was the easiest, involving only one hilarious morning in which he had to jump immediately in the car and drive to the medical labs with the precious vial of semen. He and his equipment had passed with flying colours.)

She cannot help it, she looks over to see what Casey looks like naked now, and is startled by the despondent heaviness of her hips and belly, the hanging breasts grotesque rather than voluptuous. Even in the resigned and ungainly way she removes her clothes Casey seems deliberately unsexy, as if she wants to be old and done with that business forever. Lily's own thin body by contrast seems a blessing, and she moves her hands along the ridges of her ribs and along her flat stomach with pride. Well, everything has its price, she thinks. Nothing new about that. She looks now to see Alex, who is pulling off his sweatshirt, standing behind Casey. He is even more of an ectomorph than she is, sinew and bone. She waits for him to take off his underpants, feeling ashamed of her prurience yet unable to turn away.

But he doesn't. He keeps his white briefs on and taking Casey's hand walks quickly into the lake, edgy and furtive. Lily wishes they were like the people she's read about in California, at Esalen and places like that, who would hold hands and chant mantras together as they entered the water, four bodies in one mind. She feels the need of ceremony and ritual to cleanse them of that conversation about Casey tying her tubes. A conversation that is already hooking itself into their lives.

The cool night air makes the lake seem warmer than it was earlier in the day as she slides beneath the surface, enjoying the silky texture of the water on her skin. She flips over on her back and with a gentle flutter kick steers herself out past the shoreline mist, looking up at the cloud-studded sky, the drifting stars. The life Alex has chosen for himself, the security of unobtainable galaxies.

She hears David's voice calling her softly. "Don't go out too far, Lil, there's an undertow." And she turns, with a firm and graceful breast stroke making her way back to where he stands, chest-deep. He is only a little taller than she is, a wall of a man against whom she now leans, letting her wet hair drape over his shoulder. She feels the jutting of his erect penis against her thigh and brings herself closer to him, excited.

"Help," she says. "There's an enemy submarine down there." She wraps her legs around his waist and burrows her face into his throat, playfully kissing and biting the flesh of his shoulder, and then biting again so sharply that he pushes her away.

"Hey, that hurts, Lil. Cut it out!"

"Sorry," she says, unrepentant, and swims off in a dreamy way back out to deep water. She can hear Alex and Casey murmuring—they are sitting in the shallows, splashing each other softly from time to time—but she cannot hear what they are saying. It seems to Lily specifically matrimonial, this splashing of each other. The saxophone's lonely melody slips over the water and winds itself around them. But what is the tune? She almost catches it once but lets it go, and is left with an image of neon-speckled puddles on city pavement, footsteps of a departing lover down the dark street.

The haze on the lake is lifting and the night is moonless but clear when David announces he is going back to the cottage. Lily knows she has hurt him in some irredeemable way by swimming off when he wanted her; she swims back now to where he is and tries to smooth things over. "I'm coming too, Davey," she says and stands up, the nipples on her flat breasts like small thimbles in the chilly air. They dry each other and then wrap the towels around themselves, carrying their clothes and shoes. Lily takes one of the lamps and leaves the other for Casey and Alex who have begun to swim a little, still talking.

It is only Casey's voice which is audible, and there is something brittle about it, something accusatory and plaintive. Alex's voice comes and goes in monosyllabic scraps, whetting Lily's curiosity as she walks slowly back to the cottage. It reminds her of how she used to listen to them talking in the kitchen of the flat she and Casey had shared their last year at school. Alex would bring Casey back from his place late at night and she'd make him coffee and they'd sit together at the chrome and red Formica table, talking and smoking cigarettes until dawn. Lily would hear their blurred voices through her bedroom door, not yet in love herself but on the outer shell of it, knowing the sound of it from the outside in. In the morning she'd see their coffee cups and ashtrays, proof of a complicity in which she had no part.

She sets the lamp down inside the porch and gets dressed: she pulls on one of Alex's father's old cardigans which hangs on a nail by the door and holds it around herself to stop the sudden trembling that has overtaken her. Seeing her shudder, David pours her a full tumbler of brandy, which smells strangely like rotting fruit to Lily now, vile and evil. But she drinks it anyway, needing its warmth to give her strength, and curls up in a wicker chair to wait for the other two.

First to appear is Casey, clad in a towel with her clothes around her neck, not covering her large swinging breasts. They are full—she has gone past Travis's usual feeding-time—and they seem bursting with self-importance. She clutches her clothes and towels to her body and runs to the cottage, her ankles splaying out from side to side as if she has a tight skirt on. She rushes past David who is sitting with his pipe on the wooden steps, past Lily and into the bedroom where they hear her getting the baby from his bed. When she re-emerges, in a blue bathrobe with Travis at her breast, her face has a lovely serenity and she is perfectly beautiful again. She settles into a chair next to Lily and smiles, stroking the fine blond hair on her son's small head.

The music from down the beach has stopped and the night is completely silent. There is only the uneven flutter of one oil lamp and then coming through the hedge the other one, held high by Alex. In his other hand he carries his clothing and towel; he is shining wet and bare to the night except for his white underpants. The light from the lamp reveals him, Eros and Psyche in one body.

Alex sets the lamp down in the centre of a petunia bed and piles his clothes beside it. He bows toward the porch and speaks in the manner of a ringmaster, a showman. "Ta-daa!" he says, and then again louder. "Ta-daa!"

This is so unlike anything Alex has ever done the other three sit open-mouthed, waiting to hear what he will say next. He is announcing that he will now dance a farewell to summer and will they all please hold their applause until he is through. David looks back over his shoulder at Lily and grins, shaking his head; Casey mutters to Travis, "Your daddy is drunk again, sweetheart." Lily is mesmerized, taut with expectation, wondering what he is going to do.

What he does is to leap over the lamp, making the flame waver and nearly go out, and then leap again, higher in the air, his arms straight out at his sides, his head held aloft and haughty. Clearly this is meant to be a spoof, a late-night amusement to send them to bed with a laugh. But there is also something very serious about his dancing, serious in the way he is demanding their attention. It reminds Lily of the way small boys play games as if their lives depend on it. Now he is jumping and pirouetting in a furious parody of ballet, now crouching and stamping in crazy imitation of African tribal dancing, but noiselessly. He snaps his fingers sharply every so often as if to keep in his mind some marking of the rhythms he must be hearing. The music of the spheres, Lily thinks and plans to offer that up next morning at breakfast. A good astronomer's joke.

As Alex dances the three others settle into themselves and begin to feel comfortable with the strangeness of his performance. His body is making shadows on the hedge, deformed and lacy shapes which stretch and shrink out of all proportion as he circles the lamp. His eyes are ablaze with excitement —he is obviously having the time of his life—and it occurs to Lily watching him that as long as there is a hedge between Alex and the outside world he feels safe and capable of liberating himself in their midst. With this dance he is taking them all with him into the most profound and private part of his soul, she thinks, and wonders if Casey knows this. She looks over at her old friend, awash in fondness for her after all the years they've shared, and sees that Casey has closed her eyes, has nestled herself closer to the sucking baby.

It seems to Lily watching Alex that his long bony fingers stream fire, that his yellow hair has caught fire too, and that there are tongues of flame licking the air around his face. Even his bare feet have a brightness, seem to be strung on wires of gold, threads of fire itself. He is an unexpected comet searing crazily through the August night, he is a puppet sprung free of its master. He is dancing faster and faster, he is becoming a firebird, he is burning up and disappearing into the ether.

But it is really only Alex, a thirty-five-year-old astronomer given to one moment of frenzy; thin, freckled Alex in his wet underwear dashing and prancing over the grass.

It is a dance of good-bye to more than summer but none of them know that at the time. Years later, after one of the marriages has ended in divorce and the two women have let their friendship dwindle into oblivion, Lily will find a postcard Casey sent to her after that last August weekend together. It has an old black-and-white photograph of Nijinsky dancing on the front and, on the back, only this: *Booze is bad for the heart.* Lily will be shaken when she realizes the truth of what she reads, and how much Casey had understood, even with her eyes closed.

Glowing with sweat, Alex twists himself into one last glorious leap and for a grand finale lands at David's feet, arms outstretched. "The end," he says, panting, out of breath. David claps his hands softly. "Bravo," he says. "You're a real star." His voice is warm and appreciative.

Alex goes up the steps and through the door, and stands looking at Casey holding Travis, who has fallen asleep against the blue bathrobe. Lily gets up from her chair and reaches out her hand, her fingers pointing toward his chest. She touches one of his nipples, recoiling immediately as if she's received a shock.

"You're on fire," she says, herself as breathless as if she had been dancing. She will say this again later to Alex, much later when they have finally become lovers, but this is the first time she says it.

LOSING FACE

There are times as I stand alongside the shiny kitchen range that I feel as if I am still in Toronto, as if this is the life I have always been in. Everything is perfectly familiar, every movement of my hands already known—stirring with the left and with the right scraping at a little scab of spilled and dried tomato sauce on the otherwise spotless stove top. Feeling domestic, calm, in charge. Wooden spoon, stainless steel pot, heat emanating up from the coils of the electric burner.

But what I am stirring in the pot is African tea—this frothing mixture of water and sugar, milk and tea leaves which must be boiled and boiled until the colour is a deep ruddy brown and the taste is rich and sweet. And then the tea is poured into an enamelled mug and taken out to Noah the night guard, along with the sandwich we always provide. Sometimes it is made of leftovers, a slice of ham or beef or chicken; other nights, cheese or fried egg, but never just bread and butter.

No one else we know does this, not on a regular basis. We've been advised by our Kenyan neighbours to be cautious, to limit our generosity to special occasions now and again: "If you start feeding them every night you spoil them. Food puts them to sleep, you know." But we do. Now that we've started we can't seem to stop—and sometimes I even buy cold cuts especially for Noah's sandwiches but I would never tell anyone that, not now. I am embarrassed by our soft-heartedness, maybe even a little ashamed. We have been here in Nairobi long enough to have smartened up.

And of course, as soon as I look up from the bubbling tea to the shiny blue walls of the kitchen I know where I am. I know I am not in Canada, not with this sickly-pale gecko staring at me with its drunken-poet eyes, its head raised slightly from the shelf above the stove. Not with the flies and dangling spiders, those delicate wall decorations the small gecko is here to devour, hanging from the corners, the curtain rails, the ceiling near the light. Sometimes, during the rainy season, the kitchen is infested with flying termites, their brown segmented bodies the reason for their name: sausage flies.

Sausage brains, stupid beyond belief, banging themselves against the windows and eventually crawling with idiotic determination through cracks between glass and wood or under the door. Flopping in a frenzy on the floor, flagging their wings wildly until these bits come free and lie there, unattached, like broken dreams on the blue tiles of the kitchen. Some Africans eat these termites, so I've heard. Fried, maybe they're crunchy, but I have a feeling that even then there would be an unwholesome softness at the centre. A squishiness I have come to know as my slippered feet squash them night after night, on my way from the stove to the front door where I give Noah his sandwich and tea. His *chakula na chai.*

What I feel for the sausage flies is a mixture of revulsion and curiosity and pity, a peculiar blend of emotions I seem to meet at every turn; I never feel only one way here, or two, but always three. I wonder whether I could get a termite down if I were given one to eat. Not likely to happen, since our Florence would die rather than serve me a fried bug. When Larry and I visited her village last year, her sisters had worked in advance of our arrival to prepare *mzungu* (white) delicacies, coleslaw and tomato salad, and crustless cucumber sandwiches. No, I will never taste that kind of food as long as Florence rules my kitchen. And she said, when I asked her, she would feel like "to throw it up" if anyone made her eat such a bad thing. "We do not eat *dudus,*" she said, staring at me with malice.

"I was only asking, Florence," I said defensively. "I read in a book that they were a popular food in this part of the world and I thought you might know if that is right." (And I feel my stomach heave and my mouth fill with acrid saliva at the very idea and yes, Florence, I would also throw it up.)

Florence and I are exactly the same age, and there the similarity ends. She is a small-boned but hugely strong Kikuyu woman who for two decades has been working in houses of expatriates in Nairobi. She tells me she can carry sixty kilos on her back *hakuna matata* (no problem), and I almost believe her, for I see other women on the road, women not so lucky as Florence, carrying bundles of firewood fastened by straps over their heads, bundles so heavy their backs are bent double as they walk. From behind, you can see only their thin brown legs, trotting along. Beasts of burden weighted by centuries of male oppression. And what do I do about it? What can I? Well, I hire Florence—there's one woman less lugging wood.

Instead, she cleans my house. She refuses to use the vacuum cleaner, believing that she can do a better job with a broom. It makes me frantic in a way I can't explain when I come across her doubled over, with that little brush of hers, whisking the morning's toast crumbs from underneath the table. She makes this small job look harder than it has to be and makes it take longer, I am sure of it. I rant inwardly, blaming the British. There is something so determinedly slow and inefficient about everything Florence does, it has been easy to imagine that first Englishwoman she worked for when she was just eighteen, who would have made sure everything was done exactly as it was done at home in Warwickshire. I see her—fair, with watery blue eyes and nervous hands and droopy breasts—and hear her plummy voice giving orders to Florence.

Florence, who has learned those lessons so well she has never since changed her way of doing household chores. Florence, who has steadfastly ignored all my attempts to modernize her methods. Florence, who is proud of her literacy (unusual attribute in a housegirl, as she is the first to tell me) and who thus reads anything I leave open on my desk: books, letters, diary. And then, with what seems almost premeditated innocence, tells me what she has read.

"Oh Madam, my eye fall on that book by the phone. You write down there you go to the dentist today. Do you remember?" Helpful, smiling, insatiably curious about my life. "Oh Madam, I see this letter your brother write. Your father is very sick, I am so sad." Her usually smooth and expressionless face frowning with worry, her hands clasped in a gesture of devotion.

Florence has entered my life, wants to be essential to it, so absolutely essential that I cannot exist without her. This is her protection, her only security in the world she inhabits, working for expatriates who come and go. . . . And that is her hope, that for one of us she will prove to be so essential that she will end up in London, or Toronto, or some European capital. Not forever, she says. Just for a little while.

I am increasingly aware that she observes me with a practised and analytical eye, can predict my amazements and furies—of course, I am never openly furious with her, for she told me when she came to work for us that if I ever raised my voice she would leave. That seemed fair and I agreed, little suspecting how many times there would be when I would want nothing more than to scream or to howl. I did not know how difficult it would be to have another woman in the house, a woman to whom I am meant to give orders. A woman who does things her way, no matter what I say, a woman with a mind of her own.

"Please, Florence," I say, keeping my voice neutral, thinking that I am about to solve the problem of her nosiness. "There is no need for you to dust my desk every day. You may leave that job for me to do."

"No, Madam, I will clean it," she says. "That is my work and you must not take my work from me." Here she stops, and bobs her head in a little nod towards me. "Now, Madam, shall I bring you some tea?"

My friend Cynthia, whose husband is with USAID and who has been here five years to my two, says that Canadians have the worst time of any expatriates adjusting to household help, no matter which country we're in. We just don't know how to handle power, she says. We buckle under and let them walk all over us and then wonder why they have no respect. It's a matter of not losing face, she says. If that happens then just forget it. Game over.

I spend more time with Florence than I do with Cynthia. Florence and I are bound together in an inextricable knot, each of us needing the other for different reasons, both of us knowing that and resenting it.

"You are like a sister to me," says Florence one afternoon, as she is ironing my nightgown. Her face has softened with affection, her eyes dance. "I say to my friends only the other day, that Madam of mine, she like a sister." A sly look then, sly and pointed. "And you, Madam. You tell your friends the same about me?"

The last few days Ignatius has been obsequious, that's the only word for it. Oh, I don't know, just the way he wipes the windshield of the station wagon, something in the careful angle of his elbow . . . a little extra attention to detail. This morning, for example, I had no sooner cleared the table and stacked the breakfast dishes—Florence has this Saturday off to visit her son—than he was in the kitchen door and up to his wrists in soapy water. "I do these up, Madam," he said, and I smiled and said, "Oh well, Ignatius, okay, and thank you very much."

It's the way he lets me know he wants a few extra shillings, and we all feel more comfortable if he has worked for the money. This has been our arrangement since Ignatius suggested it when we hired him at the same time as we rented this house. He had been the gardener here for seven years and instructed us immediately—all the rules and regulations are really his idea.

Then later in the day he came into the kitchen where Larry and I were just finishing the white wine we'd had for lunch—Ignatius sells our empties to a chap down the road who makes the illegal liquor called *changa'a*—and he gave me a small smile with his chin tucked under. There's a childlike hopefulness in this smile I recognize now, and I think to myself that something is up, he looks like he is preparing to wheedle.

"Yes?" I say, trying to sound stern.

"I was wanting to ask you something," he begins, directing his question to Larry whom, heavens be praised, he no longer calls *Bwana,* having finally chosen to call him nothing. Florence says Ignatius will not learn or use our names because as far as he can see white people all look alike and since we come and we go, year after year, we never stay—why should he learn our names?

"Yes," Larry says, a little wary but leaning forward in an attempt to communicate. Larry's field is communications: he's at the United Nations here, in public relations. "Yes?"

"I need to go down to the shops," says Ignatius. "Buying something extra for the children."

The children. Why didn't I think? He's going on leave next week, that's why he's been so slavishly helpful. He wants more money to buy his wife and six children "extras." Ignatius learned this word from some earlier employer and he loves to use it. "Extras" can mean anything from school notebooks to cotton blouses to medicine, to chocolates for his hard-working wife Grace who lives without him in a village eight hours from here. By the rules of protocol he has set up for us we must wait for him to tell us what these extras are. Asking would imply lack of trust.

"Of course, of course," says Larry, and gives Ignatius his twenty shillings for the kitchen work. Although he considers giving Ignatius some extra cash then he decides not to, since we have agreed privately on a system: we do not pay him until the very last minute before his leave, so that he cannot spend the money on his girlfriend Dinda who lives in the location—a small group of houses with garden plots, not quite a village—not far from here. It didn't use to matter to us what he did with his pay, but ever since we drove him home on his leave last year and saw those poor children of his, Larry and I try to do what we can to keep the money out of Dinda's pocket. It's just too depressing, those six children in that little hut. The size of Larry's office at the UN.

Off goes Ignatius on my old Raleigh five-speed brought from Canada, and Larry and I look at each other occasionally during the afternoon, wondering if he is really shopping or is having a farewell fling with Dinda. It isn't any of our business what this man does, and we try not to interfere. Still, we find ourselves wondering, guessing, playing at unravelling the mystery of Ignatius. He is so sweet-faced, so boyishly innocent, it requires an incredible act of imagination to picture him in bed with any woman, mother of his children or a good-time girl.

When he returns, just at nightfall, there is a large oblong package wrapped in brown paper balanced in the front basket, and Ignatius is steering the bicycle very carefully towards us—we are sitting now on the lawn, Larry with *The Guardian Weekly* and me with my *Collins Field Guide*. I've identified two more birds during the afternoon, a barbet and a shrike, both of them newcomers to our garden.

"Will you tell us what is in the box, Ignatius?" I ask.

"It is a lamp for my children," he says, with such deliberate and decisive pride it is clear he has looked forward to making this announcement.

"Yes?" we say, and he explains how his wife sent word that his children have come home from school crying because the teacher is angry. Angry because they have not done their school work. But, his wife says, they cannot do their work because the one oil lamp she has in their hut doesn't cast enough light for the children to see properly. In the smoky haze of the small room their eyes grow tired and they fall asleep over their books, they go to bed instead. She has said Ignatius must bring her another lamp. By some good fortune he heard only this week from another gardener on our street about a very good bargain at a hardware shop on River Road, where he has just purchased this pressurized lamp which is activated by a pumping mechanism. He will teach his wife how to use it and how to brighten the nights of his children, so that they can study, so that their teacher will not be angry any more.

He is out of breath with the effort of this telling, although in fact much has not been said so much as transmitted, gestures combined with scraps of English and Kiswahili. At the same time, we both notice the price tag stamped on the box—it is more than half his monthly salary. We are uncomfortable, unable to face this smiling man who stands before us wearing one of Larry's striped cotton shirts discarded because the collar is no longer fashionable.

Ignatius wheels the Raleigh down to his house—two cement-walled and cement-floored rooms which we persist in calling his house in a devious linguistic game invented long before we arrived here, a game in which Ignatius and his expatriate masters are equal players. Everyone is happier if illusions are maintained, and what better way than with language?

I say, "Jesus, Larry," and he looks at me and says, "I know. Christ almighty. All that extra money he's been after hasn't been going to Dinda at all."

"Do something," I whisper, but already he has risen and is following Ignatius down the path, and is stopping him. It is nearly dusk now, but I can see he's putting something into the black man's outstretched hand and I know with certainty it will be several hundred-shilling notes. I also know that

Ignatius opened his palm toward Larry a fraction of a second before Larry spoke, a fraction in which the heartache and cunning of poverty shone forth. The halo is not for Larry but for clever Ignatius, who has found a way to get a lamp for his children. I am struck by what a beautiful scene it is, the two men seeming to hold hands in the twilight, their colour hardly visible, just two men joined together. Then Ignatius is bowing, his head bobbing above his folded hands, everything in his stance servile, humble, grateful unto death. I cannot see Larry's face from here, not at all.

I had never had an obscene phone call before, not in all the years I lived in Vancouver or later in Toronto. I was completely unprepared for the honeyed voice turning suddenly to poison in my ear and I did precisely what one is meant not to do. I gasped, giving my caller the thrill he was seeking. He spoke again then, quickly. "Don't hang up. I'll only call again."

But by then I had slammed the receiver down hard. I sat for a moment on the bed beside the telephone, looking at it, a black chunky object capable of making my heart pound and my legs tremble—I can see my knees shaking beneath my cotton skirt. I get up and walk across the room, feeling as if somehow the telephone is watching me and just as I am at the door to the hall the ringing begins again. I run down the hall, calling to Florence not to pick up the extension in the kitchen.

"Let it ring, Florence. Don't answer. It's a man who is saying bad things."

We stand there in the blue kitchen, Florence and I, staring at each other while the ringing continues. Persistent, hypnotic. She is standing by the sink, her dark eyes gone dull and flat the way they do whenever she is confused by me. As if she is hiding somewhere down inside herself, waiting to see what it is this white woman wants. I see this, and I know I must calm down, explain things to her more clearly.

"This man says he is asking questions for the newspaper, Florence. And then he asks bad things. About here." I point to myself, feeling ashamed and as if I am shaming Florence by even acknowledging my crotch. She is looking at me with blank astonishment, a hand covering her mouth in embarrassment.

"Why he do that?"

"I don't know, Florence, but men do this. I didn't think men did it here, for some reason. But I guess they do."

"If this an African man, I tell him right now to stop. It is not right he do this." She goes to the wall phone and lifts the receiver as if it is hot, holding it away from her ear. "Yes? Yes? No, Madam is not here."

I watch Florence's face crease in puzzlement during the next silence, trying to catch her eye in order to gauge what is being said. But she keeps her head down, listening, listening, and then begins to speak loudly in a rapid stream of Kiswahili and Kikuyu. I can't follow—even after a year of language lessons, Kiswahili still confounds me—but I can tell from the tone that Florence is really giving this poor bugger the rough side of her tongue.

She hangs up with a flourish and strides back to the sink, her eyes ablaze, her face glowing. Fierce Kikuyu stuff.

She'd be beautiful if she'd stop wearing that headscarf— I've told her she doesn't have to dress like a servant, but she just laughs. Now, during the phone call, she has pulled the scarf around to one side and it makes her look dopey. And Florence is anything but. She may be doomed to a life of service in Nairobi households—but she is sharp-witted and astute and she is teaching me about a world I have never known before. In her knowledge of life, in her self-righteousness, she holds enormous power over me; and at this moment she is shining with righteousness. She is heroic and she has saved me.

"What did he say, Florence? Was it bad?"

"He a very bad man, Madam. He tell me he want to speak to my *mzungu* and I say you are not here. He says he want to ask you if you do it at the behind hole, and do I know this. Things like this, Madam, I cannot say. I listen and then I tell him very strong he must not say these things again. An African man talking this way—oh, I never hear such a man in my life." She looks at me sadly, as if I am not to blame for what her people do. Or perhaps as if I *am* to blame, as if my presence has caused this dreadful thing to happen. We stand in grave silence, shaking our heads as at the news of unexpected death. Grim and stricken.

"Look here, Florence, we can't let this man make us feel bad. *Sticks and stones can break my bones but words can never hurt me.* Did you ever learn that when you were a little girl?"

"No, I never know this," she says. *"Sema tena."*

So I do as she asks and repeat it, and then again, and she claps her hands to make a rhythm and we get a beat, and soon she has the words and we chant it together, Florence saying it and dancing with it, as if the old rhyme were her own. And I notice I am following her lead now, copying her movements and clapping, learning the words anew. The bad spell is being broken and I start laughing.

"Really, Florence, did he really ask that? The behind hole?" I am laughing so hard the tears are starting from my eyes and this makes her laugh, she thinks I look ridiculous when I cry at the same time as I laugh. It is not something Africans do, she says.

"Yes," she says now, "yes."

"What did you say then? What did you say that made him stop—see, he hasn't rung back!"

Florence stands by the sink again, adjusts her crooked headscarf and folds her arms across her white apron, a stance which always prefigures a moment of absolute righteousness. She smiles, savouring her power.

"I just tell him, Madam, that I put a curse on him if he call again and his man-part will fall off."

One of the things I like about living in Nairobi is our house, which is white stucco and built on a hillside in the low-slung Spanish style. The red tile roof and black iron gates seem like details in a picture book, hardly real; but then, there is an air of unreality to this entire place, too brightly coloured, too vividly drawn. The magenta bougainvillea cascading from the thorn tree has the wild vibrancy of molten plastic, its colour chemical, not natural.

Around the garden, hibiscus, frangipani, bright epidendrum orchids provide me with fresh bouquets every day if I choose, bouquets livened with daisies, roses, lilies, irises. Sometimes I tally the cost of these flowers if they'd been bought at some florist's shop back in Toronto, and I set the vases out smugly then, thinking how lucky I am.

One afternoon, as I am cutting a few stems of jasmine to freshen the arrangement on the coffee table, I notice that the walls of the house near where I am standing are filthy, especially around the side door which is set into an alcove. The stucco is stained brownish-grey, as if something dusty or greasy had been smeared along its surface. I call Ignatius, who is clipping the honeysuckle hedge at the far end of the garden, and he comes slowly, bringing his large shears with him.

"Ignatius," I say, "I just saw this. What do you think these marks are from? Why is this dirt here?"

"Noah, Madam," he says.

"Noah?" I repeat stupidly. "Noah the nightguard? But I don't understand. Why would Noah do such a thing, Ignatius, dirty the walls? Doesn't he like us?"

"Oh yes, Madam, he like you, he like you very much. He stay awake for you all night like this." Ignatius laughs and leans against the wall, bracing his feet against the foundation, rolling his body back and forth in a slow, dreamy way. His eyes are nearly closed and he is humming one of those African songs which sounds very like a hymn, probably was a hymn eighty years ago.

"You see, he do like this, Madam, not sleep exactly, he still up if supervisor come to check, he still up if robbers come. And after many nights . . ." Here, Ignatius gives a shrug and lifts his eyes expressively, international language for "what can I tell you?" What can be said about the state of Noah's uniform, the old navy serge coat which marks him as a SIMBA *askari,* a coat which probably has never been cleaned? The shabby peaked hat, the numerous rags and bits of cloth he winds around his neck and head to keep himself warm, the shredding woollen gloves. I think of Noah, keeping himself vertical during the long hours of the night, watching the cold stars overhead drift through the branches of the cassia, the gum, the thorn. What does he think? What does he hope for? What does he dream?

"Thank you, Ignatius," I say. "I see now. Well, can you wash these walls with soap and bleach to make them clean?"

He shrugs again, giving me his broad you-are-a-fool smile and says, "Yes, Madam, I will do what you tell me." He whistles as he walks back to the honeysuckle, and I imagine he's chuckling to himself—so easy to keep these *wazungu* happy doing jobs over and over, why not wash the wall? It will just get dirty again. He stands on his ladder in the sunlight, cutting back the hedge, the constant growth requiring endless trimming, endless care, that means he has a livelihood.

That night I cannot sleep. Beside me in bed Larry is oblivious, his lanky body spread-eagled, his breathing coming in raspy spurts the way it always does when he sleeps on his back. I try to shift him over, try to get him onto his side, but none of my attempts is successful. Awake, I keep thinking of Noah at the other end of the house, tossing and turning against the hard stucco house, his stomach full of hot tea and the bacon sandwich I made him earlier. I think of his solemn face as he took the thick sandwich from me, his eyes round with delight at the salty smell of the meat.

I cannot get comfortable. I keep turning over and over in the bed, desperate to find one place to sink into sleep. I see myself as from above, and watch my body flopping about beneath the sheets, something less than human, something gross. Like some kind of ugly great fish, flailing in panic, gills fibrillating, fins quivering in the air. A fish out of water. I am a fish out of water.

ORPHA KNITTING

Orpha thought she knew why she had suddenly, for the first time in her life, started to knit. The reason was, it looked good. Moreover, it made her look good, and might have the additional benefit of making her good, just the way she'd been told it would when she was a child. *The devil finds work for idle hands* and *Busy fingers do the Lord's work.* She had elected to be stubborn and lazy, had refused to learn, had deliberately dropped needles and tangled yarn in clumsy fits of temper. But now? Now she looked good and industrious and pure of heart. Who had ever thought ill of a woman knitting? Madame Defarge and the French Revolution aside, what woman knitting had ever thought ill? Knitting could make you good from the inside out. Women who knit are God-fearing, family-loving caretakers of society, keeping the feet of Our Boys warm in the trenches, fashioning baby cardigans in pale pastels, belief in the future manifest in every stitch. Women who knit make the world good.

I must be a good woman, Orpha would think, smiling. How could I be otherwise and be knitting? Impossible. Think a harlot would knit? A shoplifter, childbeater, cheater at cards, or stealer of other wives' husbands? Never. *Those* women are the sort who never lift a finger except to paint their nails. *Those* women don't care if they're good or not.

What I am doing, Orpha decided, is making something of myself, just the way my mother wanted me to. I must exist if I knit—isn't that Descartes? *Je tricote, donc je suis.* I am pulling myself together in the careful twist of wool around needle, in the looping and twisting and never letting go. There is virtue here, yes, and valour. I am saving myself by this good deed. WOMAN SAVES SELF WITH KNITTING NEEDLE. No more woolly thoughts, not while knitting knots. All for naught? Oh, surely not, thought Orpha. Surely not.

Orpha and her husband and her children live in a red brick house on an Ottawa street where all the houses are red brick. Under a canopy of tall maples (once there were elms but they are dead and gone), this street is in a central part of the city much sought after because it is well established. Even the houses have settled in, sagging comfortably into the earth. Surprising, Orpha thinks, that something made of brick should sag, and realizes how deep is her childhood belief that the little pig's house was safe from the wolf because it was brick. "You're a real brick, Orph," her friends would say because she was steadfast, never let them down, never sagged. And yet here is the brick house she lives in, with gaps and cracks in the mortar, with an enormous split in the wall of the basement where water drips in every spring. When they moved in—was that nine years ago or ten?—she and Russell had had to wedge pieces of carpet under the stove and fridge;

the kitchen slanted from east to west and if you set an egg on the counter near the toaster it would roll right along to the sink. But the house *looks* substantial. You can't tell from the outside.

Last year, on one of those educational series on television, there'd been a special on continental drift, with computerized diagrams of what the shifting plates must look like. They'd all been watching—Orpha, Russell, Stuart, and Jenny—since these science shows were one of the few things Orpha allowed; most of the stuff on the idiot box, she said, was a complete and utter waste of time. Even the news was unreliable, slanted and cut and arranged for maximum sensational value. That night none of them had said a word until it was over, had sat in rapt fascination watching great swatches of land unlock and collide, millions of years pressed into their shining tube. Time and the shape of things, the mysterious energy at the earth's core, reduced to moving dots of colour on the screen. Recent film footage gave visual proof of new chasms appearing along the San Andreas Fault—made more dramatic by a clutch of wild-eyed zealots predicting the world's end would begin in California. Earnest scientists in book-lined labs pointed at maps, documented their theories, gave support to their hypotheses, tied the whole thing up. No question, by the end of the program this business of shift and drift was something you could believe in.

"Maybe there'll soon be a new religion to sign up for," said Orpha as she flicked off the set. She had risen quickly at the commercial, knowing that the mindless sitcom following was one her children would watch if she didn't prevent them. "Something vaguely Heraclitean, I'd imagine, celebrating flux and flow."

Orpha had done her graduate degree in pre-Socratic philosophy, and it was an old joke between her and Russell that she could find a place for Heraclitus in any conversation. Occasionally, after a little too much wine with dinner, say, or if she was feeling dissatisfied with some aspect of her life, Orpha would speak the name with bitterness, aware that those years of study had come only to this, a clever irrelevant remark now and again.

"Flux might account for why the drains in the basement overflow," Russell said, stretching his arms above his head, laughing. Always ready to find humour in everything, ready to lean back and let life happen. Not uptight like me, Orpha thought.

"But things aren't moving *here,* Dad," said Stuart, his thin face so like his father's, except for the intensity of his small, narrow nose and his slightly crossed hazel eyes. He was at an age—had always been, perhaps—when he could not bear to be left out of adult banter. He would pop up, butt in, wanting to connect and be part of it all. Was it possible to be so irritated by your own child and still be a good mother? There was one to knit about, thought Orpha.

"What I mean is, we're on the Shield here," said Stuart, responding to his mother's sudden turn of the head with an urgent rise in the pitch of his voice. "*It* isn't moving. Everything is solid where *we* are."

Stuart had done a school project on mining—when was that, grade six?—and all the information he had gathered had clung like lichen to a rock ever since. He had loved the Canadian Shield for some reason and had made that the heart of his project. Maybe it was simply the heraldic connotation of the word, the chivalrous sound of that Precambrian base that so appealed to him; he was, ordinarily, a child whose interests were literary rather than scientific. On the map he drew and coloured that year, there was a wonderful sweeping strength in the way the Shield fanned out from Hudson's Bay, dipping down to where they sat in a red brick house on this tree-lined street. Ah, what Blake could have done with that, had he lived here instead of in England's green and pleasant land, mused Orpha. *Bring me my arrows of desire, bring me my shield of igneous rock.*

"Nothing is solid anywhere, like it or not," Orpha said sharply, wanting in some deep, peevish part of herself to quiet that shrill, insistent, thirteen-year-old voice. There was something about Stuart these days that reduced her to an adolescent level of response—she knew it and couldn't stop it, kept trying to disguise these feelings from him and herself. Unsuccessfully. "You've studied the atom this fall, Stuart, you know that everything's always in motion. Besides, nothing is certain, nothing is sure. Your father was right, we have flux in the basement of our lives." She was smiling, this was meant to be a little intellectual joke, lighthearted and witty; but her voice felt harsh and wicked in her throat.

Sure enough, Jenny began to cry. "That's *horrible,* Mom. You're saying we can't be sure of anything, like we could have an earthquake right here, aren't you? I'm going to have nightmares now and it'll be all your fault."

Ever searching for the dramatic moment, ten-year-old Jenny put her head in her hands and wept. There had been a heavy, melancholy cast to her chubby features since birth, something sweetly brooding in her expression even as she slept. "She enjoys crying, I swear she does," Orpha would say after one or another of their tearful arguments—they'd been meeting head-on since Jenny was two. She'd laugh and shrug to show Russell she was just kidding about Jenny's gloomy disposition, didn't for a moment *really* believe what she was saying.

Now what she did was to reach down to the floor beside the couch and pick up her knitting. It was her new gesture.

"If you say you're going to have nightmares, then you'll have nightmares," she said to Jenny in the calm and reasonable tone she'd been adopting lately. "It all depends on what you want. Don't exaggerate everything."

"Well, *you* did," said Jenny, lip thrust out, defiant, ready for a quarrel about something, anything, even nonexistent earthquakes. A curve of dark hair fell forward on her cheek in exactly the same way as her mother's and she brushed it back with an angry hand.

"You did, actually," said Russell gently, taking the edge off, the peaceable peacemaker at work. "I think it may be a family failing." He looked over at Orpha and winked, indicating he was on her side, at the same time as he reached toward Jenny and pushed her shoulder in a mocking, comradely sort of way. It was odd, when you thought of it, that Russell's field was conflict—he taught history at the University of Ottawa, where he had made his scholarly reputation with a course on revolution—and that what he sought in his own life was to avoid disagreement of even the mildest kind.

Orpha began to knit without even looking at the pattern book. She didn't care if she had to rip it out later, she had to do something now to keep from lashing out and slapping that sulky face of Jenny's. Her only female child, flesh of her flesh, and she wanted to hit her more often than not. She never had, aside from a few flash-temper spankings during the tantrum years, but her restraint was due more to Russell's benign interventions than her own inclinations. When she considered the way he interfered with her responses, always smoothing things over, always rearranging and tamping down, she could get so angry. And yet, without him, what then? What would she do without him at this moment, for example?

She looked over at her son, sitting there with his damn glasses sliding down his nose again, so earnest and thin, endlessly holding forth about how much he knew. She wanted, desperately, for him to be silent, but she did not have the same urge to slap him as she did Jenny. Something more awful and sinister, like stuffing his socks in his mouth and hissing at him, "Shut up, Stuart." And then she'd push his glasses up on his nose and fasten them to his forehead with tape so they sat properly on his face for once. Oh, imagine! Honestly! Where did these thoughts come from? I'm barely forty so it can't be the menopause yet, she thought, knitting.

Knitting, knitting, Orpha knows there is blackness in her heart and is frightened because there is no reason for it. No reason at all. It is just there. She hopes that as long as she is knitting no one will know what she is thinking. She hopes she will stop thinking if she can only knit hard enough.

Another call from Brenda. It comes, as do most of Brenda's calls, well after midnight, after the bottle of vodka is gone. Without the solace of drink, the phone offers itself to Brenda as an alternative to suffering alone. The call means the following scene takes place: Russell turning over in bed, slowly putting the pillow over his head, never worrying that the ringing means death or disaster, assuming it will be Brenda because it is always Brenda. Russell hunching the duvet up around his shoulders as Orpha is saying, "Hang on, Bren, I'll go downstairs. Wait till I pick up the phone there, okay? Don't hang up, now. . . ."

Finding her dressing gown on the hook behind the door, feeling her way out of the dark into the carpeted hallway where a nightlight makes eerie shadows float along the walls as she hurries down the stairs. In the kitchen, plugging in the kettle even before picking up the phone, knowing she will need a cup of tea while she sits there, two cups, three.

Listening to Brenda's slurry voice and her raspy intake of
breath as she inhales the smoke from her cigarettes, awful
menthol things she's been puffing away on for years, never
even trying to quit. Saying loudly, "Hang up now, Russ," and
knowing he would; eavesdropping would be the last thing
he'd do in the middle of the night. He hates knowing how
unhappy people are, he never wants details of Brenda's trou-
bles after one of these calls even if Orpha offers them in
marital fellowship. "It's a shame, a rotten, bloody shame," is
all he ever says, cutting her off, preventing her from telling.
This is not history, it is present, immediate pain and he wants
no part of it.

The reason for the calls is the same every time—the breaking up of Brenda and Nick's marriage, going on now for four,
five years. Some marriages end wham, bang, lipstick on the
collar and by god, into the courts and out again, both parties
free and ready to roll. Others take a very long time, splitting,
mending, cracking, fixing—no one ever seems to know the
right thing to do. Trial separations, trial reunions, joyful be-
ginnings, and sad, sad leavings. Marriage in remission, shifting
affections, deep hostilities, incompatible love.

No wonder Brenda drinks.

Brenda and Orpha have been friends since they were Jenny's age: with all those years collected and stored between
them, they share custody and responsibility for an enormous
amount of knowledge. What this means to Orpha is that you
have to accept the present, you have to answer the phone
when it rings, you have to listen to the hysteria and anger
and not respond in kind.

(But oh, how to respond kindly on those nights when
Brenda's thick smoky voice would slug itself through the air
looking for someone to hurt and find her, Orpha, in the dark.
Drunk and malicious, the voice would mutter and croon,

abusive and nasty. "Did I wake your hubby up? Hmmm? Did you have your man all warm and cozy there beside you and did I wake him up and make him mad? Oh, but your Russie never *gets* mad, does he, Orph? Don't you wish he would? Just once? Get really *mad*?" And Orpha would sit and listen, thinking that maybe someday she'd be able to collect this debt, but for now she would dwell on the years they had shared and wait until Brenda blew herself out like a storm. After all, if she were Brenda, she might feel this bad too. Wondering if the tables were turned whether Brenda would sit in the dark and listen to her.)

Remembering twenty years ago, Brenda's wedding—the first of all her friends to get married—and not being the maid of honour as she'd long expected. Brenda saying, "Oh jeez, Orphie, don't take this wrong but see, my mother picked these dresses and I never thought and jeez, you can see how terrible you'd look in these crinolines and all this tulle. It's not even your colour, Orph, it doesn't suit you. Oh look, you just aren't the right *size*, Orph. I'm sorry, I never thought it meant so much to you, don't cry, okay? Don't be mad. You know you're still my best friend."

Looking at her plump self in the mirror and knowing Brenda was right, Orpha smiled at her best friend who was going off and getting married and not finishing university. Brenda was so smart—she'd even had the wit to quote Pascal to her parents when they tried to dissuade her from marrying Nick—and she always won. "Sure, okay, you're right, I'm far too big to wear this stuff," Orpha had said, hating herself for being both overweight and vain. "But I want so much to be a part of your day, Bren. Let me sing, how about that? I could wear something else if I sing."

And so another girl wore the frilly dress and Orpha sang, standing in the choir loft of the small Presbyterian church, with bright spring light shining in the window and falling on her opened music as if on cue. Handel, chosen by Brenda's mother. *Father in heaven abiding, Who hears our prayers at all times, Grant us . . .*

Grant us what? Happiness forever? That's all we were asking for with our weddings, with our white dresses and bridesmaids and trailing bouquets. That's all. Orpha tries now to remember the rest of the line, with Brenda's voice raging hot in her ear, tries to find the melody, finds it, hums it in her head . . . no, the words have all melted back into time. Gone. To the music of Handel and Bach, to the strains of Mendelssohn and Brahms, they'd had it wrong. Now Brenda weeps on the phone, bitter and blaming, and Orpha sits in the dark, sad and apprehensive. Grant us what? Grant us anything, Lord, it doesn't matter what. Nothing lasts forever. Nothing lasts. Nothing.

Since she began knitting last year, Orpha has made the following items: A curling sweater for Russell with sleeves that are too long but which he cheerfully rolls up. A yellow cardigan for Jenny who says it doesn't *go* with anything, and a pullover for Stuart who complains it's itchy at the neck. Two pairs of bedsocks for her mother who is in a chronic care home and whose feet are always cold. (Her mother always has the socks on when Orpha visits; she wants to encourage her daughter in this late-blooming proficiency which she regards as a good omen. Orpha has taken a long time to settle, she thinks.) Four scarves in varying shades of blue for the family to wear in the annual Christmas photograph. Three sweaters and bonnets for newborns. (You never know nowadays who's going to have a baby next; some friends are having late ones, others have teenage daughters starting early.)

A variety of Barbie outfits which Jenny has never used since she put her dolls away last year (Orpha realizes she was trying to keep Jenny from growing up). Several pairs of mitts. Twenty-seven squares for an afghan; this was how she began the knitting and she still hasn't finished it. Nine dishcloths out of string to use at the summer cottage.

Stuart is bright enough to do well at school in everything but math. This year, in grade eight, he has been having a real struggle with algebra, to the point where his teacher suggested during a parents' night interview that perhaps Russell and Orpha should arrange for private tutoring. "I can't give extra attention to every student who needs it," the teacher had said, managing to shed responsibility and pass it on. Annoyed, but seeing he had no choice, Russell put up notices for a tutor on bulletin boards around the university. Orpha put an ad in the community paper, stuck more notices on the board at the health food store and in the window of the bookshop where she worked part-time. Within a week there were several applicants, eventually whittled down to three likely prospects among whom Stuart was told to choose, since it was important, Orpha said, that he feel *involved*. He picked the one she liked least, an engineering student named Mike.

"I don't dislike him exactly," she said to Russell. "I just have reservations. He seems, I don't know, kind of thuggish."

"You have a noticeable bias against engineers," said Russell with a laugh, picking up an armload of books to take back to the library. "You always did prefer us bookish types."

"We all have our weaknesses," Orpha said. "Well anyway, maybe I meant sluggish rather than thuggish, come to think of it. As long as he engineers some algebra into Stuart's head, the rest doesn't matter."

Mike's own head sat squarely on a short, thick neck which seemed barely to rise from his shoulders, giving him a heavy-jawed appearance strangely at variance with a soft, barely audible voice. He had his pale blond hair cut very short so that in an odd way his head seemed hairless, a protuberance of skin and muscle and bone, an extra limb stuck on his solid, stocky body. He wore sweatshirts with the university crest on the chest, a mode of dressing which struck Orpha as particularly unimaginative.

"Typical engineer's approach to fashion," she said at supper one night, describing Mike's wardrobe to Russell. "Needs the shirt to remind him where he's meant to go every day."

Stuart got up suddenly from the table, his thin face flaming with indignation. "You think you're so smart," he said to his mother. "Well, *he* can do algebra and *he* can help me get good marks. And you can't. All you can do is make fun of him and I wish you'd shut up." And before he could be told to go to his room to cool off, he ran up the stairs to do just that.

"He's right, you know," said Russell. "We do go on."

Orpha considered flinging her plate of chicken and peas to the floor and storming out, considered making a speech about the tyranny of the bland, considered bursting into tears and throwing her arms around Jenny who was sitting there watching with wide eyes, waiting to see what would happen next. But she did none of these, she did what she always did.

"I will try to mend my ways," she said, mocking imitation of a chastened servant implicit in her bent head and apologetic tone. "I do have a terrible tongue in my head, and I truly repent, I truly do."

Laughter, supper goes on, the end.

But not the end, because Orpha knew Stuart's anger was deep and had to be acknowledged by her in some other real way. When Mike arrived for his next session, there were cups of hot chocolate and muffins set out on the table, and she said, carefully so that Stuart would hear, "We really do appreciate what you're doing here, Mike. Neither of us have a head for math at all. Have you always been good at it?"

Little conversations then, Mike mumbling in his soft voice and looking at the floor while he'd answer her questions. Over the winter weeks, the habit of a few moments spent chatting either before or after the tutoring: Orpha realized it had become part of her expectations, that Mike would stop and talk to her. Sometimes, baleful sideways glances from Stuart indicated that his mother was monopolizing Mike and embarrassing him, and sometimes there were painful silences when no one could think of anything to say. Then Mike would eat and drink with gusto, making appreciative noises as he swallowed, and Orpha would stand by the stove wiping the countertops, or chopping up vegetables for supper.

"There is a rustic, primitive quality to our relationship, such as it is," she said to Russell one night after the children had gone to bed and they could talk freely. "Maybe it comes from his being a country boy, but I feel like a farm wife when he's in the kitchen. Or else like I'm in an old Bergman film, you know, long silences and heavy looks, lurking about darkly, that sort of thing. I need to get a proper wardrobe for this role, something Sveeedish."

March, and for Stuart the Easter exams coming, for Mike the end of term. Intense work and increased supplies of food and drink from Orpha, urging Mike to have a second bagel, another glass of milk, an apple to take in his pocket.

"You have to keep your strength up," she'd say, patting Stuart's thin, bony shoulder. "Both of you."

One afternoon Stuart announced he had to leave early, he was doing his friend Andy's paper route that week.

"Andy's got mono," he said, "and there are two other kids in our class who might have it too. Neat way to get out of exams, eh?"

Stuart out the door quickly with that last remark, Mike getting ready to pull his books and papers together and leave too, but Orpha stops him with the offer of more hot chocolate. "There's only a little left in the pan, Mike, you might as well finish it up," she says.

He sits at the table in the family room looking at the floor, his back to Orpha, waiting for the second cup he doesn't really want, while she stirs the milk and wonders what to say. Looks at the top of his head where the short hair swirls out from a central point—a small, flat whirlpool of fine hair that shows the skin beneath. And as she stares, she is struck by the babyish quality of his pale scalp. He really isn't very old, she thinks, remembering her babies and the vulnerable softness right at the top of their heads, and her fear of washing their hair those first few months. A deliberate strategy, it seemed, to keep new mothers anxious and sleepless, that matter of the soft spot. Dreaming at night that she, forgetful, had carelessly brushed the baby's hair with her own stiff brush and had mangled and mashed its brains. Waking from these dreams (with both children, the same dream) and patting the forehead of the sleeping infant, touching where it was safe to touch, feeling such tenderness and apprehension.

And out of somewhere comes the memory of her father's bald spot, how there had been a joke when she was a child that he was losing his hair through Orpha and her mother kissing the top of his head, day after day. The little round hairless patch grew larger with each passing year until finally there was a shiny, hard leathery dome fringed with grey. "Your mother won't let me alone, just look at this," he'd say to Orpha when she was home on weekends once she'd gone away to university, was out working, married, away. "Oh, Daddy," she'd say, bending over the chair to kiss his bald head, "I think you've had a secret harem for years. Mom and I couldn't have done this by ourselves!"

And then, sooner than she was prepared for, looking at him in his coffin, his face untroubled and dreaming, his skin powdered carefully by the undertaker so there was no shine. Subdued by death, the matte finish on his scalp was ludicrous on the white satin pillow. Wanting to laugh, or shout, or to kiss him one last time—but holding back, of course, not doing it. Why had she not made that one last gesture? How long had it been, yes, five years this spring. Had she really been so fearful of his lifeless form that she could not kiss her father, no longer her father?

Still looking at the top of Mike's head, walking over to where he's sitting, seeing that exposed place of male vanity, thinking of her father, her babies, unravelling old thoughts, she bends and kisses his bald spot. Startled, Mike turns, reaching up to swat whatever had—a fly? a kiss? this woman?—and looks at her with clear and curious eyes. He sees a woman still bending, her dark hair falling on either side of her pensive face, still dreaming. And as she is beginning to straighten, he rises, catches her hand and moves toward her. And both of them, daring, eye-to-eye, kiss.

A passionate kiss that has nothing to do with anything but itself. Unexpected, inarticulate, inevitable. His soft young mouth so unlike Russell's, nearly like a girl's, nearly like kissing her own fearful self, Orpha thinks. Opening her lips and kissing, loving the taste of hot chocolate and toast in his mouth. Opening her eyes fully now, seeing the table, the room, Mike's face, pulling apart, oh! what if Jenny . . . Stuart . . . Russell . . . ?

"And do you know what he *did?*" she said next to Brenda,

telling her all this on the phone late at night, whispering even though she was sure Russell wasn't listening, was sprawled deep in sleep on her side of the bed, keeping it warm for her return. "D'you know? He took his pulse! He did! He looked at me with great amazement and put his two fingers on his wrist. It was the most moving gesture, somehow. Oh, I don't know, as if his heart was racing and he feared for his life. Maybe he has a heart condition, who knows?" (Laughter, great hiccups of laughter.) "Or well, maybe he was testing the effects of the kiss, what kind of rush it gave him. I wonder if there's a drug equivalent to the middle-aged kiss."

More laughter, hers and Brenda's, sitting in their dark kitchens after midnight pretending their sadnesses can be dispelled by laughter, by sharing, by analysis. Women find such peculiar ways of getting through, Orpha thinks, and that makes her laugh even harder.

Stuart did just fine without a tutor, it turned out. It was near the time when Mike would have been quitting anyway, so nothing much was said when he phoned to say he couldn't come back. No one mentioned him much. He had never been part of their lives in any real way, and Stuart said now he thought he was kind of boring. Russell had only met him twice. "Nice boy, though, wasn't he? Turned out to be the right medicine, didn't he?"

Sometimes Orpha would find herself weeping when she was alone, especially in the kitchen, where she would imagine him sitting, surprised by her again and again. She would touch her mouth with her hand and imagine the softness of his lips and the swirl her tongue made in his mouth before they drew apart. Who had been more surprised, she wondered, Mike or herself? When had she ever done anything so wildly out of place, so absurdly satisfying?

A funny story for Brenda, that's all it was now, nothing

to feel sad about, but still she wept, and took to keeping paper towels in her pocket just in case. "Imagine!" she said to Brenda, weeks later, although Brenda was drunk and not listening. "I still think about him, you know. About the kissing. Everything. Do you suppose I might turn into one of those women who go around picking up teenage boys? Do you think my moral fibre is disintegrating? Is this how it starts?"

One night in June the children and Orpha are having supper in front of the television set because Jenny has a school assignment to watch the news. Russell is off at the Learned Society meetings in Vancouver and Orpha is at loose ends and enjoying it. She pours herself a glass of wine to drink with the hot dogs and flips through a magazine as her children check off the day's litany of horrors. War and famine, starvation and mutilation, hijackings and crashes, slickly and quickly into their heads and out again. Barely observed. Orpha is preparing one of her speeches about television news when her attention is caught by a woman on the screen with a long sad face. She has those mournful pouches under the eyes that give an impression of great fatigue and resignation. She is sitting in a green living room talking to an off-screen reporter about her husband, recently ousted as leader of a political party. She is being asked to comment on his downfall, and the interviewer is using phrases such as "unceremoniously dumped" in an attempt to bait her. The network wants re-action, temper, *colour*.

Orpha is struck by two things. The furnishings in the room are tasteful and forgettable except for a lampshade, directly to the left of the woman's shoulder, which has been set askew. In that orderly room the shade becomes a comic turn, the apparent flaw begging forgiveness for everything else. The other thing she notices is that the politician's wife is knitting. Her hands, which move industriously with a life of their own during the entire interview, are broad-knuckled and scarlet-nailed. "So much for my theory about women who paint their nails," says Orpha aloud, and the children make shushing noises.

Even when the woman stops to collect her thoughts, her hands are working. She seems to be making one of those Arran sweaters—there is a large heap of beige wool on her lap. She eventually speaks with candour, telling the interviewer how upset she is at the press's treatment of her husband.

"Oh, if you only *knew* him," she says, "the way we in the family do. Why, he phones home every day, no matter where he is. Always has done. We've always been a close-knit family." The needles click and loop and whirr—the fingers and the wool change place so swiftly it seems like a magic art, a sleight of hand. Of course, thinks Orpha, it is all trickery and subterfuge. The woman is clearly lying. An expert liar and knitter. An expert wife.

It is late summer and the family is at the cottage on a pretty stretch of river not far from the city. The cottage is a small, dun-coloured prefab set on cement blocks, which has slipped badly during spring thaw so that now it lists like a stranded ship. Russell explains to Jenny it has nothing to do with shifting plates and tries to enlist her aid as he lies down in the shallow space under the cottage with a jack and pieces of wood, trying to prop up the tilting side. He discusses water tables and the properties of soil, but Jenny remains unconvinced and will not come under to help him, in case the cottage may collapse. She stays at the edge, watching.

The mosquitoes are so bad this season everyone smells of bug spray, a lemony odour of citronella oil and tar and sweat that is sharp and pleasant, in contrast to the darker smells of the riverbank—dead fish and mud and rotting wood. Orpha is sitting out on the end of their small dock and beside her is Stuart, casting a line into the water, catching catfish and letting them go. He pulls his hook now and again, and there is always a fish, ugly and wriggling, caught through its mouth.

"Ugly as sin," Orpha says, and Stuart says, "It can't help it, Mom. It's only a catfish. It's meant to look that way." She does not like to see her son engaged in this cold-hearted play but what is there to say? They *are* only catfish after all, and he does throw them back.

She is knitting a very difficult, intricate pattern, a lacy dress with a drawstring waist, the first thing she has made for herself. As she knits she thinks about writing a letter to Brenda; their last call ended with Orpha slamming down the receiver in anger. "I've had enough, Bren," she'd said, in what seemed to her at the time a cold and final voice. "You sicken me with your self-pity and the way you try to make me feel as bad as you do. I hate these drunken calls of yours. Don't phone again unless you're sober." That had been two months ago and there'd been no word from Brenda. Orpha is thinking now maybe she should get in touch, and wonders what made her angry that night. Why is she so fed up? Is she actually frightened by Brenda?

She realizes, as she sits in the sunlight knitting, that even the most complicated pattern she can find is not enough to still her mind. She cannot keep the darkness out, even with this. How utterly laughable anyway, thinks Orpha, that a woman like me would knit to keep herself together. She looks over at her husband's pale legs sticking out from under the cottage, and sees Jenny crouched nearby, holding her father's bottle of beer and talking to him. Connected, but still careful.

She looks at her son's skinny frame and the ridge of vertebrae down his back as he leans away from her on the other side of the dock, watching for the slightest movement in the amber water. She looks at her own brown skin, only a few mauve veins showing through here and there, and thinks how beautiful she is now, finally at this age beautiful. It makes her happy to think that. Thinks then of Brenda, who will never be happy, ever.

She does not plan to do what she does, but she's aware that she is doing it and that it is the only thing to do. She stands up suddenly so that the knitting falls from her lap into the water. It seems like an accident. She makes no sound but stands there watching the swift current take it away, the needles floating up like masts from the bulky bundle of yarn. Slowly it submerges as it disappears around a clump of speedwell and loosestrife at the bend in the river.

THROWING AND
CATCHING

Silly and her mother Mrs. Jackson lived on the street behind our house so that their yard and ours were back-to-back. Which is how I came to know as much about Silly as I did —most people didn't see her at all, she was kept at home. My mother remembered hearing that once she'd been enrolled in kindergarten but it hadn't worked out; since then, Mrs. Jackson had taken things into her own hands. Caring for Silly must have been pretty hard but because Mrs. Jackson never complained, no one pitied her or offered to help.

Almost everything I knew about Silly I knew by observing her. (Neither Mrs. Jackson nor my mother was given to small talk and they had almost nothing to do with each other outside of belonging to the same women's group at our church; I think my mother found her neighbour a little coarse.) I spent a lot of time watching Silly in her garden throwing a hard rubber ball against the brick wall of their garage, throwing and catching, throwing and catching, over and over. I'd watch Mrs. Jackson putting out the wash, noting all the big white bloomers and strips of white cotton hanging on the line. Silly was around ten years older than I was, but it was clear these were her diapers and I knew before I was told that Silly and I were "not the same."

Her real name was Priscilla, shortened by everyone but her mother to Silly: it was the only name I knew her by, and the name she has now in memory. It bewilders and astonishes me how often children have names which can be twisted into horrid and appropriate parodies—but then, perhaps if her name had been something else, she would have been called far worse. Silly named her simply for what she was—not quite right in the head.

She was almost attractive when you saw her from across the yard, with long chestnut-coloured hair, thick and shining, halfway down her back. But her forehead was rather narrow and her face had a pointy look to it—sharp little nose and darty eyes which flicked here and there without sparkle or intelligence. And her body had the long, sad heavy look of something nearly forgotten, a shapeless appendage she dragged around, not knowing quite what to do but lug it about. Her hips were broad and her feet, encased either in men's canvas tennis shoes or big winter boots, looked enormous. Only when she was tossing the ball against the wall did Silly have anything like grace.

She was different, we explained to each other, those of us younger ones who'd gather along the garden wall and hedge separating my yard from theirs. I would invite other children after school to watch her throwing and catching the ball— not to tease or torment her, only to peep through the hedge in hushed fascination. This private viewing of Silly was my ace-in-the-hole, the ultimate gift I had to offer in friendship, and only those in favour were eligible for invitation. Silly and her ball gave me years of social power and prestige and I flourished in my role as tour guide, as documentalist and interpreter of her habits and routines. We would watch her for hours on end, fascinated by how familiar she seemed, and yet, how odd, how strange. She seemed to us like someone under a wicked enchantment, a princess upon whom a spell had been cast, to whom something awful had happened, or would happen.

The wall at the end of our yard was a little over a metre high, made of boulders stuck together with pinkish-coloured cement; on the Jackson side grew a prickly hedge nearly the height of an adult. But it was a poor thing, that hedge, with gaping holes and dead spots in it, perfect for our small curious eyes to peer through. We were nearly always rewarded by sightings, for she would be there alone in all weathers, in sundress or in navy blue duffel coat, throwing and catching, throwing and catching. Crooning little melodies to herself, little jumbles and snatches of songs we'd recognize from our own recent cradle days or from Sunday School. She loved to sing, with a voice surprisingly sweet and fine coming out of that odd, clumsy body.

My mother said she'd heard that Mr. Jackson had dropped the child on the floor when she was six months old, and she'd never been right since. My mother's friend Mrs. Petrie, who was a nurse, said that story wasn't the least bit true, you could see what was wrong with that child was never the result of a fall, it was in the blood. My father, who had known Mr. Jackson when they were boys, remembered that he'd had a sister who wasn't right and who'd been put away young. That story seemed to substantiate Mrs. Petrie's version of events, but my mother stuck to her guns and attributed Mr.

Jackson's absence from the house—it'd been several years now since anybody'd seen him—to his running away, guilty and stricken by what he had done, accidentally or . . . Maybe, she insinuated with her pause, he had dropped the baby on purpose.

It didn't matter what the reason was—Silly was dim, with a loose-lipped smile that showed her bright pink gums and small, even teeth. Like baby teeth. When she kept her mouth closed, she was rather pretty; but more often than not the lower hinge of her jaw hung slack, and sometimes little drools of saliva slid down the sides of her chin.

Silly was as much a component of my life as my parents, my older brother William, my various pets, or the actual physical environment in which I dwelled; I knew her as I knew the shaky banister on the second floor landing, or the window in the bathroom which wouldn't close tight in humid weather, or the cracks in my bedroom ceiling which could be read in such a way as to spell the names of boys I loved. Silly was a fixture, an essential detail—but she didn't know me. Oh, sometimes I would sing with her through the hedge, joining in her songs or rhymes, and once I passed her a piece of soggy cherry cobbler I didn't want to eat, calling to her: "Hey, Silly, you want some of my cake?" But we never talked or played together, which must have been as my mother wished it.

It was possible to see over into the Jacksons' yard from the dining room window, our house having a slightly higher elevation than theirs; and since that room was where the family piano was kept, I could sit at the keyboard as I practised my scales and divert myself by watching Silly with her ball. This went on for years, and I adopted a rhythm to my playing contingent on the regularity of her throwing and catching, as if she were my metronome, setting my pace at the keys.

I never thought much about it, except that it did seem to make things easier, having that rhythm in my head.

By the time I entered high school, my interest in Silly had waned considerably. I could still see her out there with her ball—but there were certainly more absorbing things in the world than spying on an imbecile. I simply ignored her, and did her no harm.

Well, that's not entirely true.

The Lutheran teen group I belonged to went carolling around town every December, singing for the elderly and sick in the congregation, the "shut-ins," as they were called. The year I was fourteen I was helping to organize the event, and my name was printed in the church calendar, which is how Mrs. Jackson must have known to come over and ask me if we would allow Priscilla to join the carollers.

Mrs. Jackson was a strange-looking person herself, not witless like her daughter but slightly squint, as if a great wind had blown her a little sideways. This effect was heightened by the way she wore her hair, heavily hennaed, in one of those out-of-date rolls from a side part; it made her head seem lopsided, on a permanent tilt. Besides that, she wore masses of makeup, dark red lipstick and high smears of rouge on her cheekbones; she was always richly redolent of Evening in Paris, the perfume of choice for my generation but somehow shocking to smell on an adult.

When my mother called me to the door and I saw that it was Mrs. Jackson I felt queasy, as if I was going to have to face something awful. And I was right, for as the early evening snowfall lightly settled on her shoulders and weird hair, she stood there speaking to me in a high, plaintive voice. It was not normal to see a grown person supplicant like this and it made me extremely nervous. I wanted her to go away.

"Well, I don't know, Mrs. Jackson, see we have too many

sopranos already and that's the problem. And like we only have three cars promised for driving us around. See, Mrs. Jackson, really we already have too many this year, you know?"

Lies, and she knew it. She made a tight line of her crimson lips and swerved away down the stairs in a silent, elegant gesture of distaste. Standing at the door hunched against the sharp winter air and shivering with unhappiness, I wondered why I had lied and why I didn't run after her now and change my story, tell her yes, of course her daughter could join us.

Because I was chicken, that was why. Scared of what the carolling group would say if I brought Silly—yet most of them knew who she was from watching through the hedge with me when we were small. Who better to bring that poor soul out into the world than the one who'd led those sight-seeing tours for years? But no, I'd be embarrassed.

Oh, what a nasty piece of business I knew myself to be. It was a shock. Until that moment on the porch, I'd had a clear image of myself as a good girl, brave and kind and all the rest of it. Now, when my soul revealed itself, I saw what a mean and hardhearted coward I was.

I stood on the step for a long time looking out into the dark night and falling snow, until my mother came into the front hall to see what was causing the draft throughout the house. "For goodness sakes, Meg, you'll catch your death!" she said. "Standing there with the door wide open! What are you doing? Come along in, shut the door, the whole house is chilled."

My mother was right, I caught a cold, one of those lingering colds that go to the chest and lodge there for weeks. Not only was I unable to go carolling, that whole Christmas season was spoiled by my being sick. I was well enough imbued with both Testaments to know that Heaven itself had visited this punishment upon me and I received it gladly. I had a rotten streak and I deserved to suffer.

During that winter when I was well enough to come downstairs to practise piano, I'd turn away from the window if I saw Silly throwing and catching. I couldn't bear to look at her, she made me feel so bad. Instead, I concentrated all my attention upon the music itself and, by the time spring rolled around, performed so well in the annual Kiwanis music festival I received gold medals in all three categories I entered. Such is life.

That spring Mrs. Jackson and Silly moved away. It had nothing to do with me but there was still a sticky, unpleasant residue of guilt coating my perception of their departure. Which, my mother said, she'd heard from Mrs. Jackson herself, was on account of Mr. Jackson getting back in touch and asking his wife to come join him in St. Mary's near London, where he now owned a service station.

We joked at the dinner table about the prospect of Silly pumping gas, about Mrs. Jackson with her elaborate and outlandish hairdo, dressed in greasy overalls, overhauling cars; we speculated whether the story was really true, whether Mr. Jackson had indeed reappeared. But within no time my family's preoccupation with the Jacksons diminished in proportion to the more immediate concern of getting to know our new neighbours, who cut down the old hedge at the end of their first week in the house. Silly was gone, leaving only the rhythm by which I played my scales.

Years passed and I followed in the footsteps of my brother William, going off to university in London where I majored in music: after my first year I confronted the truth that I didn't have what it takes for a performing career and instead chose courses to prepare for teaching music. There were several psychology courses among my options, which led to a summer job at the provincial mental hospital in London after my third year. Stanley Nichols, an abnormal-psychology professor, with whom I believed myself to be in love, had suggested that I could employ my musical talents in the occupational therapy department. I'd be categorized as a nurse's aide, he said, but I wouldn't work on the wards, I'd spend my time reaching patients with music. I'd give guitar and piano lessons and start a small choral group—he was full of ideas. He was friends with Naomi Loomis, the woman in charge of the program, and said he'd put in a good word for me. More importantly, he implied we'd see each other, since he'd be observing patients at the hospital occasionally during the summer, collecting data for a textbook he was writing.

Indeed, I was hired immediately for a four-month stint after a five-minute interview by the hospital's personnel director, and fitted for a grey uniform that same day. I was to report for duty on the morning shift the first Monday of May, and I'd be given my ward assignment and keys then.

"But I'm not meant to be on the wards," I said to the clerk passing me forms to fill out. "I'll just be doing the music program. I'm going to give piano and guitar lessons. And start a choir."

"Yes, well, that's fine, dear," she said. "But we'll need a little work from you here too."

It's easy to say now that I should have guessed how the summer was going to turn out, but I was thinking of little else those days but Stanley Nichols. I was twenty-one then and he was in his mid-thirties, an ordinary-looking fellow whose ardent nature made him seem wildly attractive. Stanley had not yet taken me to bed ("Not while you're in my course," he said) but the sessions we'd had in his office all spring promised a summer of wonderful lovemaking.

He had made occasional references to a "wife and her babies," who would not be in the city during the holidays; unseen, they had no real existence and I was not diverted by any outmoded Lutheran guilt. Where it all might lead didn't give me a moment's pause; I was obsessed, utterly, by the way he would bite the side of my neck, hard enough to make me yelp, both before and after kissing me.

Lovestruck and dreamy, I arrived at the hospital that first morning and was met by a nurse's aide at the door of the main building, who gave me a name badge to wear on my breast pocket, and a large hoop of keys on a chain I was to fasten immediately to my belt. She said her name was Cathy, and she was taking me to the ward where I'd be starting off, filling in for an absent aide. She had a brisk walk and a sturdy, low-to-the-ground body. There was something cheerfully menial about her, rather like a Shetland pony, I thought.

"You'll get over to O.T. eventually then," she said when I explained why I'd been hired, "but the supervisor says we need you with us for the moment. It'll be a good place to get your feet wet. You know."

I didn't know. I didn't know at all.

We were walking down a long gravel path as she talked; early morning sunlight shot bolts of green light through tall maple and elm trees. The velvety lawns inside the hospital grounds were perfectly cared for, unmarred by so much as an aberrant dandelion; it seemed as if we were strolling through a beautiful park, or the grounds of a private estate. I imagined myself sitting on the grass under these trees, surrounded by patients getting better as I played my guitar. It was a stirring picture, and I felt a sense of calling which took my mind, temporarily, off Stanley's lean cheeks and those fine lines radiating out from his blue eyes. Such visible evidence of his age did nothing to reduce my infatuation, more probably increased it.

"Which building are we going to?" I asked, looking around at several grey-brick possibilities. One of the oldest and largest mental hospitals in the province, it was undergoing major renovation, and near the front gates there were new, open-concept facilities, cheerful red brick with lots of glass. But here, in the centre of the grounds far away from the city street, the tall gloomy buildings among the trees seemed from another century—which, indeed, they were.

"You'll be on Ward Two over there," she said, pointing to the furthest one, the colour of lead, set off by itself as if in punishment. Small barred windows with heavy stone sills increased its sullen appearance. "Everybody calls it the Bin, because it's where the chronics are, you know, who stay forever. Two is mainly geriatric, but you have a few defectives there, and a few real crazies."

She stopped, seeing the horror on my face. "Oh, don't worry. You'll like it. They're mostly lovely old things on Two, really. There's nothing so bad about the Bin, you'll see. I'm on Four, I'll help you settle in. I've been here nearly three years, best job I've ever had."

By this point she was pulling her chain of keys out and unlocking a heavy wooden door which led down to basement level. As we entered the dim stairway, I felt deeply uneasy, nearly nauseous; in a moment I realized it was the smell of the place making me feel sick. Over the summer I grew to know it as well as my own, that peculiar smell which in itself told everything about the Bin—the fraudulent odours of Pine-Sol and Dettol masking the shameful ones of shit and sulphurous farts, and above that the fine high scream of formaldehyde and something else: lavender air freshener and bleach and boiled vegetables. Under it all, the damp stone foundations gave off their low, clammy stench—like kettledrums rumbling beneath the sharp sound of brass.

"Now, watch," said Cathy, "this door is tough. You have to turn the key twice, and then half again. See? You'll get used to it."

"Everything's locked up all the time?" I asked. My voice rose in a querulous curve even as I tried to regain my composure. "I thought, uh, treatment nowadays was kind of, more open."

"Oh, that's only over in the Main," she said, tossing her head, knowledgeable and dismissive. "You wouldn't want to let *these* ones out. Well sure, we take them out for walks, but only a few at a time. No, you'll get used to it, don't worry."

At that ominous "don't worry" I felt ready to turn and run, but it was too late—the next door opened into the ward itself and Cathy took me abruptly by the arm, pulled me forward, slammed the door and got her key in the lock in one smooth continuous gesture. Beside us—instantly—appeared a wild creature, spitting and clawing and butting against Cathy with her head and shoulders.

"Hey there, Ladybug, you raring to go this morning?" Cathy said, with one arm holding the woman's head down at waist level and with the other finishing her business with the key. "Lady wants to get out, and we don't want her to, right?" she said, holding the woman down with both hands, away from her body.

Ladybug struggled, her face contorted, her small dark tongue poking between her lips every time she spat. She had straight black hair falling down in two greasy curtains over the sides of her head, and skin the colour of porridge. Horrid—and human. Cathy took one of the woman's arms and held it behind her back, forcing her to walk ahead; it wasn't done vindictively, but it made clear which of the two was in charge. Whoever has the keys has the power, I thought, instinctively slipping my hand down into the pocket where the metal hoop lay heavily against my thigh. Lesson number one.

As if reading my mind, Cathy let go of Ladybug and turned to me. "Your authority lies in your keys," she said. "Don't forget that. Now the first thing you have to do is come meet Warthog."

Ladybug shuffled off to a chair from where she stared with dull malevolence as I followed Cathy, wondering whether Warthog was a nickname belonging to patient or a nurse. From doorways along the long hall appeared bleak faces observing our progress, old women in white nightgowns calling out and waving to catch our attention. Suddenly we stopped, and Cathy was speaking to me.

"Here now, you shake hands and tell her your name, and be nice and friendly, it cheers her up. This is Gladys. We call her Warthog but it doesn't hurt her feelings, don't worry. She doesn't understand very much," said Cathy, pulling me forward and putting my right hand on the soft old fist of a monster wearing a frayed blue ribbon in her hair, and clutching a rag doll.

I would learn later that the fleshy nodules covering Gladys, like long, hanging warts all over her head and body, were a symptom of Van Recklenhauser's disease. I would learn—within an hour, in the bathing room, where my first job on the ward was to bathe her—that these grotesque disfigurations were in addition to a misshapen spine and such grave circulation problems she'd had one leg amputated at the knee. In a perverse act of kindness, nature had destroyed her brain sufficiently so that her mind was vacant of all but the most immediate desires: her love for the rag doll, its hair of yarn rubbed off on the side she held tightly to her body, and her wish to be lathered with soap. Lathered and lathered.

Now, pushed by Cathy, I said I liked the doll and focusing my attention on it instead of on the toadlike creature herself. "She's a pretty dolly," I said. "Does she have a name?"

"Dolly," said Gladys in a deep, amphibian-sounding voice, a voice which disturbed me at the very centre of myself where curiosity and revulsion spun round in equal measure, where there seemed to be no core of compassion, no anchor of pity or conviction to hold me firm. I felt dizzy, as if the ground had given way, as if I were falling through endless dark space. . . . I hadn't known such ugliness was possible, and I hadn't known how empty my heart would be.

Cathy said we would go meet Quale, and I wondered if this one would look like a plump little bird. Quale, it turned out, was the head nurse on the floor: "Agatha Quale, R.N., here in the Bin since the Year One," she said of herself on introduction. She was a big, garrulous woman with blue-grey hair and eyes, and a very large nose, an intimidating beak of a nose overhanging full and sensuous lips. Her face seemed too full of its features and her voice, when she spoke, sounded too full of saliva; there was spittle at the corner of her mouth after only a few words, and just listening to her I felt myself needing to swallow.

I would get used to that voice, as I would get used to everything. I would even, within weeks, be so fond of old Gladys I could hug her without flinching, could rub the soap under her great flapping breasts so gently she would hum with pleasure; but on that first morning Quale seemed as hideous as any of the other strange beings around me.

By the time I came off the shift at three, I felt as if my skin had absorbed the odours of the place. Even after a shower and great clouds of talcum it seemed my nose was full of the earthy reek of Gladys, and the others—fifty of them in all, crowded into a ward built for thirty. Fifty women who wouldn't know a guitar from a piano from a hedgehog. Or a warthog.

Stanley phoned at six, from his office at the university; he wanted to know how my first day had been. The invisible wife had not yet departed, so he couldn't comply with my plea to come by the apartment I was sharing with my cousin. Either as a result of that disappointment or simply from fatigue, I burst into tears during my gloomy recital and Stanley, no doubt feeling responsible, promised he'd be free by the weekend.

"Keep your spirits up, Meg. I'll make a couple of calls tomorrow to see what the hell's happening because I've talked with Naomi several times about you coming, and I know she's expecting you in O.T. Don't worry, Meg. Think about what you'd like to do on the weekend."

I thought about that—in vivid detail—for the next few days working the morning shift in the Bin. But I also thought how betrayed I felt by Stanley, how no one named Naomi had come to my rescue. If I tried to bring up the topic of music with Quale or any of the other nurses, conversation would lurch into another gear and off we'd go in some different direction; I started to suspect Stanley had no pull here after all—he was just a professor doing research who happened to know a few people—and I wondered whether I *really* found him all that attractive.

That got settled very quickly when he came to see me on Sunday afternoon; my cousin was out for several hours, I said, and we could just stay at my place and have tea, if he liked. Stanley was not obtuse and, after a polite cup of Earl Grey while I complained about my working conditions, the serious biting began.

I had been correct in my assumption that lovemaking with a mature, experienced man would be far more interesting and satisfying than with fellows my age: Stanley made it a long and complicated affair, his entire concern to delay our climax. Just as our bodies would be swelling and rising together like waves ready to break, he would move down the bed where he'd kiss the arch of my foot, or he'd turn me over and nibble my spine slowly and carefully. By the time he ultimately made his way into my body he held my arms down on the bed so tightly there were imprints from his fingers afterwards.

Nor were those the only bruises to show for our passionate afternoon—my neck was ringed with bright red lovebites, as were my buttocks and thighs and breasts. The next day I looked as if I'd come down with some allergy or contagious disease. I was absolutely smitten.

Cathy raised an eyebrow when she saw me in the stairwell a couple of days later, looking pointedly at my neck. But she didn't know me well enough to comment, and I said nothing. Later that day, as I was interviewed by Naomi Loomis, head of the O.T. unit, it seemed to me she was staring in a very cold and aggressive way, as if she knew exactly what had happened and who had done it. A blonde woman of perhaps thirty, she was crisply attractive, explaining without apology that her program was not yet fully under way, and until the piano was tuned properly—the tuner hadn't kept his appointment—there was no point in giving lessons. As for guitar lessons, if I wanted to bring my own instrument I had better understand that it might get badly used.

"We thought we'd have two donated this spring," she said, shrugging slightly, "but as usual, what was promised was never delivered. As for a choral group, we might get something going, let me see, could you come over from Two on Wednesday, for an hour, say? Right after lunch?"

I went back to the ward dejected and angry, feeling trapped in a rotten job I hadn't reckoned on. Besides being physically hard, it seemed oddly degrading—I had never before experienced the disconcerting intimacy of tending another woman's body, wiping her bottom or fastening her Kotex to its elastic belt; I hadn't ever lifted incontinent old women in and out of bathtubs or changed their clothes and the stinking sheets on their beds. Now I had backache from leaning over their chairs to spoon disgusting slop into their mouths; I had pounding headaches from the perpetual bedlam of the ward. I understood little but my own exhaustion and frustration and a deep feeling of futility: I couldn't for the life of me see purpose or design in what any of us were doing there.

The one thing I didn't mind—I admit, I rather enjoyed it—was helping Quale dish out drugs twice a shift. My part in this was counting and recording the number of pills in little paper cups and checking to make sure they were actually swallowed (Mrs. Sneak, for example, was able to gulp while retaining pills in her cheek). During drug-time the ward was calm and happy since most patients lined up submissively for their doses to keep the devils away. The job made me feel so useful I gave no thought to the implications of constant sedation.

Having decided that I was the best summer help she'd ever had, Quale negotiated with personnel and obtained my services until I was due to leave in September. She told me with such glee, patting my cheek so I should feel her genuine pleasure, that I could hardly do anything else but act flattered.

"You're just wonderful, Meg," she said. "You've fitted in

much faster than I expected. Now, I've made arrangements with O.T. for you to drop over there from time to time. I said, this girl is a treasure and I want her on my ward." She smiled at me enthusiastically, a great friendly gargoyle of a woman, the corners of her mouth flecked with white foam.

I reconciled myself, figuring that when it all balanced out, a summer of making love with Stanley a few times a week was going to be a summer well spent. What the hell, I said to myself. Two's not going to kill me. In a few weeks I'd be back in real life, studying music again.

I saw Cathy later that week and told her the news and she didn't look surprised. "You're the type Quale likes, Meg," she said. "Big and strong and sweet-natured." She said she'd show me the rest of the Bin, would take me up to Four where she worked, and to see Six and Eight as well. "They'll send you to help up there eventually so you might as well have a look beforehand."

The other wards were similar to mine; lined up against the dull green walls were wooden restraining chairs in which old women drooped and dozed. Not all of them so old, actually—some were in their twenties or thirties, but severely deformed and mentally defective.

On Eight there were fewer patients and it seemed more peaceful, almost pleasant; on the floors below there was a constant zoo-like noise of nonsense being shouted and screeched. I pointed out this difference to Cathy, saying that maybe working this ward wouldn't be so bad. She laughed.

"Don't let anybody hear you say that," she said, "or you may find yourself here. It's quiet because this is where they keep the catatonics. And it's where the padded cells are, where the real crazies get put when they go round the bend. Ladybug's up here every few weeks, she must be about due.

And," she went on, in that brisk and pony-like way of hers, "this is also where they do electroshock. You'll be asked to come up and help sometimes, we all take turns."

"But I'm not a real aide, I'm only here for the summer," I said, thinking that I had better prepare some arguments in case Quale ordered me up. I didn't want anything to do with so barbaric a practice. In Stanley's course last term we'd had two lectures on shock treatment—he had described the procedure and its effects as "stone age" compared to sophisticated drug therapies now available.

"By destroying memory you destroy the soul," I had written on the margin of my notes, watching his blue eyes seek out mine in the lecture hall as he spoke. He was remembering, I felt sure, the way my breasts had felt in his hands as we'd embraced in his office an hour before.

I turned from Cathy and began looking into rooms where I saw some women rocking back and forth, some standing rigid against the wall and others crouching animal-like in corners. All of them wore the same cotton dresses as the women down on Two, a shapeless garment with a large V-neck so it could be slipped over the head easily. Cathy said if you put any of *us* in one of those sacks for a day it'd make us bats too—still, they must have been more comfortable than our stiff uniforms made by Pollyanna & Co.

As we approached the nursing station where I was to be introduced, Cathy stopped and patted the head of a patient sitting on the floor with her legs straight out in front of her. She had a small, nearly bald head dappled and mottled by tufts of dark hair. "Hey there, Jackson," Cathy said.

To tell the truth, I wouldn't have known her had Cathy not spoken the name Jackson. And even then, it took a few moments to realize who this pitiful soul might be as I looked down at her, propped up against the wall as if she were the Warthog's rag doll. Slowly, my brain registered one detail after another, until it seemed likely that this could be Silly.

"Do you know what Jackson's first name is?" I asked Cathy. "Is it Priscilla?"

"You *know* her?" Cathy said, her little Shetland face one frown of incredulity. "How could you know Jackson?"

"If she is who I think, she lived in the house behind mine most of my life," I said. "We called her Silly. I wonder if it could be her."

"Well, her name's Priscilla all right," Cathy said. "She's been in for a while, she was here when I started. The reason I know her is I helped take her to the infirmary when they did her teeth."

"Teeth?" I had a sudden sharp memory of the prickly hedge around my face as I watched Silly yawning one day in the summer sunshine, seeing those tiny teeth shining white in her bright pink mouth, and the dribble down her face catching the light.

"I guess she's never been as violent as some of them, but after a while she started biting anyone who came close. It was a real hazard if you had to feed her, and of course she wouldn't feed herself."

"Why not?" I asked, looking down at Silly again—her arms and hands looked perfectly capable, although they were pale and limp, as if they'd been kept under water.

"She's catatonic, Meg," Cathy said, in that tone of hers I was growing to hate, the one which implied that while *I* might have the fancy university courses and was here for the summer on my way to better things, she, Cathy, had actual experience and knew what was what.

I was disbelieving. "Silly's never a catatonic, Cathy, her

intelligence is too low for a start. Autistic, maybe, but honestly, I watched her for years, she's not a schizo, I know she's not."

"Maybe she was crazier than you knew," said Cathy, in the same condescending tone. "That's how she's diagnosed and she certainly fits the bill, a zombie for months and then hyper as hell. And when Jackson's hyper, she bites. After a couple of nurses got seriously bitten, I mean, this little lady here drew blood, they pulled her front teeth."

She took my hand, an odd little comforting gesture, as if she thought Silly mattered, as if Silly were family. "Look, it was a lot better than keeping her in restraints or drugging her just to feed her. This way, she's not a danger and she's still got her molars for chewing. There are days she seems pretty bright, as if she's getting better."

"But Silly can't get better," I said, feeling curiously argumentative. "She just is who she is. What's she doing here? Where's her mother? Where's her ball? No wonder she wants to bite people, she belongs at home. How did she get here?"

"Quale knows everything," Cathy said, her voice tight in her throat. "Ask her."

I did bend down to make sure it was Silly—in all the years I'd known her I'd never been this close, had never smelled her breath or touched her dry white skin. There was no hedge between us now, and here she was: leaning against the wall with her gummy mouth partly open, her small black eyes flat and unresponsive.

"And her hair?" I asked. "She used to have the most gorgeous hair. Did they take that off her too?"

"No, she does that herself when she's excited," said Cathy. "Rips it out by the handful. Last year they kept her hands in mitts and it kind of grew in, but as soon as the mitts were off she went at it again. But I'm telling you, Meg, she's one they've given a lot of shock to, and it's working. Her phases are getting shorter and that's a good sign."

Cathy knew so much about everything here, I thought resentfully. It was to be expected, of course, but secretly I felt offended that she actually did know more about poor Silly than I did. Silly had always been mine to show.

I bent over again, and spoke to her, watching closely to see if there was any reaction. "Hi, Silly, it's me, little Meg from next door. Remember?"

Nothing.

Back on Two, I agreed that what Cathy'd said was true; better to be working down here in the thick of it than on Eight where life had trickled to a halt. I stopped and hugged old Gladys Warthog as we passed her chair—not only she, but the entire ward seemed adorable. It occurred to me, as we walked down the long hall to see Quale, that not only was I getting used to the chronics on Two, I liked them. I knew them in ways I'd never known anybody: drying them after their baths, I knew their private flesh, the patchy pubic hair, the saggy labia hanging like earlobes, the wrinkled thighs and buttocks—and somehow this awful intimacy demanded respect and affection. I still didn't see any purpose to keeping them alive, but I'd begun to think that purpose wasn't essential and maybe pure existence was enough in itself. I was beginning to feel differently about drugging them—one day Mrs. Sneak managed her pill trick and she was enormously funny all afternoon, doing a send-up of Quale that had us all, even Quale, howling with laughter.

I described this new turn of mind to Stanley later that week, after we had again made love in an extreme and passionate fashion and were lying naked and exhausted on the floor of my bedroom in a rumple of clothes and sheets. Making love with Stanley was more and more like making war, as if our torsos and limbs were working out some terrible, wordless argument. We had gone on until both of us were glistening with sweat, and then Stanley had licked me all over as if he were a cat, until i was frenzied with longing, thrashing around like a mad thing.

Stanley cautioned me not to get too involved on Two; he said if I allowed personal emotion to cloud my vision, I'd start making judgements without fully understanding what was going on. "You've got to see the Bin for what it is," he said. "It's a garbage heap, Meg. You're lucky you've got Quale as a model. She may be a dinosaur but you can learn a lot from her. There's not an ounce of sentiment in that old dragon."

I told Stanley how upsetting it had been to see Silly again and it turned out he knew her too but, like Cathy, he called her Jackson. "Basically, the study I've been doing the past couple of summers has been comparing the effects of drug therapy and electroshock—that's how I know Quale, since a number of our cases were from her ward to begin with. But we found the appreciable changes in behaviour too minimal to bother with. And the data was totally useless from patients like Jackson. We're only charting females from the Main now."

As I rode the bus to work early the next morning, I felt distressed, rather as I felt during difficult piano sight-reading exams when quarter-notes threatened to wriggle away like tadpoles. I preferred life to be orderly and without discord: I had excelled at playing Bach from the time I was a child. Now, just when it seemed I had come to terms with the Bin, I was getting confused about Stanley.

I despised that cold, clinical tone in which *females* sounded as if they were laboratory animals, and I feared I might not admire him as fully as I had in the beginning. Admiration had always seemed a requisite for love and so I felt confused—I was sure I loved him because I craved him, was always hungry for his body and the sensations it gave mine. I allowed him to try what he called "little experiments" when we were in bed together, and he was endlessly inventive, persuading me to do things I hadn't ever imagined doing. I never knew what to expect, and it made me feel stirred up and anticipatory much of the time.

Silly had been dumped, Quale said. Mrs. Jackson had found one of Mr. Jackson's garage mechanics fondling her and had realized if she kept Silly "out" there was bound to be trouble. Mr. Jackson had urged this course of action, she said. Now the Jacksons had moved to Alberta where they managed a big gas station on the David Thomson Highway. They'd been back to see Silly once but the visit had made her so much worse it'd been decided they shouldn't return. They were probably rich as thieves by now, Quale said, but that doesn't do Silly much good, does it?

"Classic case, the Jacksons," she said. "I've seen hundreds of them. Keep their retards at home for the first twenty or thirty years, and then something happens and they realize the problem they've got on their hands. So they bring them in here, and of course the poor things miss the only people they've ever known, and some go right off like your friend Silly. Now, her case is a little different, Meg. We think maybe that mechanic caught with her wasn't the first one. We think she'd been in a bad state for quite some while. I even wondered about that mother of hers, but that was none of my business, was it? Just as well she's in here, just as well. Don't get yourself worked up, Meg, she's all right."

Predictably, as the summer passed I became stronger, able to heave even the leaden weight of bedridden old Babyshit, whose favorite activity was rubbing excrement in her hair. I was no longer thrown off my stride by Lady's flying tackle when I came in the door, nor fearful of tall, gaunt Griffin, who had once tried to strangle Quale. I had become blithely efficient and tough, and I believed Stanley to be completely wrong: the more I became emotionally involved, the closer I came to accepting the Bin itself. What I couldn't come to terms with was Silly.

I went up to see her every day at the end of my shift— although I knew it was pointless, I felt an obligation to my own memories to try to bring back hers. Silly and her ball were part of who I was, and it would have been unthinkable to pretend otherwise, to act as if she were just anybody. I bought a hard rubber ball, the same kind she'd thrown against the garage wall—but when I placed it in her hand, she let it drop; when I tossed it toward her, she made no movement to catch it; when I threw it against the wall exactly as she used to do, she closed her eyes.

Quale, when she heard from the head nurse on Eight about my regular visits, cautioned me to lower my expectations, adding that the only thing that really worked was shock, no matter what I'd been led to believe "by that Nichols up at the university. I've been here a long time," she said, "and I've seen more Sillies than any of those professors can imagine. And I'm telling you, Meg, that's what does the trick."

Stanley, too, said I should let go of this idea that I could find some key to unlock Silly's memory. "That's a very limited intelligence, Meg, as you yourself recognized. And she's been so zapped I doubt she can remember much. Leave her alone. There are a lot better ways to spend your time. What's happening with the choral group Naomi Loomis scheduled?"

The choral group. Euphemism for a little band of patients from the Main who wanted to believe they were only in some kind of rest home—a restorative facility, as one witty nurse called the place. Strangely, although music had been the reason I'd come to the hospital, I hated that weekly hour in the O.T. unit; it seemed a bogus activity, singing these cheerful old songs and hymns. Like the piano, still untuned, the patients' voices were never in pitch and achieved harmony only by accident. Those who volunteered to sing in the group were supposedly normal people who had suffered "breakdowns" or depressions; they spent time in Naomi's department in hopeful preparation for the outside world.

But they made me feel uncomfortable. It was as if they themselves were off-key, not quite in step—you could tell just by looking at the rancid glitter of their eyes they were drugged to the hilt—and I didn't believe any of them would ever get out. The more they tried to act sane, it seemed, the less sanity was within their reach.

What was sanity anyway? Surely it did not reside in these awful sessions when even a simple alto line was enough to make Tommy, a young depressive ablaze with acne, sob with anxiety. Every attempt at singing harmony ended in sympathetic suffering from the others who knew Tommy's misery as their own. The sound of their wretched voices irritated me so acutely it took great discipline not to run back to Two.

I was beginning to see what kept Quale and Cathy with

the chronics, the ones Stanley laughingly referred to as the Dregs. In the Bin there were no expectations to be crushed; there was only existence, day after day after day.

I saw Stanley from time to time within the grounds, as he'd promised, but there was never an opportunity for intimacy—he was either with his student assistants, or with the senior hospital psychiatrist who was supervising his research. At the university there'd been his office, the shut door against the world and his lips against my skin—but here there was nothing like that. Once he saw me across the lawn as I played my guitar for a small group from Two taken out for some air; he waved but he didn't come over to where I sat with old Gladys clapping her hands.

Another time I was having a smoke in the back stairwell with Cathy when Stanley burst in with a group on their way up to Eight where, under the wings of the hovering psychiatrist, they were to observe that morning's electroshock lineup. He saw me, and put his finger to his lips in a provocative and disclamatory gesture. He was a married man, the secrecy of our affair was of course necessary—but his caution made me feel unclean.

Stanley had never actually said he loved me. He said he found me irresistible, which I had taken to mean the same thing. I thought I must love him—I still thought love and sex were synonymous. He always came to my apartment when my cousin was out and never took me to his home, for which I was glad, supposing that I wouldn't have felt comfortable. I tried to imagine his house, the children's toys scattered around, the wife's perfumes on the dresser, family photographs on the mantel, in order to test myself for guilt. But all that would happen is I'd feel angry at Stanley for being the kind of man who cheated on his wife. The anger increased as the summer wore on but I continued to see him every time he called; I hadn't suspected love could so easily accommodate hostility but I was discovering that no matter how angry or disillusioned I was, sex was still thrilling. In fact, it sometimes seemed my ambivalence made it even better.

The day came when Quale told me to take two patients up to Eight for treatment; my protest was overruled since the ward was understaffed that week. "There's nothing to it," she said. "I think it's about time you saw it's not the torture you imagine. In any case, there's no sensation of pain. You've helped with Sally Thule—well, it's no worse than that. And up there you're all set when the convulsions come, everything's in place. You just hold them down, Meg, same as you've done down here."

Quale was right—handling old Sally, who was prone to epileptic seizures, had been good preparation. And in the electroshock room, everyone knew exactly what to do, even the docile, tranquillized patients who lay quietly on the table while their foreheads were rubbed with vaseline, while electrodes were attached, while their arms and legs were bound down with soft rubber straps, and a rubber baton was fitted in their mouths so that they wouldn't chew their tongues. It was all very humane. And after the current had run through them, and their bodies had jackhammered against the table as if they were having a *grand mal,* and after they'd been lifted back onto a gurney and wheeled down the hall to sleep it off . . . after all that, maybe they'd wake out of their madness or sadness. Eventually. There was as much a chance for this to work as anything else. Maybe Quale was right.

Naomi Loomis had had a brainstorm, she said: the newly formed hospital choral society would travel from ward to ward the last two weeks of August, bringing music to the rest of the hospital. Poor Tommy was not ready for this kind of public exposure, and his fears infected the rest of the choir, who broke out in a rash of psychosomatic complaints which depleted the soprano section. Nevertheless, our little group rallied and after much rehearsal trooped around afternoon after afternoon, singing "Down by the Old Mill Stream" and "Love Me Tender." We were a hit, a social and cultural phenomenon on the nut house circuit. No one had ever seen the like, said Quale.

The day we sang for the Bin was one of those hot, muggy days you get every August in southwestern Ontario, the air too heavy to breathe. My hair hung in limp strands down the back of my neck and as I walked across the grounds with my choir I had the sensation of moving under green water. I felt as if I were drowning and wondered if this is how people like Tommy felt when they were depressed. My body felt steamy and thickened with longing, as if my blood were congealing with sexual need. I wanted, more than anything in the world, the ecstatic release of an hour with Stanley, but I was afraid that he and I were finished. It had been a week since I'd seen him: our last time together had ended badly.

He'd brought soft braided cords with which he wanted to tie me, and as he began winding the silky rope around my wrists I suddenly, and strenuously, objected. It was going to be like being zapped on Eight, I said, struggling in a panic to get my arms free—desperate, determined that he not pin me down. When I did finally slip my hands out of the rope, I began slapping him, and hitting with my fists. It seemed to him to be another of our games, for we often tussled naked, and he was aroused and laughing, until in my agitation I struck him very hard against the side of his head, the crack of my knuckles against his skull making that awful sound of bone on bone. He looked startled, as if he had been torn from a dream, and he backed away, his eyes blinking and tearing from the severity of my blow. I hadn't fought like that since my brother William and I used to wrestle a decade before, and I was shocked by how strong I'd become over the summer. "Oh, I'm sorry, Stanley," I said, and reached out to touch his face but he pulled away and stood up.

I sat on the bed and pulled a sheet over my nakedness and watched him put on his clothes and slip his feet into white canvas tennis shoes. I thought that once he was dressed we would sit together and talk and forgive each other; but instead he gathered up his cords and walked from the apartment wordlessly, as if he suddenly found me tedious. I wanted to explain that I preferred the way we'd been in the beginning, before his "little experiments" became all that there was, but I was too proud to run after him, and as days passed and he didn't call I was too nervous to phone him in case the reason for his absence was the return of his wife. In the end I was powerless, the newfound muscle in my arms counting for nothing. What I wanted—sex—had been taken from me.

My despair did not prevent the choir from being a grand success on Two, where we had a captive audience in every sense. Their chairs arranged in rows at one end of the ward, the women (all but Babyshit) sang along in enthusiastic cacophony. The deep bellowing of Gladys and the wild screeches of Mrs. Sneak vied with Quale's churchy quaver, and Ladybug sang her own brand of gibberish. Four and Six gave us the same happy response, and then we went up to Eight, where my hopes were high for Silly.

She was in her usual spot on the floor near the nursing station, and I instructed the choir to stand directly across from her for our first songs. We began with "Jesus Loves Me" and other childhood hymns I remembered she'd sung in confused fashion on the other side of the hedge. I watched her carefully for any clue that she was listening, but her thin face was immobile, her arms limp against her body. Over the summer her hair had grown in and covered her head, more light-coloured than I remembered. For a fleeting moment I had the crazy hope there'd been a mistake and this wasn't Priscilla Jackson at all.

"C'mon, Silly," I said, crouching beside her, "we need you to help us. What shall we sing?" Behind me, the group had begun their spirited rendition of "She'll Be Comin' Round the Mountain," which usually enticed our audiences to join in. Out of doorways stared curious grey faces, and a few women came hesitantly toward us—but there was no participation. As Cathy had joked, singalongs are not a normal feature of catatonic life. Silly sat like a block of stone.

After a few more songs we moved down the ward to the sun room, where we were given glasses of lemon Kool-Aid and a plate of cookies—a tea party put on by the nurses of the Bin to thank us for our visit. Because this was the final day of the choir's tour, Naomi had arrived to make a small speech about the importance of music and to show her appreciation with several items made by patients in her program (placemats, an ashtray, a belt). I made a speech in reply, but I made it short for I could feel tears welling in my eyes. I was disappointed that the singing hadn't roused Silly and angry at myself for thinking it would—but the tears flowed from a different, bitter source. At the edge of Naomi's pale blue collar four small red welts gleamed on her ivory-coloured skin.

I went back to Eight later in the day after I'd finished my shift, still hoping that the music might have had some effect on Silly. I'd had a cry over Stanley in the back stairwell but it hadn't lasted long; maybe I didn't care as much as I thought I had. Maybe I was even relieved he had moved on although I wasn't quite ready to admit to myself that what I'd felt had never been love at all.

She was in her room sitting on her bed, looking at the wall. Her thick legs hung over the side, her big feet in blue felt hospital slippers swinging gently as if there were a tune in her head, but her face was expressionless, her eyes dark and remote.

"Silly," I said. "Nothing I've done has worked. What should I do? Don't you want to get better? You could go down to Two with Quale if you snapped out of this, you know, and you'd like it down there. Really." I stood by the door, talking on and on, telling her how much it mattered to me that she sing.

"Don't you remember?" I said. "You'd be in your yard singing and I'd be behind the hedge and we'd sing together. Maybe you didn't know it was me but it was. I've known you all my life. And you'd throw your ball against the garage, don't you remember, and I'd be at my house playing the piano, didn't you ever hear me? You must have heard me, you did, didn't you?" I came toward her, fraught with the need to make her remember, to bring our shared past into the present, to make this summer mean something. There had to be some reason I had come to this place—it didn't seem possible our paths should cross without there being some meaning.

In one swift movement Silly flung herself off the bed and against me, pushing me towards the door. Although she was smaller, surprise gave force to her weight and I was knocked back awkwardly, unable to prevent her falling on top of me.

That is all that happened, nothing else—she simply rose up and fell against me, and as we toppled to the floor I cried out loudly, calling for help.

The head nurse and another aide came running, and within seconds the event was over—for me, a glass of water and comforting from the staff: for Silly, the confines of a white cotton straitjacket, sleeves pulled around her body and tied tightly. She was sedated and placed in a confinement room where I looked in on her before I left the ward. I had explained that she hadn't hurt me at all, but with her old history of biting, the head nurse said they couldn't be too careful. There she was, on the floor slumped against the wall, but her eyes were like two small shining coals, and her mouth was moving ever so slightly, as if she were singing to herself.

Quale told me not to go back up on Eight for the duration of my last week, and in an uncommonly harsh tone said she meant it. "You stop this business before you get hurt, Meg. Look what you've accomplished by wanting Jackson to sing or bounce a ball or whatever it was you wanted. Nothing!"

In fact, according to Cathy, who made a point of checking for me each day, what I'd done was disturb poor Silly sufficiently that once out of the straitjacket she'd begun pulling her hair again, singing nonsense as she did so. The doctors decided to try another series of electroshock to see if that would bring her round, and by the time I left the hospital the treatments had begun. Cathy said it was making her calmer, and that I shouldn't be upset.

"Look," she said, in her brisk and sensible way, "be glad you're okay, it could have been worse, it could have been like Griffin trying to strangle Quale. It's just too bad it had to happen when everything else has gone so well."

She said she'd miss me and gave me her phone number so we could get together, maybe go to a movie—something we'd never done during the summer and I felt sure never would. But from time to time during the next months, until I left London the following spring, I'd call to say hello and ask how things were going, what news she had of Quale and her ladies down on Two. For some inexplicable reason I couldn't bring myself to take the bus out to see for myself, couldn't bear the thought of smelling that place again. I told myself it was the smell. I told myself I would go back someday, I knew I ought to—but I couldn't face it quite yet.

Less baffling was my decision to take no psychology courses in my final year, in order to avoid seeing Stanley Nichols, who, another student had divulged in September over a chummy beer, wasn't married at all. "That's just one of his sick routines," she said, grinning, and made the motion of tying her wrists together above her head. "Sex maniac," she said, stretching her body in a long, lazy slide, as if she were remembering the feeling of his tongue on her legs. I felt better about having hit him so hard.

Cathy would always, without being asked, tell me that Silly was much better. "I took up that ball you left," she said when I called in November. "I threw it to her and she caught it, Meg, and now they let her bounce it in the sun room whenever she feels like it. You did her a great favor, don't forget that, coming into the Bin the way you did—oh, but old Warthog's the one who misses you. She really does. She calls her doll Meggie now, did I tell you? You should come visit her someday—Quale would be thrilled if you turned up, you know, everybody on Two misses you. And maybe we'd go up and see Silly as well. They couldn't stop you, Meg."

I didn't entirely believe Cathy's stories of Silly's improvement, but I thought it was good of her to tell them, trying to make me feel as if I'd done some good, as if there'd been some purpose to my coming into Silly's life again. Cathy, I slowly discerned, was more sensitive than I'd given her credit for being, she understood everything, she knew the right things to say. I felt sorry I'd never really returned her friendship—I'd been too obsessed by Stanley for one thing —but it seemed too late now to do anything.

She had come with me one afternoon to Naomi's department, and had listened to me trying to play a prelude and fugue on the old piano that never got tuned. We'd both laughed, because it really did sound awful, enough to make Bach turn over in his grave, but I had to play the whole thing out once I'd started. You have an obligation to the music, I'd explained, you can't stop a fugue in midair. And she'd said, "That's like how you describe the way Jackson used to bounce her ball against the wall, all that throwing and catching she couldn't stop."

"Right," I said, secretly amazed that I'd never thought of that before. "That's exactly right."

SKIN THE COLOUR
OF MONEY

The first time, you feel a little awkward and self-conscious, horribly aware of not only your pale skin but your fine clothes, your watch, and the gold bangle you forgot to take off before coming here. You feel unjustly assessed by the eyes watching you from every corner, you want to stop and explain: "Look, I'm not as rich as you think I am." But here inside the walled market of Kariokor no matter what you do or say, you look like just one thing. You stick out like a sore thumb. A white thumb, more precisely. You seldom see people your colour inside these walls.

You come here on this first visit with another *mzungu* woman who is showing you where to buy decorated gourds for half the price you would pay downtown at the African Heritage shop. The young man who incises the gourds is called Boniface; he has a small stall in which he sits on a low stool so he is looking up at you, his face tilted at a humble angle in order to answer your questions. Even as he talks—he speaks English very well—he works steadily, unswervingly, his sharp tools cutting precise and delicate lines into the hard brown skin of the calabash. He is maybe twenty-six, at most thirty, and you would like to ask him something about his life, how he got here, where he learned his trade, how he bears the cramped quarters where he works. But the woman who brought you here has warned against too much conversation. To be overtly friendly is to invite confidences of the sort which end in requests for money to pay for children's schooling, a mother's medical bills, a brother's bail . . . the less you know about them, she says, the less they can ask of you.

She really is not a hard woman, your friend Bertha. The opposite, rather. She's one of the few compatible women you have found in Nairobi, with a warmth and humour you have come to depend on. But sometimes she says things like this that *sound* shockingly hard and cruel. Because, as she often explains, she knows more than you do. She has lived in Africa for fifteen years—west, south, and now east—and her experience has consolidated itself into attitudes you can see she is trying to pass on, to save you from making the same mistakes she once did.

It is simply a matter of not letting yourself be used, according to Bertha. You must never forget for a moment that people will try to use you for their own ends, as a way of meeting their own needs. Within that framework, you can still communicate, give and take and learn from each other . . . but you must remember: There is only one thing black Africans see when they look at you. They see your skin, and your skin is the colour of money.

"Even the Kenyans who have doctorates from Oxford or

Harvard or McGill," she says. "You have to remember that. Of course they know better, of course they know that not all whites are rich. They've seen the slums in Boston, they still subscribe to *The Guardian Weekly* and they know the world as well as you do, probably better. But they see you in *this* context, and here you mean one of two things. Either you are a taker or a giver. And they took back their country from the takers a generation ago. Which means there's only one category left, honey!" Bertha laughs as she says this. She laughs whenever she is making outrageous statements which she means you to take very seriously. Her laughter seems to be a signal to pay attention.

Boniface is showing you an extremely large gourd on which he has carved three different pictures, each one framed by traditional designs of leaves and flowers. Almost the entire surface of the gourd—probably over a metre in circumference—is covered with markings made by his knife, and has been polished over and over again so that it shines with a deep ruddy glow. The three pictures are representations of African animals mating: a male rhino humping a weary-looking female, a wild-maned lion roaring in ejaculatory ecstasy over his spouse's supine shape, and two zebras caught by Boniface's knife *in flagrante delicto*. It is so clearly and exactly what the tourist trade demands that there is something astonishingly likable about the gourd. It is what it is, something to sell to someone who will take it away as a souvenir. This gourd will never be used as it might have been in days gone by as a container for milk or water; it is simply an object made with one thing in mind—to obtain money from someone with skin the colour of yours. "Do you think for one minute an African would buy such a thing?" asks Bertha. "And set it on a shelf and fill it with dried flowers? Don't be daft!"

You think of your housekeeper Florence the day you and

Larry came home from Kisumu with a carload of clay pots. You had gone crazy over them in the market there, made light-headed by the heavy, damp heat of Lake Victoria and a little dizzy from the rich odour of decaying garbage and jostling people. You were astounded by the pots, the incredible number of them—pots of every sort and size, so simply made and so . . . yes, what you thought was, so primitive. You were quite moved by that aspect. You stroked the round sides of rough soot-blackened henna-brown pots and went on and on about the purity of their line, the uneven texture and lack of uniformity, the innocence inherent in designs unchanged over ages, naive and wise at the same time. You even quoted William Blake.

You could have bought them for much less money if you hadn't gone into such raptures, but once you'd let the hawker see your enthusiasm for the pots the price went directly and proportionally skywards. No matter. Cheap at half the price. And that was a long time ago, last year in fact, before you'd learned to keep a straight face in the markets, to fake indifference while making a deal.

You bought seventeen pots in all, some of them for planting ferns and ivy along the wall of the house, some for decoration (actually, they're so badly fired you cannot use the casserole in the oven without it cracking or make tea in the teapot without it leaking, so much for primitive . . . but they do look wonderful on the dining room sideboard) and some to use as vases for (yes, admit it) bouquets of dried flowers. When you arrived home after the long drive across the country, Florence met you at the door, ready to assist with the carrying in of luggage. You began unloading the pots from the car and her face was a study in amazement and disgust, but she helped you bring them inside without a word. When she set down her final load inside the living room, she stood up straight and adjusted her headscarf and her apron, movements you have come to know precede a righteous speech. Florence is a feisty Kikuyu, fearless in expressing her opinions.

"This big pot for making beer," she said. "All these other for cooking over the fire. What you want with these pots?" You see her expression and imagine she thinks she is going to have to prepare the evening meal in one of them, and that would be the last straw. She'd hand in her notice in a second if she couldn't use your Calphalon or Crueset. One of the joys of Florence's life has been the high-quality kitchenware you brought with you from Toronto. Better, she says, than what you find in the Asian shops in town—which is not exactly true but you cannot persuade her to think differently about anything concerning Asian merchants whom she hates ardently, and you no longer try.

"Oh heavens, Florence, I don't mean to use them for cooking," you said, laughing so she could understand there was nothing to worry about. "We just bought them because they're so beautiful."

She looked at you with disbelief, rolling her eyes to one side, the way she always does to indicate her total rejection of whatever you have proposed, and then coughed a little, low in her throat. "These not beautiful," she said. "These cooking pots. Beautiful is this"—she pointed to a ceramic lamp base—"or this." Again, her finger stretched out to indicate something else of real worth; a pewter figure of Merlin holding a crystal ball. Florence has worked in Nairobi houses long enough to know without question that beautiful and valuable mean the same thing.

You tried right then, at that very moment, to have a discussion about aesthetics, and for several minutes you felt as if you were making headway, as if you were getting through. You explained how beauty is in the eye of the beholder, and how for someone like you, the pots from Kisumu are a new way of looking at the world. You see all of Africa in these pots.

"I look at these pots and I see stirring and smoke and cooking *irio,*" said Florence, aggressive and suspicious at the same time. "No beauty, just work. Burnt food over the fire, another pot broken from the flame. Work and trouble."

"We see things differently, you and I, Florence," you said brightly, trying to smooth over and put a nice face on things. Trying to eradicate the antagonism you felt radiating from her. You wondered why she was so put out at you for buying these pots. Maybe because you're in a life which doesn't need them, you realized with a guilty shock, suddenly feeling your point of reference shift and alter. Maybe because you have the exquisite privilege of looking, simply looking at them. Yes, that would make you mad, too. But it seemed too elaborate an idea to get into with Florence and so you let it go.

They sell clay pots here in Kariokor, and charcoal-burning *jiko* stoves, and brooms and baskets and plastic buckets, and sandals made from old rubber tires, and a host of other things all meant to be used and used and used again. Used by Africans, that is. Boniface's decorated gourds are definitely an exception in this marketplace—everything else made or sold here has a practical reason for being. Even the sisal bags called *ciondos,* woven by women sitting on the ground outside the market walls; even these things now made for the tourist or overseas market are meant to be used—they were used initially by African women and still are. The last decade has seen their traditional patterns in brown and ochre mutate to brilliant fuchsia and turquoise and scarlet, better for catching the eye of foreign buyers.

The production of *ciondos* is divided between the sexes at Kariokor, a careful marriage of mutual labour and benefit.

After the women have finished their weaving, the baskets are brought inside the walls where young men attach leather straps. There's a stall next to Boniface's where several of them work from dawn to dusk, listening to taped music as they secure leather strips to the woven bags or sew zippers across the openings. Like the bright colours, zippers signify a changing world. So much theft on the streets of Nairobi, the streets of New York and London and the world . . . zippers are crucial now for tourist sales. Without a zipper, a *ciondo* sells for half the price. Zippers mean profit.

The day that Bertha brings you here, you tell Boniface you would like to buy one of his gourds, perhaps the very large one. And you ask, as she has instructed you, what is the best price he can give you since you cannot possibly pay the amount on the sticker attached to the neck of the gourd. He smiles and says you should tell him your price, and then the two of you will come together to find a middle way. You suggest something less than half the sticker sum—this is what Bertha has told you to do—and he shrugs. Then, looking up at you from his stool, he says loudly so that everyone around can hear, "What do you take me for, a fool?"

Bertha is as startled as you are by the sharp edge of his voice. You had only meant to initiate the bargaining process as is always done, you had certainly not meant to insult him. Bertha raises her eyebrows at you and you understand you are now to suggest another, larger figure. You do this and Boniface laughs, slapping his knee with delight. He sees he has the upper hand and that you are a little worried, even a little frightened of upsetting him. Of doing the wrong thing.

And yes, you are also aware of the eyes and ears of all those young men in the *ciondo* stall next door, who have been openly laughing at this last interchange. You are anxious about what they will think of a white woman haggling over coins she can well afford to spend. You are lost, you do not know which moves to make to restore your dignity. Which moves are yours, which moves are theirs? How is one ever, ever to know? You let Bertha take over for you and she, with skill and gentle persuasion, buys the shining gourd for you at half its sticker price.

You have come a long way since that first session with Boniface. Months have passed and now you visit frequently, bringing him new customers just as Bertha (who has moved to Geneva where her husband has finally got a top-level job no longer "in the field") once brought you. He greets you always with that special African handshake in which you twist your hands three times, and he calls you *"rafiki yangu,"* Kiswahili for "my friend." You know he also calls you "mzungu yangu" (my white person) to the leather workers next to him. And you thought you heard them call you *"memsahib shillingi"* one day. Mrs. Money.

Mrs. White Person with skin the colour of Boniface's hopes and dreams. If only he could make enough money, he could stop this business and then . . . and then, what? You buy as much from him as you can and you sit on the stool beside him and smile your friendliest smile for, really, what else is there to do? You cannot help who you are, and nor can he.

"Na wewe ni rafiki yangu pia," you say to Boniface as you settle your pleated cotton skirt around you, proud of your bits of Kiswahili in which you say he is also *your* friend. Proud of how accepted you feel by him, and by the leather workers next door. Without Bertha to chide you for such naiveté, you have made great strides with Boniface—and he has not ever asked you for help the way she'd said he would. Today you are not here to visit him but you will sit and make conversation for a little while, inquire about his work, refuse the offer of a soda, and then move on. Today you have come,

as you do regularly now, to visit his grandmother, old Mercy.

She is well over ninety, wizened and perfectly shrunk down to essence of woman, a tiny dark brown crone missing her top row of teeth but none of her wits. Sharp and quick and still able to sing celebration songs from her Machakos girlhood, she is losing her sight now, slowly—one of her old eyes is clouded over with skim-milk blue but the other is still glittering jet-black. Some days she seems to see perfectly, and other times, when it suits her to, she acts as if she is blind, touching your face and stroking your arm with her thin dry fingers; they feel like whispers on your skin.

Since the day he called her over to come and shake your hand, you and this ancient Kamba woman have formed an attachment. It's the oddest thing that's ever happened to you and you can't explain it, nor do you often try to. You just let yourself feel affection and openly accept hers back—for she does seem genuinely fond of you, and calls you her "young girl." You call her Mzee Mercy, having learned in Kiswahili class that the prefix Mzee before the names of elderly people shows respect. The old man who ruled this country long before you arrived was eventually known only as Mzee, and he gave the word a status it still carries. In this culture, being old is not a negative attribute the way it seems to be back home. For one thing, here it means you've survived.

It was on your third visit, the day you first came to Kariokor alone, that Boniface called Mercy over from where she was sitting in a group of women drinking *chai* together and talking. "Here, *memsahib,* this is my own grandmother," he said, pushing the old lady's shoulder a little so that she'd move toward you. "She is more old than anyone in this place and she knows many things. She cannot speak English or Kiswahili, but if you wish to talk with her, I can tell her what you say."

You shook her hand and told her how honoured you were

to meet such an old person and then you couldn't think of anything else to say. You stood there speechless, staring at her shabby dress and ragged headscarf, noticing the way she was "dressed up" with a necklace of pink plastic poppets and a rhinestone brooch. But you were unprepared for conversation and it made you feel lacking, as if you were letting your side down. (What to say, what to call across the great divide of age and race? What to offer, what to ask?)

You wished Bertha was with you, she'd know what to do, she wouldn't be standing here paralyzed by cultural incompetence. You felt your cheeks and neck flush with the awful certainty that Boniface was waiting for you to make some move and you couldn't imagine what you were meant to do. You knew you were red with embarrassment, as pink-faced as a mortified child would be—you could feel the dark splotches of heat rising under your skin and even your ears seemed to be burning. As you looked over at Boniface to see if he might give you a clue, you heard the old woman saying something to him, and begin to laugh. Boniface started laughing too and his loud "haw-haw-haw" was picked up by the strap-boys next door and the women who'd been sitting with Mercy. All around you the sound of laughter, African-sounding laughter you did not understand, but you knew it was because in some way you had made a fool of yourself.

"Oh, do not look so sad, *memsahib*," said Boniface, finally able to contain himself. "It is a very funny thing my own grandmother has said. She has looked at your face and has wondered if you are trying to change your colour." He had to stop there to catch his breath before going on with more laughter, more slapping of his leg while urging everyone around to join in this grand joke. A *mzungu* turning from white to red. What next? Maroon? Copper? Mahogany? Chocolate? Coal?

Beside you, the old woman's shoulders were shaking with laughter, and she hopped up and down in a little dance on the spot, perfectly delighted by the merriment she had caused. She reached over and took your hand and laid it against her face and said something else which Boniface did not translate for you but you sensed it meant that she wished you no harm; her wrinkled skin, hardened into ridges and folds, felt oddly pliable and tender beneath your fingers.

You left that day as soon as you could gracefully make an exit, and did not return for nearly a month; but when you came back (you had to buy a going-away gift for someone in Larry's office and one of Boniface's gourds was ideal) she was seated on a stool beside her grandson, and welcomed you with great enthusiasm, as if she'd been waiting for your return.

In fact, since then, you come to see her, not Boniface. It amuses Larry—he loves telling people this—that although you feel ill-suited to the East African Women's League, and you will not put your name on the waiting list for the Muthaiga Club, you seem to have formed an alliance with the Old Ladies of Kariokor. "An exclusive little group," he teases.

You have learned, over time, not to make any special effort other than bringing the occasional gift for Mercy: a cardigan you don't need, a silky headscarf, a necklace of imitation pearls, sometimes a bit of cake or soft cheese. What she gives you back are her old songs, none of which you understand without translation by Boniface, whom you suspect of dramatic elaboration—according to him, all her songs feature copulating lions. When Mercy sings, it is easy to think of copulation. She waggles her thin old hips and tosses her narrow shoulders and her milky eye seems to look far back into her head, far back into the Africa you can never, never know. Her good eye glitters at you, daring you to try.

She is happy singing these songs, you think. No one but

you ever seems to sit and listen to her, and it occurs to you
that maybe she is one of those boring types who go on and
on, and that Boniface is using you to get his grandmother off
his back. Perhaps, but you don't care. You feel very peaceful
here, sitting on a stool sipping orange soda and listening to
Mercy's quavering voice gather strength and become a pierc-
ing wail threading its way along the stalls, pulling all of
Kariokor together.

In order to get to Boniface's stall you must enter by the
doorway where women are selling honey in clear glass bottles
placed out on the ground in bee-beset rows. As soon as you
are inside the market walls there is a heavy and overpowering
sweetness in the air, but it is only a passing sensation; for as
soon as you pass the honey-ladies there are other, far stronger
odours. Sharp, sour, acrid. The smell of rubber tires being
sliced, the bright, woody aroma of sisal, the sweaty stench of
leather, the complicated richness of rotting fruit . . . and over
it all and through it all smoke and burning meat and the salty,
green reek of people and urine and labour. You know how
work smells now, you told Larry after one of your early visits;
it doesn't smell like his office in the United Nations compound
one bit.

In the beginning, you wore strong perfumes before coming
here, as a kind of olfactory shield—it was a bit of a joke,
the way you'd spray on Opium before going to Kariokor.
Now, you no longer bother. It's not that you don't notice
the way the place smells; you like it. You like having your
nose assaulted, your senses beat upon. You believe, even
knowing it can't be true, that here in the market with Mercy
you are part of Africa.

Whenever you think this (you don't say it aloud, not even
to Larry) you wonder what comeuppance will be yours. This
is dangerous pride, this feeling as if you belong. Hubris, asking

for trouble. One of the last pieces of advice Bertha gave you before she left for Geneva was this: "Don't fool yourself," she said, in a voice resonating with concern and foreboding. "You can never be one of them and don't forget it."

This afternoon in the kitchen, like a dim and distant echo, you heard Bertha's voice underneath Florence's. She was standing at the sink, wiping her hands on her apron and glaring at you, angry and not afraid to let you know. She discovered you wrapping up an almond cake she had baked this morning and when she said, "What you doing, Madam?" you tried, too quickly, to explain about the little treats you take Mercy. You only succeeded in enraging Florence, who had baked it especially for Larry, and who considers the Akamba people deeply inferior to her own.

"You take this food I make to some old Kamba?" she asked, her voice sharp as scissors. "You think it not good enough to eat?"

"Oh no, Florence," you began, wanting her to understand, her of all people, how wonderful it is for you at Kariokor, sitting with the old lady and listening to her songs. But you saw her face and you knew it was impossible and that language would fail you if you tried. And so you set the cake firmly on the counter beside Florence and walked from the kitchen.

You decided on the way to the market you'd simply have to be careful from now on about taking things to Mercy, you don't want Florence upset and resentful. You can just as easily buy little cakes from the bakery. Or maybe, you think, you should just give her some shillings, and then she could buy what she needed. Yes, that would no doubt be better. But you must be careful not to insult the old lady with cold cash replacing your usual personal gifts. You will sit with Boniface a while, and ask him what he thinks of the idea.

IN TRAINING

O ur mothers had been in training together—that's how they always put it, when what they meant was that they'd studied nursing at the same hospital—and had formed such a strong bond they'd become as close as sisters, perhaps closer. For years I believed Sophie was another of my cousins, and it came as a great relief to discover, around the age of eight, that I called her mother Aunt Mary as a convention, not as familial requirement. I really wouldn't have minded being related to Aunt Mary, nor to Uncle Ralph whom I adored, whose rich tobaccoey aura lingered in the nose long after we'd been visiting. But Sophie I just couldn't stand.

From our earliest encounters she made me frantic with her soft and puddingish way of moving and talking, her passive and indecisive personality. The first time I called her Sofa it was purely from the childish joy one finds in words which sound like other words; but as we grew up, I called her Sofa to tease her into tearful rages, to see if I could really make her mad. It was true, she *was* like a small, overstuffed, and lumpy sofa, with odd, sharp bits of things stuck down behind the cushions. The grown-ups were forever speaking of what a lovely child Sophie was, so sweet, so placid; but I knew she cheated at cards and was capable of hard, brutal pinches to my arms when no one was looking. I knew I drove her to it, but somehow that just made her more culpable in my eyes.

I was as different from Sophie as "chalk from cheese"— our mothers had used that expression about us for as long as I could remember, and I was vexed by it, since both chalk and cheese have a blandness that was Sophie's and not true of me at all. I was, in my own mind at least, tough and brittle and thorny; "a wiry little thing" Uncle Ralph once called me, in what seemed a wistful voice, as if he wished his daughters were more like me. Or so I imagined.

Fortunately for Sophie and me, we didn't have to see each other often since we lived a good seven hours apart. Still, our mothers arranged as many visits as possible—wedding anniversaries, Christmas holidays, Thanksgiving weekends— and we were also forced to spend weeks together every summer (until we reached the age when we went off to camp) because our mothers wanted us to be *friends* as they were. Our mothers were always ecstatic in each other's presence, hugging and kissing, laughing merrily at things that weren't funny to anyone else. My mother's name was Betty, and Aunt Mary used to say it over and over again, with a syncopated rhythm, whenever they first saw each other again: "Betty, Betty, Betty, Betty, Betty!" We children (I had a younger brother, Gary, and Sophie had two younger sisters, Lizzie and Judith) generally ignored them and went off on our own, knowing we were peripheral to their happiness and not minding at all.

Our fathers got along well enough to make conversation on their own without the wives present, but it was clear they'd never have chosen to sit in living rooms together if they'd had any say. My father, called by Sophie and her sisters Uncle Evan, was a high school teacher, geography and physical education; Uncle Ralph was an editor on the *Free Press,* which meant we usually went to their house rather than they to ours, since it was more likely that my father would have weekends or holidays free. Uncle Ralph was not above mentioning a relevant detail such as long vacations if the conversation moved round to teachers' low salaries (as it often did), but it was understood by us all that Uncle Ralph was argumentative on principle, and enjoyed his reputation for being abrasive and cantankerous. He always had the air of being on the brink of some disaster, or worse, of missing some disaster. Later in life I would learn this is a common affectation among journalists; but at that point, Uncle Ralph's headline-chasing style seemed authentic and generated an appealing excitement. He treated each day as a new venture, and when it was over, and the paper was out, he would pour Scotch whisky in a cut-crystal glass and collapse in a maroon leather armchair, a man who had yet again met a deadline, and won. He would sit there and smoke cigars as he held forth on that day's news, blowing marvellous smoke rings if we children were watching.

Uncle Ralph had greying fair hair, and the same pale skin and pale blue eyes which so offended me in Sophie. He had a thick yellowish-grey moustache which did not entirely disguise the peculiar cast of his face, that startled look of the hare-lipped. The disfigurement was slight and his speech im-

pairment minor, noticeable only in a muffled nasal tone and
now and again in his pronunciation.

I felt sorry for him, not being perfectly made, and wondered
if he ever felt sorry for himself under that brusque, busy way
he had. He was always ordering his family around, in much
the same way he must have done reporters in the newsroom,
and when Gary and I were there we were treated exactly the
same way. No quarter given, no feelings spared. "Get me a
clean ashtray!" he'd bark, and we'd all rush off, anxious to
please, because in his gruffness there were also fine traces of
affection and humour.

In the living room stood a low oak lectern upon which
lay open an enormous dictionary. Every day before breakfast
Uncle Ralph would turn a page so that a new selection of
words was exposed to the air. Then at the evening meal he
would quiz us, bearing down on whichever unfortunate child
happened to warrant his attention, asking the spelling and
the meaning of one of the words on the open pages. It created
a constant tension in the house, a unifying pressure and worry
among us as we would hurriedly scan the pages at the end
of the afternoon, trying to figure out which obscure and
difficult word he would choose. There was no way of knowing, and Sophie, Lizzie, and Judith had long ago accustomed
themselves to failing; but I always felt compelled to try very
hard, and so I was often lucky. Victory was sweet, for it
meant Uncle Ralph noting my triumph with great ceremony,
using his fountain pen to write my initial beside the learned
word: eponymous, Quadragesima, umbrageous, deterration,
shibboleth.

Sophie and I had been born three months apart and the
year we turned ten our mothers decided to hold a joint
birthday party on the middle weekend between the two birth-
days, which fell at the end of September. We drove from our

house to theirs on the Friday evening, Gary puking as usual every few miles into a paper bag beside me on the back seat. I was convinced he did this on purpose as a demonstration of how much he hated going to Sophie's house; there were only girls to play with there, he'd whine, and my father would chuckle and say some day he wouldn't mind that so much. I think my mother simply didn't hear his protests; she'd already be smiling to herself, anticipating the hours of talk ahead, seeing in her mind's eye Mary out on the front steps, welcoming us in. Standing there in the porch light, her plump face shining with love, she'd open her arms wide, as if to encompass and soothe us, tired and cranky as we'd be after our long journey.

On the Saturday evening Aunt Mary and my mother prepared as festive a celebration as they ever had, decorating the dining room with yellow and white chrysanthemums on the table and the sideboard, and Aunt Mary brought out her white damask tablecloth and the crystal and china and silver we usually only saw on very special occasions. Sophie and I were both given wine glasses for our ice water while the younger ones had the usual striped tumblers; and there were ribbons tied round our chairs with enormous bows fastened to small cards on which 10 was painted in gold. Since I had already had my birthday I tried to achieve a casual nonchalance about all the fuss but it was no use—this was wonderful.

Sophie and I (both of us resenting, privately, the sharing of the event) scrubbed ourselves until we glowed and dusted ourselves with Aunt Mary's talcum before putting on our best dresses, since Uncle Ralph had said we were to look good for the photographs he'd take. By late afternoon our mothers were deliriously busy in the kitchen, getting things ready and sipping sherry out of translucent teacups. They were slicing cabbage for coleslaw and stirring the gravy and bumping into each other every few minutes in the long narrow space of Aunt Mary's kitchen. You could feel their enjoyment and their sense of a remembered past, the remembering of our births. Sophie and I crept down the back stairs that came out into the kitchen and sat there listening to them, whispering back and forth ourselves about babies coming out.

Although our mothers were not what you might call "modern" in their views, they *had* both trained as nurses and that gave them a certain no-nonsense stance about all things concerning the body. Between us, Sophie and I believed we knew just about everything there was to know; certainly we knew more than any of our friends did. My mother had always insisted that we call parts and functions by their correct names, and there were no cute words in our household for vulvas, bowel movements, or breasts.

"That is not your dickie, it is your penis," she instructed my brother when he came home from kindergarten with a new word. "And this is your scrotum, in which your testicles are housed." *Housed,* I would muse. A soft little wrinkled house where two small nut-like things hung mute and blind, unable to see out. The penis had the window, I supposed. My whole body, then, was a house in which my uterus dwelled, ready to house a baby someday. We were all little houses of one sort or another.

When our parents were together, we would hear them telling jokes in low voices which always rose in uproarious laughter, Aunt Mary getting hiccups more often than not, gasping for breath. It seemed as if the jokes were just too much for her, although she was often the one telling them —and the words were often the very ones we were forbidden to use. "Medical humour" my father called it.

"You two are as dirty-minded and as foul-mouthed as a football team," he'd say, but in a jolly, appreciative way. I think he liked the rawness of my mother when she was with Mary; there was a bawdiness, a delicious earthiness that was absent ordinarily. On the way back home, they'd be sitting in the front seat in the dark, talking over the weekend.

"Honestly, Betty, the one about the orderly and catheter, I always think 'Oh lord, if I hear her tell that one more time' . . . and then she does, and it's still funny!" And he'd laugh, a reminiscent kind of chortle, and my mother would lean her shoulder against his and look back to see if Gary and I were really asleep. And if she thought we were, she'd laugh too, a throaty, husky sound that made the car seem like a shell. The four of us, encased by her laughter, safe against the outside night. I'd lie there, cuddled up against Gary (who never threw up on the way home), wondering exactly what the joke was about. And what the secrets were that couldn't be shared with children.

With all the explicit naming of parts came a moral attitude which seemed to have permeated our mothers' nursing experience. God was omnipresent in all discussions about the body and its purpose, and we were given stringent sets of rules, and a sense of deep personal responsibility. Rule: "You must never let anyone touch you there and you must never touch yourself." It seemed as if they gave us information only to stifle our curiosity about sex, to quell our natural nosiness and inventiveness; had they really forgotten what it was like to be us?

With all the facts precisely in mind, there was still the mystery. What did it mean that we had squirmed our way out of their bodies ten years ago? Of course we didn't ask the question in exactly that way—sitting in the twilight of the stairway in a rare moment of companionable complicity, Sophie and I merely collected our thoughts. "Imagine," we said. "Imagine." And we imagined badly, and without knowing which side of the image we were on; as babies, we had no memories, and as females, we did not yet know about the blood and the pain. That part had still been kept from us.

I liked Sophie at moments like this because there was a feeling of being in the same life together which there never was with Gary, who was four years younger and not given to speculation about anything more interesting than whether I thought our parents had hidden the Christmas presents behind the furnace again this year. Sophie was the same age and as bright as I was, although her talents lay in other directions from mine; she could play the piano and was good at drawing and painting, the sorts of things that drew high parental praise. All I ever wanted to do was to sit and read. My mother would throw up her hands sometimes during these visits and say, "Honestly, Ralph, she should have been yours. She looks like Evan but I swear to God she'd rather read than eat."

Although with my dark curly hair and narrow, freckled face I was the picture of my father, I did feel much more akin to Sophie's. I liked his crabbiness, I liked the way he smelled. And the way he would pat my head approvingly when he found me reading, and would argue with my mother when she'd say I was an antisocial introvert. Often when we were visiting I'd curl up in the living room with a book after supper; Sophie would be playing the piano and showing off for my parents, or else organizing the younger ones to put on a play, dressing up in boring costumes just to get attention. I would sit as quietly as I could and hope my mother wouldn't urge me to join the others. And if I looked up and caught Uncle Ralph's eye he would smile his rabbity smile and I would know he was on my side.

The night of the birthday party: children spilling things on the good tablecloth and Aunt Mary not getting cross because it was, after all, a special occasion; the fathers at each end of the table trying to keep order; Sophie and I in the two middle chairs, with paper hats and necklaces made that afternoon by Gary and Lizzie and Judith. One enormous cake iced in yellow and white, the two of us blowing the candles out, everyone singing and clapping and cheering. Presents to unwrap— matching nightgowns and rolls of Life Savers. Speeches by the parents, clinking of glasses, laughter, hugs and kisses, tears in the mothers' eyes, my father getting his handkerchief out, more laughter. Abundant, abounding love.

It was maddening to have to share it with Sophie this way, but I knew this was a thought that could never be uttered, it was too dark and ugly and mean. Still, it was there, even though I liked her better tonight than I had in some while. We looked at each other across the table—she in her pale blue nylon dress with a lace collar, her fair hair French-braided back from her round face, and I in my peach-coloured calico dress my mother said set off my large brown eyes— and between us there quivered suspicion and affection and malice.

In the morning there was the inevitable Sunday School at Aunt Mary's United Church. The fathers, both self-proclaimed free-thinkers, were allowed to do as they liked and stay home, but we children were marched off, as always, with never a question of whether *we* believed or wanted to.

Lunchtime brought the usual question of whether my family would leave then and get back to our house in time for a late supper, or spend the afternoon and drive home at night, with Gary and me bedded down in the back seat. It was a perfect autumn day—crisp fresh air, splashes of early colour in the maples along the street, gloriously blue skies. There was no real debate at all: we would stay.

Sophie and I were allowed, as it was our birthday weekend, to spend the afternoon without the company of the little ones, and as soon as this edict was delivered we made rapid preparations and raced from the house. Uncle Ralph and Aunt Mary lived near a large park which stretched along a wide, shallow river; the younger children weren't allowed to play there without supervision, so it was the logical place to escape to. We each took a bag—for me, a new book, and for her, new coloured pencils and a pad of creamy drawing paper; for us both, apples, the first Macs of the season—and set off down the street, feeling very nearly glad to be in each other's company.

We slowed our steps as we began to talk about school, how we hated it for different reasons, and about our teachers, contesting with each other for the craziest, the weirdest. I was not above exaggerating for effect ("When she thinks nobody's looking, Mrs. Slater picks her nose, she really does. And then she eats it.") but I suspected Sophie's stories to be of the same elaborate manufacture, so it all seemed permissible. We exchanged information about the subjects we took and what we were "getting" ("What'd'ya get in social studies? What'd'ya get in arithmetic?"), a comparison in which I came out very well since my grades were always higher than Sophie's. But she remained cheerful, and said with enormous conviction that she didn't think marks mattered. They were only marks, after all, they didn't tell you anything about the real person. Just marks on paper, so who cared?

Something in my memory was suddenly triggered. I remembered a joke I'd heard about marks. "What goes 'Mark, mark'?" I asked, in that specific tone one gives Knock-knock or Little Moron jokes. Walking along, swinging my plastic bag, happy in the sunshine, oblivious to everything but this new idea, that we'd probably get along better if we told jokes and didn't talk about school.

No answer from Sophie and so I say, "Give up?" and look over at her, to see if she is ready for my reply. And there is her face, livid and shivering, pale eyes icy-cold with animosity as I say, "A dog with a hare-lip," and it is too late, *now* I see Uncle Ralph's face. And at that moment she spits at me, then turns and runs. The spit misses me, but the quick flick and curve of white spittle caught by the sun is alarming, a venomous arrow meant to penetrate my heart.

"No!" I cry. "No, Sophie, I never meant Uncle Ralph!" Knowing immediately that that is why she is running, that this is a joke she has had to face before. I am running after her, my mind a burning tangle of questions. Wondering why, why did I do that? How could I have been so stupid? I've never even told that joke to anyone before, I never thought. . . . I don't mind hurting Sophie's feelings particularly, I insult and tease her as a matter of routine . . . but the idea of hurting Uncle Ralph! I love him more than any of them. I love him even more than my own Dad if it comes right down to it. That terrible knowledge flashes before me, a secret truth, even as I am running.

I am yelling her name at the top of my lungs as the sidewalk ends and we enter the park, but Sophie, who is ordinarily not a very good runner, is so fuelled by indignation that she is well ahead of me and won't turn back.

"I love your Dad," I am crying. "That joke wasn't about him, it was just a joke. Just because you kept talking about marks, that's all. I was only trying to be funny, okay? I'm sorry, Sophie, okay? I'm sorry! Wait up!"

Eventually she slows down but I have ruined the afternoon. That in itself does not especially alarm me either, since one or the other of us usually messes up the good time we are meant by our mothers to be having. No, I have spoiled something precious in myself. And I have to really think now about Uncle Ralph's peculiar mouth, his cover-up moustache, the way he says some words.

But of course there is no way to talk about this out loud. And, least of all, not to Sophie, who has become solidly sullen and hostile. She closes off and becomes inanimate when she is hurt—a piece of furniture, a sofa. She is well ahead of me when she stops and sits down on the bench of a picnic table, her back to me. She is opening up her bag, taking out her pad of paper and pencils, and looks up at me as I advance to a point about ten feet away, out of range. Her face is tear-stained, as mine is, but there is an awful coldness in her eyes.

"I hate you," she says simply. "And I am going to tell my father what you said."

I have no recourse but my usual tactic of abuse. "You sofa!" I say, in as disdainful a way as I can. "You fat sofa!" But she has won and that knowledge alone is chilling. After all these years she has instantly, at a stroke, achieved real, total power over me. She is untouchable, unhurtable, protected by the true righteousness of her position. I retreat to the shade of a nearby copper beech, and open my book.

Eventually the afternoon sun begins to slant, streaking gold across the summer-brown grass, making long blue shadows slide out from under the trees. We have been here for hours, and I have been so engrossed in *The Sword in the Stone* I have forgotten until now, when I look up and see her back, that she hates me. That she is going to tell on me. As if she feels my eyes upon her she gets up and makes an announcement as if speaking to the park. "We are supposed to be home so you can leave at five." She turns then, and looks at me with distaste.

"I said I was sorry, Soph," I say, knowing this is not even a last chance, I have used all my chances up. My tone of voice is ungracious and insincere, the sound of someone who is beaten. She ignores me, as I expect her to do, and begins walking to the far end of the park which will take us on the longer route home. That's fine with me. There is no one else in the park now, although earlier there'd been some little kids by the swings and slides, and the *whap-whap-whap* of some people playing tennis in the distance. There'd been a few old men and ladies walking dogs, and some boys on bicycles, and one family who were clearly foreigners, who sat on the grass for their picnic instead of at a table. They were noisy, much the same as our families had been last night, and I was glad when they left. I like this park much better when it's empty.

We are coming near the river at this end of the park— it is shallow and muddy. The lowering sun glints in my eyes as I walk, and there seems to be a kind of sadness in the light itself. Along the river the row of weeping willows have begun to yellow, tired old trees leaning heavily over the water. That is where we always played in the park when we were younger, making forts or playing tag or catching frogs down under the shady hanging branches.

I am looking at the trees, remembering hiding in their leaves only last spring. That seems a hundred years ago and a time that will never come again. Everything is broken now. Then I see something red and blue among the yellows and greens of the willows. It is a man's plaid shirt. It is a man, standing still, but beckoning to us with his hand. He is making a chucking motion with his fingers, the way old people some- times tickle you under the chin, but there is something wrong with the way he is doing it. I know immediately that it is a dirty thing he is doing: I know where he means his hand to be. And then he calls out to us: "Girlies! Here, girlies, over here!"

Girlies is a bad word. I do not know exactly how I know this, but there is something more nasty than old-fashioned about it, something threatening. Because of "girlies" I know he cannot persuade me to come any closer; nothing he can do can bring me to him under the willows. I look at Sophie, who has stopped and is staring at him, her face a bright crimson.

"Don't worry," I say, "we don't need to go near him."

"But look," she says, in a low voice, and I look again, the shape of his body clearer now as he has stepped out of the shadows a little. He is very pudgy, and there is a pasty look to his nearly bald head that reminds me of a lump of dough. Reminds me of the little retarded boy who lives on our street at home. Something soft and addled, not quite formed. He has opened the fly of his trousers and his hand is making a sliding movement around the thick beige-coloured knob sticking out. It is much bigger than my brother Gary's. It seems sickening, stupid.

"Girlies, you come here," he calls again, his voice thick and disgusting. But there is something odd in the air, an invisible net falling down around our shoulders, a filigree of fascination snaring us and pulling us toward him, making me forget the dangerous sound of "girlies." And then he begins to move toward us and, all my senses alert again, I grab Sophie's hand and say, "Run!" I feel as I if I am saving her, saving us both from something more frightening than I can even think.

We run breathless down the long stretch of the park, across the grassy baseball diamond and up an incline to the gates which open out on a quiet street where there are houses and cars and people. Safe.

There are several blocks to walk to Sophie's house and we do so in absolute silence, on opposite sides of the street. All I think of is that when we get there, Sophie will finally get me back for all the wrongs I have ever done her, and although I know I deserve to be repaid this way, I cannot stand the idea of Uncle Ralph looking at me with eyes full of sorrow or anger, or hate. Sophie's hatred is a small thing compared to the pain there will be if Uncle Ralph despises me. This makes me cry, and I scuff along tearfully, the dreadful man quite gone from my mind: this fear is far worse, because there is nothing I can do to save myself. I wipe my eyes and nose only at the last minute as we come up the walk to the house.

Our parents are sitting out in wicker chairs on the porch, drinking coffee as they always do before we make the night drive back. Uncle Ralph has his feet up on the railing and is smoking a cigar with his eyes closed; my father is reading Uncle Ralph's newspaper, and my mother and Aunt Mary are talking, don't even notice our arrival. It is a scene I know as intimately as a dream, and all I can think as we approach is that it will never be like this again. Sophie is running ahead of me, up on the porch to her father.

"Daddy, Daddy, I've got to tell you something!" She takes his hand and says, "Privately." He laughs and shrugs as he gets up from his chair and says "Sure, kid," in the tone I think he might use with one of his best reporters. I am crushed to hear him using such a chummy tone with Sophie, especially when I think what is to come. She has led him through the screen door into the hallway and I can see him bending down a little as she is talking. I am coming up the walk as slowly as I can, waiting for my mother to see that I've been crying, to ask what's wrong, when Uncle Ralph and Sophie emerge from the house. On her face, as she glances at me, is an exultant look of absolute triumph.

"Evan, Betty, Mary, this is serious. Girls, I want you to tell us exactly what happened." He looks down at me coming up the steps with such affection and concern, I suddenly know what Sophie has done. She has told him instead about the man in the willows. I burst into tears of gratitude and relief, and the adults take my howls for hysteria, the result of terrible strain. The shock of seeing "the pervert," in their words. The event becomes a perfect crisis.

Hours later we were finally on the road after an evening of high drama; Gary and I were battened down with blankets and told to sleep all the way home, we'd not be there till daylight. Sophie had already fallen asleep on the living room floor, curled round a pillow, so we never had a chance to say anything to each other at the end of it all. But I wasn't sure of what we might have said, anyway.

Lying in the back seat snuggled up against Gary, I couldn't sleep. I watched the lights of cars flashing by through the steamy windows, and listened to my parents talking in careful voices. Uncle Ralph had had the wit to call not only the police but also his top young reporter who was there, on the scene, when the man was caught and taken to the police station. It turned out he *was* retarded, a man in his late thirties who had lived all his days with an elder sister who refused to admit he was anything other than a little "slow." She'd had complaints about him from time to time in her neighborhood, and had been "keeping a good eye on him" for the last few months. But that Sunday he'd got out of the yard, and wandered off and she didn't know where to look (it turned out in subsequent investigations he had often been seen by other children in the park but never officially reported).

Both Sophie and I began to feel a bit panicky about the poor man once the wheels of justice began to spin that night; we tried to explain to our fathers and the police that he hadn't really *done* anything, we'd just been scared. (I wanted to say that it was his calling "girlies" that had been the worst thing and had alerted me that what he was offering was vile—but it seemed too complicated to go into.) But the grown-ups all said that for his own good, as well as for ours and other little girls and boys, he must not be allowed to run around loose any more.

The whole thing turned out to be a marvellous coup for Uncle Ralph. He got a lot of mileage out of it and even wrote several editorials (which he ordinarily didn't do), lashing out at municipal policies regarding parks, lambasting provincial facilities for the retarded, sermonizing on the need for education in the schools about the dangers of molestation. He often took a very personal note in these pieces, which Aunt Mary always sent to my mother, and when I read his words on paper, the episode became even more vague and flimsy in my memory: "My daughter and her friend, little girls barely ten years old, playing in the park that Sunday afternoon, might have had their innocent lives changed forever."

That sort of thing, the irony of which I could never articulate to anyone. But oh, it was a feather in Uncle Ralph's cap, it was all grist for the mill.

For Sophie and me it was a turning point. Although by some unspoken agreement we never in later years talked about our quarrel—that awful, awful joke—we did sometimes talk about the poor retarded man, and where he was now, and what we had done. And what it meant, seeing him. What it meant, in the same way that we tried to work out what it meant to be born, have babies, be us.

What it meant, in the long run, was that we became exactly what our mothers had always wished.

SITSY

Afterwards she said it must have been the walled town of Aigues-Mortes itself that brought on her claustrophobia. She was not ordinarily given to scenes of the sort that had occurred in *La Crêperie*, her distress so apparent that the waiter, a young man with large glistening eyes, had rushed to the kitchen to bring her a pitcher of water and in his excitement had upset another waiter's tray of crepes. That had caused a huge commotion at the table where it occurred, as well as the smashing of three wineglasses which fell to the floor along with the ill-fated plates (two with spinach, one *au jambon et fromage,* and one *Camarguaise* featuring a tomato sauce laced with squid).

Emma, suddenly and inexplicably, had been unable to breathe. She wasn't asthmatic, John explained to the family at the next table who inquired if their cigarette smoke had created the problem, a degree of neighborly concern, he noted, unusual in this country. No, it hadn't been their smoke, he assured them in his smoothest Berlitz-learned French; his wife was only feeling a bit *ourlé*. They had looked at him oddly, but it was not until he and Emma were out the door that he recalled it had not been *ourlé* he wanted to say, but rather *entouré*.

"I told them you were feeling stitched up instead of hemmed in," he said to Emma with a laugh. He really didn't like admitting mistakes—mistakes do not get you far in a company like IBM—but here was something amusing enough to distract her and change her mood. Besides, they were establishing a routine, after nearly three months in Montpellier, of confessing to each other the foolish errors they made each day in this impossible, intricate language.

Emma looked at him with a sideways glance he felt was deliberately wan, acknowledging his laugh with a small forced smile. She wasn't quite ready to give up the event and her own traumatic place within it—the entire small restaurant in an uproar, the family whose *crêpes* had been spoiled stumping out in a rage, the cook emerging from the kitchen red-faced and sputtering, in a temper himself at their bad grace in leaving, and both waiters crouching, shamefacedly wiping up splinters of glass and shards of crockery from among long stretches of stringy cooked cheese and tomato sauce. And she, Emma, back against the wall in the corner, ashen, eyes tightly shut and hands clasped against her chest, the clenched white knuckles of a woman in pain.

The thing was, Emma admitted later, there had been no pain involved. Just the overwhelming sensation of smothering, as if all the air had been drawn out of her lungs and no more allowed in. As if the stuccoed walls of the room had advanced ever so slowly, and enclosed her, pushing her into that corner so that she couldn't move. "I felt absolutely helpless," she said. "As if I'd been completely taken over."

John was the soul of kindness in the restaurant and later too, guiding her outside into the little square and over to the grand statue of Saint Louis who led crusades from Aigues-Mortes more than seven hundred years ago. He stayed calm and efficient, dealing first with his wife and later with the cook. As if this were something which occurred regularly, he helped Emma sip water, murmuring comforting words and mothering her until her breathing eased and deepened, and the look of terror in her eyes diminished. He paid for their meal (which they'd only begun to eat when Emma had her *crise de nervosité*) and tipped twenty francs to the waiter who'd brought Emma water, promising they would return another day when Madame was well.

But even as they were walking around the bronze statue to admire it properly in the brilliant November sunlight, Emma said, "You said we'd be back, John, but honestly I never want to come here again. There's something about this place, bad vibrations, I don't know. But even out in the open, I still feel very tense. Isn't that bizarre?"

"Maybe you're being contacted by the ghosts of your ancestors in the tower," he said, joking, squeezing her arm and drawing her closer to him as they walked away from the square; restaurants along two sides, and the old Gothic church of Notre Dame des Sablons on another, it was the ideal little spot for *les touristes,* they'd agreed when they first arrived. A little French culture, and a little French lunch. What could be more perfect?

Before setting out this morning, they'd read all about the town, its ancient walls and its tower, in the narrow green *Michelin Guide de Tourisme.* John had gone out to the nearby boulangerie, as he did most mornings, for croissants to have with their coffee, and they'd spent a leisurely hour in research, sipping and eating. As Emma had read aloud in her halting and badly inflected French, John had flipped through a large French-English dictionary, kept in the kitchen for such occasions, in search of this word or that. Together they had slowly translated several paragraphs of densely written prose: *Un peu d'histoire, les fortifications, et autres curiosités.*

Sometimes it seemed as if these preparatory moments were the best part of living in France, even better and more satisfying than driving around taking photographs. The reality of travel involved sore feet and never being able to find parking or a proper toilet anywhere. Too often, as a day of sightseeing wore on, they found they were barely speaking, irritated by each other in a baffled, numb sort of way. But beforehand, cheerfully engaged in the act of acquiring information, they'd feel compatible and perfectly in tune.

About six or seven weeks ago, they'd got no further than translating the section on Avignon when John's long, searching look across the table had meant they'd ended up back in bed making love well into the afternoon. They had gone to Avignon the following weekend and had had a wretched time, finding the papal palaces oppressively dull. Today, as was their habit, they'd pieced together everything they should know about Aigues-Mortes, an old fortress town whose name, meaning Dead Waters, had sprung from its location on the edge of the Mediterranean, surrounded by salt flats and brackish lagoons. "A landscape of melancholy," translated John.

But by misfortune they'd chosen the Sunday of *la fête de Toussaint* for their visit, and the ramparts (according to the text, the best existing example of thirteenth-century military architecture) were closed for the holiday. Emma didn't much care whether they walked on the stone walls, but to her great disappointment they'd been unable to enter *le Tour Constance,* the enormous circular tower in whose dungeons, century after century, prisoners had been confined until they died. She'd been especially taken by the guidebook's tale of a Huguenot woman named Marie Durand, who'd never lost her spirit during thirty-eight years of captivity in the tower, who'd carved on the stone floor one word: "Resist." The name Durand figured in her family tree, Emma told John, some-where on her mother's side; she thought it had been a great-grandmother. She'd seemed absurdly pleased by such a tenuous link with the Huguenots, John thought, but he didn't say so.

Leading Emma away from the square, John was uneasy, knowing that they had to pass through a narrow street lined with souvenir shops to get back to the parking lot outside the town walls. The street had seemed cramped on their way into the town—given this recent attack, he feared Emma might feel claustrophobic again. But instead, her attention was taken by a row of postcard stands on the sidewalk, and she pushed the racks round and round looking for exactly the right card to send her brother Charlie. It was a custom of hers to send postcards from various places they visited, sometimes to friends back home but always, without fail, to Charlie.

"I'm going to send one of these," she called to John, who had crossed the street to browse in the outdoor magazine stalls of a tabac. "If I just write 'Sitsy' he'll crack up."

As Emma paid out her francs to the shopkeeper, John watched from outside the shop, trying to see her objectively, as if he had just come across her here, an American tourist in the south of France. Her thick hair had blown around her face as they walked, making her look more tousled than usual, and the striped cotton shirt she wore most of the time hung loosely over her denim skirt. Around her shoulders she'd thrown a large floral scarf as a last-minute attempt to look fashionable, but it had twisted askew in the restaurant and she hadn't thought to straighten it. Her girlish appearance had always been part of her charm, but here—in contrast with Frenchwomen her age who appeared to be immaculately coiffed and perfectly dressed—she often seemed simply dishevelled.

John himself was more and more frequently being taken for French as he added to his wardrobe at good boutiques; today, for example, in his olive-brown cashmere pullover, with a small leather bag slung over one shoulder, he looked, and indeed felt, European. He should have been born here, he thought: his long nose wasn't a facial flaw in this context, it gave him a slightly Gallic air. His dark complexion and wavy hair added to an image he was consciously cultivating, and he enjoyed those small conversations in shops or cafes when he would have to say—with a shrug of surprise at being taken for a Parisian on holiday—"*Ah, mais non, je suis americain!*"

Not so his wife. There was no mistaking her mode of dress, her way of walking, her accent, her personality; her rumpled and casual youthfulness was distinctly New World. Although she was over thirty, her freckled, open face radiated a childlike desire to please, a quality which so eclipsed her terrible French he could see she was charming the sour-faced old woman at the cash register. Emma was "user-friendly"—she had described herself thus on their first date. When they met, she'd been taking an evening course in database systems to upgrade her job as a university librarian: John had been one of the guest lecturers. He'd found everything about her so foreign to his own behaviour, his more formal and carefully reasoned approach to life, she'd been irresistible. He couldn't stop thinking about her, trying to figure her out as if she were some programming problem he had to solve; what was this woman, who looked to be a creature of impulse and disorder, doing in a library?

Emma, for her part, had been just as fascinated by him. It took John only a few weeks to realize that he had fallen in love with her and that he would never understand her. She had not wanted what she called a limiting legal arrangement, declaring that she preferred to live separately, but over time he found that his closet was cluttered with her shoes and clothes and that his bathroom shelves were crowded by her contact lens solutions. He had gradually persuaded her that only by marrying each other could they be perfectly happy, and had given so many convincing, logical reasons she'd eventually agreed. On the day of their wedding she had told everyone how difficult it had been to get him to propose, and John could not tell whether she was teasing him or whether indeed that was her version of the truth.

Now, at this moment in the shop, she was glowing and animated, bearing no resemblance to the waxen-faced and shaken woman she'd been half an hour ago. How was it possible? She was chatting away to the old lady as if they were *des vieilles amies de coeur*. He'd seen this kind of change in her often and he always found it bewildering. He had a placid disposition which seldom varied, a maritime climate; but Emma was all ups and downs, dark gloomy despair followed by clear, sweet sanity, turbulent storms and sudden forgiving rainbows. "I blow hot and cold," she'd say, without apology. "That's the way I've always been. My brother's exactly the same."

She showed him the postcard for Charlie as they strolled past the remaining shops. It was a photograph of several white horses dashing through shallow water, head-on towards the camera. The colour was intensified to enhance a blood-red sunset in the background, making the card dramatic in that vulgar way paintings on velvet are, but there was nevertheless something stirring about the photo, John thought, something very touching. The reckless lift of their heads, their glinting eyes and flying manes, the symmetry of all those sturdy white legs splashing together, the idea of wild horses made real. It was the idea that saved the picture itself from complete decadence, he decided. One needed romantic visions from time to time as a counterweight to orderly existence. Perhaps especially in this over-civilized country, one had need of bad postcards of wild horses. He would tell Emma his theory another time, for he could not discern at what level she was struck by the photograph, whether her appreciation of it was genuine or slightly mocking.

"That old lady in the shop said if we drive down to the sea we'll see lots of them, John," Emma said, holding the postcard away from herself to look at it again. "I thought we'd have to go over further into the actual Camargue but she said no, the white horses are everywhere here."

"Now, about the Sitsy business," John said, as they settled into their small Renault, belting and buckling, unfolding the map and putting another Mozart in the tapedeck. "Say the poem again that goes with it, okay?"

"How could you forget something so easy?" asked Emma, astonished. "God, you've heard me do it plenty of times. *Lucky lucky white horse, lucky lucky lee, lucky lucky white horse, give your luck to me. Sitsy!* And then you make a wish on the horse."

"But you have to say 'Sitsy' before anybody else to get your wish, right?" said John. Emma had had this odd word in her vocabulary for as long as he'd known her, which would soon be three years. They'd been married for nearly two and were still discovering things about each other's earlier lives

—yes, of course he'd known how to wish on a Sitsy, how could he have even momentarily forgotten?

"Good for you," said Emma warmly, patting his knee in approval. "And besides that, it's like birthday candles, you can't tell your wish or it won't come true. It's one of those things Charlie and I share from our childhood." Her eyes opened very wide as she smiled at him, encouraging him to join in the pleasure of her nostalgia.

Maybe, he thought, it annoyed him a little that she shared so much with Charlie; maybe he forgot things like the silly poem unconsciously because her clinging to the past affronted him. It didn't seem right, somehow, that she should still be so connected with a former life in which he had no part— as if her real existence predated this one. Well, it was her brother, not an ex-husband or ex-lover. And she and Charlie seldom saw each other—the only time he'd met his brother-in-law had been the day of their wedding. Charlie had flown in from Bangladesh, where he worked for UNICEF, and then had flown off somewhere else the following day. They'd gotten on well, and John thought he and Charlie would probably be friends if they ever spent any time together. He had the same easy and familiar manner as his sister, and they were so similar in appearance they might have been twins although Charlie was younger by two years. Still, John admitted (but only to himself) that Emma's devotion to her brother rankled somewhere deep in him, somewhere he could not access easily.

They decided to take the route to Saintes-Maries-de-la-Mer on the coast, which the old lady had promised would provide white horses. Emma studied the map for a long time, as if she were looking for them, as if they'd be marked there, between this road and that. She and John drove in silence for one side of a cassette, *Concerto for Flute and Harp in C Major,*

K. 299. Early in their relationship they'd discovered a shared passion for Mozart—they'd brought their entire collection of cassettes for the six months John would be teaching his course in Montpellier and they'd bought several more in the past few weeks. It had become a joke between them that the little Renault now needed Mozart as much as they did, and wouldn't start unless there was a fresh cassette in the tape deck.

"It's funny, isn't it, how there are things that stick in your head from when you were a kid," Emma said as the music ended. "I really don't know why this thing has stayed with me all these years. But I have it in mind from when I was little, how we'd be driving in the car, my father at the wheel and my mother beside him, Charlie and me in the back. We'd pass the time just fine, Charlie and me, singing songs and playing games, we never poked at each other or started fights the way most kids do. Every so often Mum would call out 'Sitsy!' and we'd look out the windows and there'd be a white horse in some field we were passing. It didn't happen often that you'd see a completely white one, so it was out of the ordinary, you know, something special. She had sharp eyes and whenever we tried to find one before she did, it was impossible. She wasn't the kind of mother who would let her children win just to make them feel good. If she saw a white horse first, it was hers and no mistake. You didn't have to say the whole verse aloud in our family, saying 'Sitsy' stood for the poem. But you had to be fast to make your wish before anyone else said anything, or the wish was no good."

"I remember all the instructions," John said with a laugh. "But the little poem somehow got wiped."

"Well, that just shows you don't listen to me carefully enough." Emma spoke in a joking way, but there was an edge to her voice. Why was it, he wondered, that whenever he'd be feeling they were totally united in the present (as he did now, after having gone through that lunchtime embarrassment together), that she'd have one of these fits of reminiscence?

"I've been looking for Sitsies for years," Emma continued, ready to fill out her story to amuse him. "I grew up thinking everybody did it when they went driving in the country, but I've never met anyone who knows the word except Charlie and me. And we have no idea where it came from except that our Mum said she'd learned it as a little girl. Once she died, there was no one to ask, Dad had been gone for years, and he probably didn't know anyway. He used to snort, like laughing through his nose, whenever she said 'Sitsy,' as if she were a real idiot. I loved her so much for keeping on doing it, even when he was laughing at her. Honestly, I can re-member that. I loved having a Mum who believed in making wishes. That's what makes this postcard so wonderful. It isn't just these white horses thundering around the Camargue . . . it's as if we've come to where my mother would be in heaven, all the horses she could want and all her wishes coming true. I can hardly wait to share this with Charlie. Do you see?"

John had that uneasy sense he often had that he didn't really see but that he had better pretend to see or else everything would turn sour. Emma would become distant and cold, would say that clearly he was incapable of ever being on her wavelength. "Oh, just forget it," she'd say, and toss her head.

Of course he understood the story about her mother, and the wishing on horses—the white horse was a magic animal in just about any European-based culture you cared to name. Why, if she wanted a *real* Sitsy, they should go see that enormous chalk horse on a hillside in Wiltshire. No, he had no problem seeing. But with Emma, that "do you see?" always seemed to have a twist, a curve, a hidden meaning. Did he see? Did he? Why had Emma's mother been wishing all those years—she must never have gotten what she wanted, he thought, and had to keep at it, over and over. Did Emma see that?

"Why did you fall apart in the restaurant, Emma?" he asked. He didn't know quite why, but it seemed the only way he had of replying to her question.

Emma looked at him with a sudden full turn of the head—usually she kept her eyes on the road as he drove, as if she had to look out for both of them. It bothered him a little, as if she didn't fully trust him or find him capable, but this quick turning and facing him in the front seat of the car was more ominous than if she'd simply kept staring out the window. He felt his fingers tighten on the wheel.

"I don't know. I honestly don't. I've only had something like that happen to me a couple of times before, and not for a long time. I guess in some part of myself I must feel kind of, what did you say it was, *entouré?*"

"Is it being here?" John asked, feeling now that he'd started he had to keep going. "Is it being in France?" After all, she didn't have a job here other than some volunteer work at the American Library and she had found few people with whom to be friends. She'd started French lessons at a small private school in the centre of the city, but she'd lost interest after a few weeks—she said it was because her classmates were all young au pair girls, and their conversations never went anywhere interesting. Tedious. She said she'd rather stay home and learn French by reading the newspapers than waste money on classes. Accordingly, she spent a lot of time by herself.

Too much time, John thought. It would be a reasonable explanation for this hysterical breathlessness; she felt over-whelmed, confined by a life in which, without fluency, she was not really free. But he tried to say "Is it being in France?"

in such a way that she would understand he was also asking, "Is it being married to me?"

"Look!" Emma cried, pointing ahead to where several white horses grazed in the distance, carved ivory figures against the deep blue sky. Her face was flushed, radiant with happiness. "Look, John, look at them! Sitsy and Sitsy and Sitsy and Sitsy! Oh, aren't they beautiful! Wouldn't Mum have had a field day here!"

A field day. Another of her quaint expressions carried forward from that rural upbringing she and Charlie still cherished in their speech habits and in observances like this Sitsy thing. Who'd credit a woman her age with such fervent excitement over a few white horses off in a field? Whatever this was about, John thought, it was much more than just these horses. Hardly white anyway, if you took time to look; the muddy flats on which they grazed had darkened their legs and flanks, and their bodies were the soft dove-grey of early morning clouds. Very pretty, actually; solid and compact, but graceful. Yes, they're beautiful, John decided. Sitsy, and Sitsy again. Emma was going to ignore his question which, in an odd way, gave him an answer.

About half an hour earlier they had left behind the vineyards and the trademark *Listel* painted in large letters on buildings along the road. Sunday, none of the winemaking cooperatives were open for *la dégustation* and they couldn't stop and sample the light, dry rosé of the countryside, *le vin des sables;* they could only admire the grapevines themselves, the remaining leaves transformed by the first fingers of frost. Gold, scarlet, burgundy, rich autumn colours swirling along the rows above gnarled old rootstocks—the vineyards gave this bleak flatland a mathematical beauty, vanishing point after vanishing point down the rows as they drove. Eventually they'd arrived in these marshes created by centuries of Rhone silt, not good for anything but tall feathery grasses and stunty little trees and wild rice. Here lay the ranches where black bulls were raised for the bullfights in nearby Nîmes; only an hour's drive from these corrals to the Roman arena and certain death.

But nowadays, more profitable than black bulls, the tourist trade. At intervals along the road *les auberges* and *les hostelleries* offered low off-season rates on their CHAMBRES/ROOMS/ZIM-MER. And adjoining most of these places (besides the small restaurants advertising fresh local beef) were ranches offering the attainment of fantasy: a chance to ride the white horses of the Camargue.

The horses Emma had seen, when they were able to look more closely—John stopped the car on the narrow shoulder so they could get out—were certainly not wild, and were definitely not galloping in a blizzard of white. They were standing in little groups of three or four in their muddy, trampled paddock, flicking their tails now and again in a fitful, bored-horse manner. They wore bridles, they'd been bred and broken for bearing tourists into the marshes; signs in several languages advertised excursions on horses taught to pose for cameras or for videotape recorders, horses trained not to snap at children or nervous urbanites who'd never mounted a saddle before in their lives.

Wordlessly, John and Emma watched a few of the horses coming toward them, heads raised and ears perked, unques-tionably anticipating food—who knew what awful gunk peo-ple might offer these animals across the barbed wire fence separating them from the road? The bleached, silvery grass in the ditch was littered with plastic bags, candy wrappers, the same ugly garbage thrown by travelling yahoos every-where. As the horses drew near, the afternoon breeze brought their distinctive smell ahead of them, and John felt his nostrils fill with the earthy, warm odour—a noble smell. What was it Swift had called his civilized horses in *Gulliver's Travels*? Surely something more suitable than Sitsy.

"How sad," said John finally, patting the warm, moist nose of one of the horses, who was trying to chew on his sleeve. She was a lovely creature, her coat grown long and thick with the cold weather coming, her large dark eyes glowing with intelligence and humour as she kept trying to work her soft lips around his wrist. Her bridle was a pale robin's egg blue, she was clearly a favourite of the stable. "How sad for these poor horses, this riding business."

"But only because we'd expected to see them free," said Emma, looping her cotton scarf back around her neck after one of the horses had tried to jerk it away with his teeth. It had not been a friendly gesture, Emma decided. She backed away from the fence, annoyed at the horse, disappointed by the reality of these shabby animals and ready to leave. She'd had enough disillusionment.

"It's my fault," she said, "for buying that card, and not asking that old woman properly what kind of horses we'd see. She was right, I suppose, these *are* white horses. Still, for that matter, my mother's Sitsies were always farm animals —she would never have seen a wild one in her life. It's that damn postcard that's making us feel bad, John. Let's go." She moved away and got in the car quickly, without looking back at the horses by the fence. Her face had closed itself and become expressionless.

John tried to make sense of his emotions and thus dispel them but the interior of the car seemed heavy with his sorrow and anger. Emma was fiddling now with her big scarf as if she were trying to get rid of something around her shoulders, as if she were trying to prevent his sadness from coming down on her, and for some reason that was irritating him unreasonably. He knew it was ridiculous to feel as he did and worse, that he couldn't find a way to say what he was feeling past repeating the word "sad." It wasn't that he was inarticulate, he told himself, it was a matter of being too careful, trying to express too precisely what he meant.

He wished he had Emma's relaxed abandon with language—she'd say the first thing that popped into her head, she always let words jumble and rush any which way—and he wished that she understood him well enough to speak for him. Seeing these docile creatures pushing their long faces over the fence made him want to howl with outrage and grief. He needed language more harsh, more desperate than "sad." But that language was not in his nature, nor was howling, and he knew that.

"Houyhnhnms," he thought, calming himself by searching his memory for Swift's wonderful word. Going through the files was a mental trick he'd had since boyhood, a way of restoring his equilibrium. When in doubt, try to remember something, anything. "That's what he called them. Houyhnhnms."

Emma had become coolly detached from the horses, urging John to start the motor and get going again. These same horses over which she had been, only minutes ago, ecstatic —this was so like her, John thought. Quite as she described herself, blowing hot and cold, her mood entirely dependent on some invisible emotional thermostat which measured her inner life and had nothing to do with how he felt. Nothing. He was finding her increasingly self-centered, and this was a perfect example. Since these particular horses didn't have to do with *her,* she didn't care about them.

Her vision of the world, John judged, was limited to perceptions directly related to her memories—her other life.

Looking at white horses was only useful as an entry to her childhood with Charlie, or as a way of remembering her long-dead mother. She had no interest in seeing them with John, or seeing them through his eyes. Or even simply seeing them, relating to them as fellow creatures getting a raw deal. These animals only existed for her as markers along her own path into the past.

But if I told her what I was thinking, she'd say I was arrogant, he thought. She'd protest, she'd say I was presumptuous and that I was misreading her again. And that my ego is the one that needs attention all the time. We'd have a quarrel, and she would weep and I would say I was sorry. And I would be.

They were both quiet the rest of the way down to the sea, neither of them commenting again about horses along the road. Neither of them leaned forward to turn the cassette over, neither one spoke as they looked out over the subtle shades of grey and green and brown, blending, almost without definition, into themselves. The monochromatic flatness had an absence of detail John found deeply appealing; by entering this landscape he was leaving behind the sad horses. Finally, stretching along the horizon to their left, clusters of apricot-coloured stucco houses appeared, newly built on the edge of the village of Saintes-Maries-de-la-Mer.

One had only to read about this place in the *Michelin Guide* to expect there'd be all the trappings of the travel trade, John thought; the town was being developed to keep pace with the rest of the tourism industry along the coast. It was one of the best sites in France for wind-surfing—he knew this from reading local newspapers—and that seasonal influx was clearly paying off for the developers. It hardly mattered where they went on these weekend drives; it seemed that every town within an hour or two of Montpellier had new suburbs with seductive names redolent of pleasure and leisure and ease.

On the skyline above the low-lying buildings stood the triple-bell tower of the church. Here, forty years after Christ died, a boatload of his persecuted followers landed after a voyage down the Mediterranean from the Holy Land. As near as John and Emma could make out from the confusing guidebook text, there had been at least three women named Marie, but only two had stayed here, Marie-Jacobe and Marie-Salome. With them remained Sara, a dark-skinned slave girl, now Saint Sara, patron saint of the gypsies. In the village church, a reliquary held what was left of her bones, sacred and silent, giving off miracles like electricity; the guidebook further promised that they would see the statue of this humble black woman, venerated by generations of *les gitans,* the gypsies of France.

The bells in the stone tower were fully visible, hanging from metal racks. The tower made an easy landmark to follow from the car-park by the sea, where they had walked for a little while looking out at the cold, rolling water, laughing in amazement to see wind-surfers dressed in black rubber body-suits, hanging on earnestly to their gaily coloured sails whipping across the waves. "Madness," muttered Emma, and John agreed.

"One hundred percent," he said. "These guys are certifiable. Why would anyone want to be out there this time of year?" Emma shook her head in companionable disbelief and they huddled together in the wind, watching the sailboards skim like enchanted birds over the surface. Funny, John thought. Even as he was being disparaging, he knew he envied these guys their craziness, envied them the sensation of freedom they must feel flying silently across the water like that.

He wondered if Emma were thinking the same thing. But he didn't ask. She was the one who had made those long involved speeches about freedom before she finally agreed to marry him. He couldn't bear a discussion in which she might start talking about these things again. Not now, not today. It was disturbing enough that he wished himself out there.

Walking toward the church they crossed an open space, a flat square of dry mud dotted with dog turds, where several knots of men and boys were playing *pétanque*. As often happened on their excursions, both of them were struck by the picturesque quality of scene before them. Hardly possible there'd be so many old ruddy-faced men wearing black berets in the whole of France, let alone in this tiny town by the sea. And yet, here they were, discussing and disputing the distance between their silvery *boules* lying in the dust.

"Just waiting for us to come along," said Emma. "And of course we left the camera in the car. Never mind, it'd be embarrassing trying to take pictures anyway. Let's go see the church and then have a drink or something. I'm getting hungry. Aren't you?" She took John's hand and wound her fingers through his in a tender gesture undoubtedly meant to restore harmony between them, to make him feel loved. It bewildered him how, just when he'd be feeling most separate from her, she'd do something like this which would seize his heart fiercely. It was as if, he thought, he were adjusting himself to her uneven and passionate rhythms . . . but why was that? Why wasn't Emma becoming more like him, instead?

The old church built of sandstone was a creamy colour outside, its surfaces roughened and pitted by centuries of wind and water; but it was dark and cold inside, smelling a little of the morning's smoky frankincense and of the afternoon parade of visitors. The damp stench of stone hung

around them as they let their eyes grow accustomed to the
dimness of the nave. Right by the doorway stood a revamped
candy-dispensing machine, containing pamphlets about the
church, its saints, and its faithful gypsies, *"éternal pélerins sur
les routes du monde."* They'd begun a collection of religious
literature from other churches, so Emma quickly inserted a
five-franc piece to get one of these, choosing *"Les Gitans"*
because of the quirky black-and-white photograph on its
cover—a young woman kissing the stomach of what appeared
to be a large doll, the statue of Saint Sara. Here and there
along the stone walls, glass cases of religious treasure shone
and glimmered—silver chalices, golden crosses, sacred scrolls
and letters, the jewelry and paraphernalia of belief, the necessary credentials without which people would not come to
donate their coins in the pamphlet machines or in the poor
boxes by the door. In one large case hung several paintings
from the nineteenth century, all illustrating miracles attributed
to the two saintly Maries who had settled here with their
Sara. There they were, a blissful and bosomy pair of ladies
draped in Biblical garb, sailing through the skies in a wooden
boat, far above sin and suffering below.

Walking forward down the central aisle and merely glancing at the displays, Emma and John approached the underground crypt at the front of the church from which warmth
rose in shimmering waves. It felt, John said later, as if they
were being pulled along that aisle by a force within the crypt,
and as they descended shallow stone steps into the small
narrow room, he felt weightless, light and luminous himself.
He was not ordinarily given to extreme reactions, and the
sensations surprised him, took him off guard. The soft, blurry
glow given off by tiers of burning candles in metal racks along
the walls produced such a stifling heat he was suddenly nervous and looked towards Emma to see if there were any signs

of her earlier fears of enclosure. But she appeared to be enjoying herself completely, smiling incredulously at her surroundings.

There was a handful of other visitors, some there out of curiosity and others praying audibly to Saint Sara whose bones (a few brown splinters barely visible through the window of the wooden reliquary) were on the central altar, and whose statue stood off to the right, near a wall covered with marble tablets thanking her for intervention and assistance. The small saint was, as promised, dark-skinned, with eyes painted in such a way they seemed to be glittering. Indeed, Saint Sara herself was sparkling all over—her pearl tiara studded with bright rhinestones, her many layers of costume heavily embroidered with metallic thread. These dresses of tulle and satin and silky polyester caught the candlelight, creating a subtle but discernible halo around her figure.

Primitive magic, pure and simple, John thought. Of course. Why had it taken him so long to see? That's why Emma clung to these memories of her mother making wishes. At some essential level, she still needed magic. And, to be honest, so did he. So did everyone, one way or another.

Around the base of the statue lay a few pathetic built-up shoes no longer needed by once-crippled children and in the nearest corner crutches and canes leaned against each other in silent testimony to the power of prayer. A glass box stood on a small pillar between the altar and the statue, with a slot in the top through which one could drop supplications written on paper. John snapped the fastener on his leather bag and took out a small day diary and a pen. Ripping out that day's page, he folded it in half and ripped again.

"Here," he said, passing one half to Emma, who had moved to a rack of candles and was preparing to light one. "This is even better than candles, Emma. Make a wish to Saint Sara and we'll put it in the box. Let's see if the small black hope of the gypsies can answer prayers as well as those Sitsies of yours."

She looked at him with amusement. "I had no idea you were such a superstitious heathen," she said softly. "You're as bad as I am, John, playing with holy stuff like this. What's got into you today?"

"Saint Sara," he said, and handed her the pen. He watched her carefully as she wrote, using the palm of her other hand as a surface for the paper; it was something very short, and quickly done.

"Do I sign it?" she whispered, sensing that some of the others in the long room were watching them with disapproval, as if they could see that what Emma and John were up to was sacrilege. "Do I give her my telephone number so she can get in touch?" Laughter was bubbling up at the improbable sight of her sensible husband carrying on this game with such intensity. But that was typical, too. If John played at anything, it was with his whole self, and here he was, devoting himself to the business of asking for prayers to be answered. Making wishes, asking for miracles, all the same thing.

John took the pen from her and wrote on his own scrap of paper just as quickly, his message to the saint as brief as Emma's. Together they moved toward the glass box, bowing their heads slightly in as reverent a manner as they could and, knowing they were being watched by the others, they knelt while putting their separate papers through the slot. Then they turned together, as one, and holding hands left the crypt, still feeling the suspicious eyes of believers upon them.

"Oh Johnny, lightning will strike us, it really will," said Emma, laughing openly once they were outside. The afternoon was drawing to a close, the sky beginning to take on the lustrous colours of mother-of-pearl. The square where the men had been playing *boules* was deserted now, and they walked across it quickly; a chill wind coming up from the sea blew at them and made them stride heads down.

"Really, that's all it is, isn't it, religion?" said Emma into John's ear as they hurried against the cold. "You know, asking for things and saying thank you."

"Tell me what you wished," he said, stopping, holding her shoulder with one hand and brushing the hair from her face with the other. "You must tell me." He loved her so much at that moment, her freckles, her wildly blowing hair, everything about her. He wished he could say what the day had meant to him, what he thought he was discovering. All this sharing of events, all these days they were spending together, a reliquary of memories richer than anything they had ever experienced apart—all this still needed magic, still needed wishing. Things could come true, but they needed wishing to stay true.

"Oh come on, John, you know I can't. It's the same rule as Sitsy, I'm sure. You're not allowed to tell." It had all been a game, they'd just been fooling around . . . now, abruptly, Emma was serious, as if what they had done mattered, and John himself was solemn, earnest in his request. He felt the same uneasy fear he had in the car when she'd turned and looked at him fully.

"No, you must tell me. And then I'll tell mine. And then Saint Sara will bless us for trusting each other and grant us our wishes." John heard himself and wondered where all this was coming from, it was not his usual style. The church had affected him somehow and he still felt as if his feet were made of sponge, as if there were light emanating not only from the pearly clouds but from the ground and the buildings around him, as if he himself had absorbed light from within the crypt.

"Stop, John, you're pinching my shoulder. Let go, I'll tell you. It was just a whim."

"What?" He waited, porous and expectant.

"I just wished that Charlie would come to see us while we're here. So I wrote 'Please send Charlie.' That's all. See, nothing so big. But if it doesn't happen I'll blame you!"

Emma had tried to speak lightly, but her voice had fallen flat and heavy, and she looked startled herself at what she had said. Would she ever blame John? Blame all of a sudden seemed enormous, full of dark portent and omen. "So then, you have to tell me yours," she said. "What's your wish?"

John threw back his head and laughed, a sharp, bitter sound. "Well, this is your lucky day. I wrote 'Please give Emma whatever she wants.' And now we have only to wait to see whether old Saint Sara reads her mail."

He put his arm around her shoulders and pulled her close for a moment and then, letting her go, continued walking across the square. He no longer felt as if he'd been enlightened. He kept his head down against the wind and slightly turned from hers, so she wouldn't see his face.

OBSERVING THE
NICETIES

Opening a packet of Peek Frean biscuits I open a room I have not visited in years. In the room, on a walnut coffee table, sits a china plate—pale blue with a fluted edge—and on the plate are several Nice biscuits arranged in a fan. Nice. A city in the south of France. At some point in my childhood, I learned (can't remember how or why I knew it must be true) that these biscuits were named after the place and pronounced the same way: *Neece*. This knowledge made me feel remarkably clever and superior to my mother and her friends who simply liked to have a nice little cookie with a nice cup of tea in the afternoon. When I told my mother how she should be saying the word, she kissed my forehead and said, "Good for you, dear," and continued to call them nice as she always had.

They *were* nice, those flat oblong biscuits sprinkled with

sugar and tasting of coconut, each with its name impressed firmly and reassuringly in the middle. They were nice women, too, my mother and her friends who used to sit in our living room, sipping tea with milk or lemon, nibbling cookies and talking together year after year after year. My mother served tea every day at four whether or not there was company, a habit she and my father regarded as genteel.

My father was a general practitioner with an office and examining rooms in the basement of our house and very often he would make time in his schedule to come upstairs on the dot of four for a cup of tea with Mother. His nurse, Miss Tobias, never joined us: she said she preferred coffee and used to make herself cups of instant with hot water from the downstairs bathroom tap, a habit my mother declared un-wholesome. But, she would add, who was *she* to tell Miss Tobias what to do? Miss Tobias was a professional nurse, was she not? And taste was, after all, a matter of personal pref-erence. Nevertheless . . . The sentence left hanging meant her unspoken censure was severe.

My brothers and I usually came in from school shortly after four o'clock and were included in the tea circle as long as we "behaved." And as long as Mother didn't greet our arrival at the living room door with an odd little frown and a quick nod of the head. Those small gestures meant that the present conversation was "adult" and not for our ears.

It usually involved one of the women who visited regularly, breathless and tearful, in the throes of imparting intimate details; but occasionally she would send the same signal when just she and Father were alone, side by side on the sofa. There would be a sudden silence and she would say, "Go along to the kitchen, children, make yourselves some chocolate milk," and Father would stare into his teacup until we had gone. The wonderful thing was that our mother managed to make us feel, by her secretive nods, as if she wished she could let us in, but, didn't we see, this other person needed her attention terribly, and, well, we could always have tea with her tomorrow.

We liked having tea, my brothers and I, not so much for the tea itself or the predictable cookies (Mother never baked and they were always store-bought) but for the way we *felt* there in the living room with her presiding over the silver tea tray. She called this four o'clock ritual "observing the niceties" and trained us early in the manners required for entry into her realm. By the age of five we each had our own porcelain cup and saucer, mine with hand-painted daffodils, my brothers' with cornflowers, roses, and violets. We held our cups carefully, full of cambric tea we'd sweeten with as many sugar cubes as we dared. We took pride in not spilling, we didn't even mind that there were so many rules involved.

We weren't allowed to slurp from our saucers the way some children did, and were never to dip our cookies in the tea. "A vulgar practice," said Mother, "which I find offensive."

When we were permitted to join the grown-ups, I noticed that their conversations would fragment into particles, meaningless little murmurs and nothings, arched eyebrows, the occasional broken phrase or half word here and there . . . a silly sort of code. As if they thought we cared about their doings or wanted to hear their gossip! Why, we simply endured Mother's women friends as a necessary aspect of afternoon tea.

Unable to continue with their real conversations, they'd turn to us politely and question us about school—Mother approved of having children drawn into discussions as a way of preparing them for later life. This was especially true if Father was "up for his cup" with the visiting ladies, since he evinced a lively interest in us; but I suspect it was also true he liked to turn attention toward us out of devilment, as a method of damming up the natural flow of female chat. There'd be questions about what books we were reading, perhaps a request for one of us to play the piano or to recite a verse. We always complied, having been so imbued with the notion that this was the way things were meant to be that it never occurred to us to rebel, to pout or say we didn't want to.

After our social duties, we were able to finish our tea, palming biscuits off the blue china plate as fast we could before we'd be told we could leave. And then the adult voices would bubble up again, we'd hear them even as we left the room, animated and natural once the children had gone.

While we observed the niceties, light coming in the west window of the living room would catch the dust motes forever swimming in the air. Whether it was the age of the house itself or its ancient coal-burning furnaces, the overstuffed furniture or my father's pipe smoke or the shedding of our countless dogs and cats, there was always dust in the air, settling on our lives. Only for a few hours on Thursday afternoons, just after Muriel the cleaning woman had come and gone, were there any surfaces free from dust.

I was allergic prior to the medical profession discovering the fine fortunes to be made by diagnosis of such ailments, and my distress due to dust, animal hair, and feathers was unlabelled. It simply existed. In his role as physician, Father went no farther than to tell me I had sensitive mucus membranes and that I ought, as a well-bred child, always keep a handkerchief close at hand.

Over the years I learned that whenever I was in the living room I would sneeze. Frequently, and often with vigour. I wore glasses, and my reddened eyes were attributed to my

reading in poor light without them; my sneezes, to a disposition which sought attention at any level by any means.
"She just does that," my brothers would obligingly explain
to any visitors who didn't already know my habits. "Don't
look at her and she'll stop."

In fact, I couldn't stop. Nor could I stop going into the
living room, the centre of our lives and the place in which I
sneezed more than any other. It was my favourite room in
the house, made somehow more cozy by dusty old pillows,
the mess of crumbs round the chairs where my brothers and
I usually had our tea. One of our tabby cats would be curled
under the piano lamp, whether it was turned on or not.

Before the tea tray was brought in, a place would be made
for it on the low walnut table by Mother's hand sweeping
the magazines and newspapers and books into a woven grass
basket kept by the sofa for just that purpose. But by next
day they'd all be out again, ready to be pushed aside in that
deft gesture of hers.

My mother was not in the least domestic and should have
led a life in which all her needs were anticipated by servants.
Somehow she had been born into either the wrong class or
century, for it never occurred to her to wipe or sweep up
between Muriel's weekly visits. Like the sprinkling of sugar
on the biscuits, dust in the room layered itself gently day by
day, a grey film falling sweetly, like age, over us all. And now,
like the speckles of dust drifting through sunlit afternoons,
my memories bring me the fragrance of Earl Grey tea, of
lemon zest droplets in the air, of crisp sugary wafers in our
hands. . . .

I bite into a Nice biscuit at this very moment and sneeze.
A loud, resounding, satisfying sneeze, a whopper. The kind
that would have had my brothers rolling on the floor in
simulated shock, as if blown into smithereens by the force of

it. The dry, oversweet flavor of the cookie is a little stale and sickish—even fresh from the package there is something about it tasting of dust, making me sneeze with longing and desire for that room, for those women with their tea cups in hand.

The sneeze has been severe enough to bring tears to my eyes, and I feel my cheeks damp as I stand here remembering my mother in her primrose yellow afternoon dress pouring tea from the silver pot with its carved ebony handle. Her head would be bent to one side, her elbow raised in a graceful gesture both poised and supple, like a violinist's, her other hand held out, fingers flattened against the teapot lid; she would usually tip her chin up during this ceremony as if inquiring something of great importance, but what she would be asking was, "Milk? Lemon?"

The picture of elegance, my mother. Her hair was brushed up and away from her forehead in a style she must have adopted in her early twenties and never changed, for in every photo taken over decades she looked exactly the same. She had a cultivated, patrician appearance, and a manner of bearing herself that commanded attention and respect. "Junoesque," my father once said, hoping to flatter her, "a true goddess of the hearth."

"Juno was never goddess of the hearth," said Mother, pleasantly contradicting Father as she so often did. "You're thinking of Vesta if you're thinking of the hearth. But if you mean Junoesque, that usually implies statuesque and stately. Although I take exception to stately, Oliver. Stately has always meant overweight in my family, the old aunties who wore corsets were stately. Perhaps you had better just say you like the way I look and leave it at that." Smiling but very firm, a large Junoesque woman.

Being a doctor's wife is never easy—even the most devoted

of them will tell you over tea (and in possibly more detail over gin). My mother, whose name was Margaret, never complained about her life in any whiny, self-pitying way, for after all, she had chosen it by marrying Father; but she did make it clear that hers was not an easy row to hoe, and she regarded her wifely role as akin to a real job.

She had calling cards made for herself; although few people still used them in the fifties, she kept a small silver case of them in her handbag and another leather box of them in her writing desk. Embossed on the creamy paper was *Mrs. Dr. Oliver W. Greenwood.* And she had her writing paper engraved the same way, her name and address centred at the top of the page in flowing Tiffany script.

"But your name is Margaret," I said, having been allowed to use one of her sheets of paper to write a Christmas thank-you letter to her sister, my Aunt Katherine. I must have been seven or eight, that age of tender sensibility when everything begets questioning. "This name doesn't look like you."

"Margaret is my given name, dear," my mother said pleasantly. "But my chosen name, the name by which the world knows me and by which I live, is this one here. Mrs. Dr. Greenwood is my title of occupation, do you see? I can still sign my letters Margaret if I choose, but under the banner of your father's name."

I didn't see, but I pretended I did. For my immediate understanding of occupation was as I saw it in the *Life* magazines scattered on the table in the living room. *Occupation* meant soldiers stationed in Germany, or American troops living far away in Japan, or Russians taking over all those countries and making them Communists too. It meant powerful forces keeping you under control and making you give up things, dominating you entirely. Now I knew my mother didn't mean that, she meant it was the work she did . . . but my brain filled up with an image of Margaret being taken over and losing her name. It was far too silly an idea to say out loud, and so I never rid myself of it as I might have if it had been aired and laughed at. Instead, I kept it to myself and continued to wish she would call herself by her own name.

She was such a strong-looking woman, Junoesque was indeed an accurate way to describe her, whatever my father meant by it. She came from a family in which few of its members grew to less than six feet, and in which physical prowess was prized and rewarded as much as academic endeavours. Her particular enthusiasm as a child had been swimming, from which she developed those wide, muscular shoulders so stunning on tall women. Her enlightened parents had encouraged their daughters and sons equally, and Margaret had been sent to the University of Toronto where she'd excelled at languages—but her real passion had been leading the women's swim team to a string of victories. Although she might have gone on to a career in translation or perhaps the civil service, she had met Oliver Greenwood when he was still in medical school and married him in the spring of her sophomore year so that she could follow him to Montreal, where he was going to do his internship. In those days, one did not consider possibilities other than marriage if one was serious about a young man, she explained years later. Marriage to Oliver, she said, had seemed far more important than finishing her degree.

She still had the strongest crawl of anyone who swam in the small Muskoka lake where we had our summer cottage, and she easily beat Father and everyone else consistently, summer after summer, in the cottagers' race across the bay every August. She wore a black swimsuit of some thin, elastic fabric; she was startlingly unlike the other mothers in their floral suits with little pleated skirts and draped bosoms. And she always strode into the water—on race day and on every other too—as if she were conquering the lake simply by entering it.

She'd pull a white rubber cap over her thick hair but it was never sufficiently large to cover her entire head and strands of wet hair would curl down her neck and along her cheek. Mother loved to swim. She seemed an entirely different person when she was slicing through the dark water, her long arms lifting and sweeping, her feet keeping up a steady flutterkick of foam behind her. A different person, that is, from her formal presence in the living room, that gracious woman in a pale silk dress, head on one side, judging the stream of tea from a silver spout.

Tea made in silver has a different flavour than tea brewed in crockery, and Mother much preferred the sharper taste she claimed came from her silver pot. She always swore she could taste the difference, just as she could tell whether the pot had been warmed properly, and whether the water poured over the tea leaves had been bubbling. I recall this guiltily as I plug in the kettle and place two Red Rose teabags in one of those little British teapots, round and squat and glazed shiny brown.

The kettle is in a kitchenette down the hall from my mother's room; she's not permitted to have electrical appliances which heat. It says so in the contract my brother Randall and I signed when she came here. When we brought her here, rather. Calmed by sedatives and rum-laced tea, not able to understand what was happening or where she was going, Mother was admitted with a minimum of fuss and bother. It is a small, two-litre electric kettle, and as soon as it boils a mechanism turns it off so that it can't boil dry. These safety devices are a great boon to the forgetful, and to the overworked staff here who stride purposefully along the corridor every now and again, carrying things, looking preoccupied and efficient.

They do not wear uniforms but you can tell by the way they bustle they are not visitors, as I am. They are nurses, here in this place to care for the elderly who, like my mother, have lost all sense of themselves; who, for reasons ranging from stroke to Alzheimer's to hardening of the arteries, inhabit the world in an altered state. Still a noble figure of a woman, Mother is large and heavy and potentially dangerous not only to herself but to those around her. We have all had to concur in this evaluation, finally, all of us but Margaret Greenwood herself. For some reason this sensible kettle offends me and I wish it would boil its head off, wish it had a whistle and would blow itself silly.

I am making this pot of tea for my mother and me, and have brought a green paper packet of Peek Frean Nice Biscuits to have with it. I am hoping she (Maggie, they call her here) might recollect something, anything, when she bites into the cookie. Might she suddenly see the cat curled on top of the piano, or the magazines needing to be moved before she sets the tray down? Might she hear the confiding voices of her friends, might she hear me playing "Für Elise" with no mistakes, not one?

"Oh please," I whisper, and I hear myself, realize I have spoken out loud. Dear Jesus, I think, I'm not in this place ten minutes and I'm as openly demented as the rest of them. But what does it matter, there is no one in this tiny kitchen to hear me. "Please remember something. Remember observing the niceties."

My voice sounds oddly like a child's, the child I am still in my mother's presence although I am older now than she was in that dusty living room I am remembering. And she has become the one who is a child, whose existence depends on being taken care of. Once our father died, she could not stay alone; we hired Miss Tobias to begin with, but she's really too old herself to look after someone as difficult as Mother. And it became apparent that without Father—or perhaps, because of him, because of some earlier, unmentionable event—the two women were unable to get along in a civil fashion.

(It was true that Miss Tobias seemed to delight in deliberately infuriating Mother; she'd make her tea by sticking a teabag in a mug and delivering it with the tagged string dangling over the side. Mother would dash the whole thing to the floor and chase Miss Tobias from the room, who would then telephone one of us that "the patient" was being a handful again.)

Sometimes Mother's eyes flash with a dark, raddled anger as if she knows what's happened to her and blames us, hates us, hates herself to the point of madness. Hates being here, an old loony in a home. A *home*. That word has suffered so many indignities it has lost its sense as much as poor old Maggie has. Preceded by an article, it suddenly means its opposite, not *home* at all but a series of small rooms off a brightly lit corridor where the shifty smell of wilting chrysanthemums mixes with that of rubber-soled shoes. There's a glassy coldness at the window pane, a jangling bell announcing meals, a nasty stiffness to the cotton sheets. Sad old bodies stuffed into a space from which they will be removed in order to be placed in coffins.

Language creates such intricate traps, transforming itself through us and because of us and still alarming us with its changes: The Home. A Home. "We're going to take you home, Mother," does not sound like what we did: We put her in a home.

Old Maggie doesn't speak now, not at all, so we can't have a witty conversation about the meaning of words the way we might have, long ago. Oh, she loved fiddling with language, arguing with Father for the pure joy of the sound of it. "Either a home is a home or it isn't," she'd have said, if the subject had been raised over tea. "Define your terms and stick to them, Oliver, fuzzy thinking in a physician is a worrisome trait. You can't go changing the meaning of a word simply by whether you've put an article before it or not. For goodness' sake!"

The colour in her high cheekbones would have risen and her spirit would have visibly soared as it did whenever she challenged her husband to meet her strength. Oh, how she loved an argument, little caring if she were right or not; she'd pick a fight just for the fun of it, for the rush of adrenalin and the chance to use her brain, for the marvellous clarity there'd be all of a sudden, the way everything seemed to come into focus in those moments of verbal battle.

I couldn't keep her with me—I travel a lot in my job and I live alone, you know, there'd be no one to look after her —and Randall tried but his wife Laura nearly went crazy, Laura who is the most placid of any of my brothers' wives. Besides, she said, it wasn't good for their children to see Granny this way. We agreed, all of us, the other two on the long-distance lines assuring Randall and me that whatever we decided was all right with them. "Whatever you think best," Jim said, and Gordon said essentially the same thing. "We feel fine leaving everything in your hands," he said.

Randall comes Sundays and I come Wednesdays whenever I can, but it is hard to know if it matters to Mother. The nurses encourage us to visit, they speak of stimulation and change of scene and they want to perk us up by assuring us we make a difference even though we can see, plainly, she does not know who we are.

I carry the plastic tray with the tea things into my mother's room and she doesn't look up. She is slumped in her chair by the window, her long legs straight out in front of her. She is dressed nicely (the staff see to that, especially on the days family is expected to visit; this kind of care is what we pay for, isn't it?) but the collar of her dress is all twisted to one side and the skirt is runched up around her hips. "Please, Mother, please Margaret, Mrs. Doctor Greenwood, remember me. Remember Jane, your only daughter?" I don't know whether I am speaking aloud or not, half the time I'm here I feel crazy myself.

Life is meant to offer solutions, if you look hard enough you are meant to find the way out of things, the forest paths and mountain tunnels miraculously offering escape in all those stories Mother used to read to us night after night and . . . but there is no way out of this. She will never come back. She will never know me again.

"Remember the light coming in the west window?" I say. "The way it would make the teapot shine?"

I break off a piece of biscuit and slip it between her dry lips, taking her chin firmly in my hand so that her eyes, deep in their bruised old sockets, look directly into mine. Her hair is no longer brushed back from her forehead in careful waves; it has been cut and permed into a parody of hair, nothing like that shining auburn crown adorning my Junoesque mother. Nor even a marvellous mess of curls the way it would be when she came out of the water, dripping and triumphant, after beating the pants off at least thirty other swimmers in the race across the bay.

I wish I could take her up to the cottage and out on the

lake again, let her remember swimming across that stretch of water, let her swim again until fatigue and age and her sad old body would drag her down under, into the dark. That is the way she would like to go, I know it is. I know in my heart this is what I should do, but how? I would have to do the whole thing myself, Randall would never have the courage or the sense of moral symmetry to help me, I could never ask him.

There is no one but me, her spinster daughter Jane. I would have to think of a good enough reason to take her out of the home for a day, I would have to do such a lot of planning. Oh, I don't know. I really don't think I could, but . . . for the moment, I am here. I bend forward, bringing the teacup close to her face, smiling for all I am worth.

"I love you, Mummy," I say. "Here now, sit up. Have a nice little cookie and a nice cup of tea."

FINE TUNING

My little sister and I have just been on the transatlantic line for more than an hour, and I am totally exhausted. Lying here in an early morning tangle of blankets, my head aching and spinning as it so often does after a conversation with Lennie, I want nothing more than to have a cigarette between my fingers, and to see her face coming near mine as she flicks me a small flame with that sterling silver lighter she's been using for years. Ever since I gave it to her, back when we all smoked, when giving someone a cigarette lighter could not be construed, as it would be now, as a gesture of latent hostility.

Well, of course here in France it would still be completely acceptable; the air is as blue with Gitanes and Gauloises as ever, or so it seems. Last night when we had dinner out, Martin and Lucy and I watched a woman at a nearby table puff her way through the courses—seven cigarettes between the hors d'oeuvres and the *poire au chocolat*.

I told Lennie about this, trying to think of amusing things to pass along during the conversation. It had been pretty funny at the time, watching that woman, but it didn't seem to translate on the phone. There was just silence at the other end, that silence that means Lennie is thinking "So?"

It used to drive me crazy when she'd go "So?" with a slight lift of her eyebrow and shoulder, not enough to be a sneer or a shrug but just enough to suggest disdain. Because she was so much younger—of five in our family I'm the eldest and she was last, the baby—we were only in the same house together for a few years. That meant we never quarrelled the way we might have if we'd been closer, for there were a lot of irritating things about her, like the "So?" business. In my opinion she was a spoiled brat but it wasn't often a problem I had to face; I went off to college the same year she entered primary school. Years later, when Martin and I got married, she was my junior bridesmaid, carrying one of those wicker baskets full of babies' breath, and stephanotis, and ivy. Darling, really darling.

Martin says he's noticed in the last year or two I lose my train of thought more often than not. Neither of us is worried that it's serious, you know, not Alzheimer's or anything like that. I just think possibly my brain is wearing out like the rest of me, or maybe it's my befuddlement since we've been living in France, where trying to think and speak a foreign language is like being in forward and reverse gear at the same time. Or the marvellous wine, it could be the wine.

The thing about Lennie's call . . . I was talking about her lighter. I had it engraved with her initials, LC for Lenore Christine; in those days, one didn't ever engrave a single girl's last initial, in the expectation her family name would change.

This was the ultimate compliment, leaving off that initial—
I knew this because I had come of age reading *Seventeen*
magazine and had absorbed all its rules and rituals, retaining
them well into later life. Lucy, my daughter, who has read
up on the fifties and claims I am a classic case, says she
sometimes sees me roaming from room to room as if I were
still looking for a crinoline to starch or a pair of saddle shoes
to polish. True, I say. True enough.

I gave my sister the lighter when she was eighteen and
had failed her first year at university and was feeling rotten
about it. She'd been smoking steadily since she was fourteen,
and her fingers already were stained nicotine yellow; I wanted
to do something to establish my acceptance of her, to dem-
onstrate my affection for her no matter what. Sure, she was
a brat but she was, after all, family.

I still smoked occasionally then, one of those slow quitters
who takes a long time to break the habit, and it happened
that Lennie came to stay with Martin and me in Ottawa that
summer after she'd failed. I would have been thirty-two then,
too removed from her age range to be a *real* friend, and the
lighter was an inspired idea. It meant that in the late afternoons, when I got home from my job at City Hall and she
came in from classes (she was taking two transferable university courses, our Dad had paid her way on the condition
she make up her failures), we'd sit at the kitchen table by
the open window and drink mint tea and smoke filter-tips,
and she'd light them with the pretty little silver lighter.

We talked a lot about our parents, which was one thing
we had in common. Yet what we had to say about them
differed enormously because of that age gap and neither of
us really wanted to hear whatever truths the other had to
tell. We both knew our mother was killing herself with booze
but we each had invented our own reasons for that, reasons

we couldn't alter without altering ourselves. Memory is a hazardous game, better not to play unless you're willing to take the consequences. So we'd light another cigarette, or pour more tea, and look out from the highrise across to the silent Gatineau hills, in what seemed a wonderful unspoken complicity. Looking back now, I wish we had talked a little more.

Lennie was so pretty that summer. Now she's glamorous and everyone is knocked out by her—but then, she was simply beauty itself, even with a cigarette hanging from the corner of her mouth. Really. Of the five of us, she got the looks, there was never any quarrel about that. So Celtic-looking you could die, black hair and cornflower eyes and skin the colour of milk. And it turned out she got the brains, too, although that's been a bit of a surprise. She always made herself out to be an airhead—if not intentionally, at least she made it easy for the family to take that view. The rest of us went through school and into responsible jobs without a hitch but it took her a decade to get through and settle down. Of course, given Lennie's luck, she's had a lot of success. You've seen her, Lennie McCormack?

You must have seen her, everybody else seems to have. She's had offers coming in from all over the map since the Gulf War, after only a handful of on-air reports. CNN took some clips from the station where she's been working only a few months—she covered that big protest demonstration on the coast, you would have seen her then. They always use Lennie on-camera instead of voice-over because that stunning face of hers keeps people tuned in even while they consider changing channels.

Lennie, who is more cynical than I am, says the real reason we saw her face was to divert viewers from what she was reporting; none of the top brass, she says, wanted any of those "unpatriotic" demos given air time but if they'd cut them entirely they might have laid themselves open to accusations of censoring. So they put Lennie in front of the camera and hoped the protesters' placards wouldn't get noticed.

"It stinks," she says, "but the fact is, I'm a face now, Julia, and I'm getting a name as well. That's the terrible thing about all this. I let myself be used and I feel I'm losing my integrity, maybe I've lost it entirely, who knows. The peace movement went under in that bloody war, but all of a sudden I'm on top. So what good does it do me? I feel like shit."

I've seen her twice during these past weeks—we get CNN in our apartment here in Paris—and I saw the strain in her eyes, the lines around her mouth a little more defined, as if she were under some stress. Now, that's not entirely accurate, or even true. Until this morning when she called I had no idea how bad she was feeling. I shouldn't make myself out to be wiser than I am as if I were one of those intuitive sisters who "knows" when something's wrong. To be honest, I'm already unsure of what Lennie was telling me this morning, what I thought I heard or what I imagined she said.

When she called—sun not even risen here, well after midnight her time—Lennie's voice was ragged and there was a clink now and again on the line, a clink I know very well. Ice against glass translates itself through the magic medium of Mr. Bell's invention and pierces the heart. And of course, when I ask her midway through the conversation (after she's said "Julia, you have to listen to me, my life is a mess") whether or not she's drinking, she says she's not.

"Why are you asking?" she says. "You must be at it again yourself, right? It takes one to know one." And we have a good laugh, because it's true, isn't it? My head is splitting after last night's Chablis in the restaurant and the Cognac we

197

drank once we got home. Martin likes to have a nightcap in front of the fireplace no matter what time we get in—one last look at the papers, one final drink, his habits so set and ingrained I know them by heart. I turn on the lamp by his chair as soon as we're in the door, go over to the cabinet and take out the crystal glasses without being asked.

He was already in his shower when the phone rang this morning; Martin gets up at six no matter how late we've been the night before. He likes getting into his office by eight, he says, because in that hour before his staff arrives he can accomplish the whole day's work. He's always been like this, no matter what country we've lived in; he has his own rhythm and his own way of doing things and hates having embassy underlings interfere.

It's an odd trait to find in a man who's made a career in the diplomatic service, this crankiness. You'd think he'd be happier in his work than he seems to be—this posting to Paris is meant to be a plum, a reward for those other, less prominent places where we've spent our lives. Lucy accused him last night at dinner of a negative attitude toward the French after we listened to him recite his complaints of the day but I don't think it's the *French* he hates. Martin finds fault with everyone.

None of us are well or happy any more, and I think I said this to Lennie, not meaning to downgrade whatever's wrong with her but it's true, we're all sick at heart one way or another. Even this war so quickly won by the forces of truth and justice, this war we're meant to feel great about, makes me ill. Such ugliness, such monstrous ugliness. I told Lennie how Lucy went right off the deep end one night when we were watching some coverage—good word, that—of the oil spill in the Gulf. Those poor birds coated with black guck, those innocent creatures dying horribly because of . . . because of *us,* Lucy said, people like Martin and me, because of the way our generation has let hers down.

Since that night when she stood in the living room shouting at us (as dramatic a performance as I can recall since her childhood tantrums), more of that story has come to light, and we've been hearing about those birds. Hearing that it was the same footage used over and over, that pathetic cormorant long dead somewhere else, maybe in the Alaska spill, who knows, do they have cormorants there? No, I don't think so. We've heard that much of what they showed wasn't from the Gulf at all. Came from the files.

Lucy says it hardly matters where the film comes from, the very fact that it exists rests on our shoulders. There's no arguing with her, if she wants to blame Martin and me for the world's ills she will, and that's the truth. But what do you suppose they call those files—EDVs? Ecological Disaster Visuals? Dying Creatures? Oil Spills, Various?

Lucy's the age now Lennie was then, when I gave her the lighter; odd to think about that connection because there's little else similar—they're such different people, my sister and my daughter. Lucy would go wild if she ever knew I was still smoking that summer when I was pregnant with her. She rages here in France at the way her schoolmates smoke, she won't put up with it at all. If they ask politely if she minds—they're in the living room, say, listening to music, or at the table working on old test papers for the Bac—she absolutely rants at them. I've seen her take one of those blue paper packets of cigarettes and mash it underfoot on the floor. She's become a Green, an environmental fanatic to the point of being really unpleasant—I'm surprised she has any friends at all, the way she goes on. But she does, she's incredibly

popular at her *lycée;* French teenagers seem much more phleg-
matic than Lucy, strange to say. I'd imagined it'd be the other
way.

Lucy. How different she is from Lennie. From different
planets, different galaxies. She's pleased enough to have an
auntie turning into a media star, and she approved of her
positive reportage of the anti-war demonstrations, but she
doesn't *really* care about Lennie, not in a warm or personal
way. Martin says she's issue-oriented, one of those people
who thinks about the big picture.

Lennie, on the other hand, always gave the impression at
that age of being such a scatterbrain she wouldn't have known
an issue if it'd leapt at her. Ideas didn't interest her much,
but she was always involved with people, usually in some
intense, complicated, knotted-up sort of way. Lennie was
forever getting herself tangled in some awful relationship, and
then would have the devil's own time getting free.

She failed again after that summer with Martin and me—
she didn't even bother writing the final exams—and her next
few years are generally not spoken of in the family. I think
basically she just buggered around. She told me recently that
when she was using her silver lighter it wasn't for tobacco,
and she figures she was stoned for something like four years.

She said she thinks it was wonderful, but she can't remember very much of it, her memories are wavering and
kind of mottled, as if whoever was in charge of the darkroom
made a mistake in mixing the developing fluids and all her
negatives turned out slightly blurred. Well, not so much
blurred as kind of overlapping and stuck together, she said.
God, I said, I understand that, my brain's been double-
exposing for years, my problem starts as soon as the film goes
in the camera. We had a good laugh over that, me who's
never had more than two joints in my life more dopey than

Lennie. There's nothing wrong with her now, she's sharp, I'm telling you, Lennie McCormack is very sharp.

For some reason none of us in the family ever understood, eventually she had a massive change of heart, went back to Ottawa and got her Master's in journalism. She made the move to television after a long spell on a Toronto paper and now today she's walking the fine edge of fame. Richard, the man she lives with, has been part of this *volte face* of hers, but as far as I can discern he's a result rather than a cause. I'm glad of that, for Lennie's self-esteem, her sense of having turned her life around herself. It'd be awful to owe all that to somebody else.

You know, I preferred long-distance telephone calls before this satellite business. I loved the idea of voices travelling underneath the ocean through coral-encrusted cables, loved the notion of whales and squid swimming near my words, maybe listening in. Cable-link gave you a sense of your words being grounded in reality, whereas this other stuff, ricocheting off metal objects floating above us . . . well, it's all up in the air, isn't it? No sense of getting down to the bottom line. Conversations lack substance. I said all that to Lennie this morning, too, and it only annoyed her.

"Julia, you've said that so many times before, it's not fresh or amusing any more. Why can't you just stick to what we're talking about?"

"What *are* we talking about?" I say, indignant, wounded by her impatient tone. I was only trying to lighten things a bit.

"We're talking about me," she says. And the eldest-child voice still rampant within my psyche rears up resentfully, wanting to snipe, "Yes, well, so what else is new?" But that would be spiteful and counterproductive and I have the sense to keep my mouth shut.

"So then tell me, Lennie," I say. "This is costing you money, this call. Tell me why you're phoning. What's wrong?"

She starts again with the war, and what's been won and what's been lost; she's being philosophical and political, and even sounds a little like Lucy as she goes on about the Big Boys in their silk ties, meaning the men who control the networks, the men who steer the government, the men who have the power. Power over the way the war was run and won, over the transmission of information on the air, everything. Phallic power.

"Jesus, Julia, this whole thing was about their cocks, and nobody seems to see that," she says, and her voice is tired and lifeless, not her television voice.

"Sure they do," I say, trying to jolly her a bit. "It's always been measure, measure, that's how history is made, inch by inch. Men have been playing this game forever, right? Mine is bigger than yours, but his is bigger than mine so I'll cut a little off his and sell it to you and that's how it goes. C'mon, Lennie, this is not news to either of us."

"You'd be surprised," she says, "how few people share our sentiments. When I proposed this theory to my producer he hit the roof and told me I was a stupid cunt."

"So sue him for sexual harassment," I say, more flippant than I usually am this early in the morning. "What's going on that's making you so upset? You're tougher than this. A little language has never worried you—what's the matter?"

"Richard," she says, and her voice is so low I can hardly hear her.

"Richard? You're having problems with Richard? Is he fooling around? What?"

"No," she says, "but I am. I don't love him any more."

"Richard?" I ask stupidly. "I thought you were crazy about him."

"That's all an act," she says. Her voice is dulled—whatever she's drinking is taking the edge off, but it's also dragging her down to that deep awful place where voices, even those being bounced off stars, sound as if they are under water.

"An act?" I ask, nervous now, as if we are on the outer edges of a dark and dangerous territory I don't want to enter. I avoid women who tell me marital secrets, I have enough myself, thank you very much. She and Richard have been together long enough for Richard to seem like family and I catch myself wanting to take his side against her. Lennie says I've always done that with whomever she's living with, sided with the men rather than her, but it's not true. In this case, honestly, Richard is a lovely guy. Gentle, intelligent, good-natured. Perfect for Lennie.

"That's what I'm calling about," she says. "What I want to know is how long an act can last. I'm serious, Julia, I want to know what the limits are. I've never forgotten you telling me, back I can't think when exactly, that there were times you acted your way through with Martin. That's your phrase, acted your way through. Do you remember that? Do you remember saying that?"

"To be perfectly honest, honey, I don't," I say, trying to sift quickly through memories of talks she and I might have had in which I might have said such a thing. "It sure as hell sounds like something I might say, though."

"But do you ever *stop* acting? Can you define the line between what you feel and what you pretend?"

"I've never faked an orgasm," I say, sure that's where she's heading and deciding we can save some time if we just get down to it right away. "And if I were you, I wouldn't ever do that."

Lennie is laughing, her first real laugh of the entire call, a slow, dirty laugh—the kind that follows one of her particularly raunchy jokes. There's also something indulgent in her laughter, as if what I've said is terribly naive, and indeed, it probably is. Given the differences in the lives we've led, Lennie's a lot more worldly-wise than I am and the idea of my giving her sexual pointers is ludicrous. But I am in the dark about what she wants me to say. Why is she calling to ask about how I handle my marriage?

"Okay, Julia," she says, finally settling down. "Let me put it this way, one question with two related parts. Outside of raising Lucy, why have you stayed with Martin and to what degree is your marriage *real*?"

"Well, in terms of Lucy it has been necessary," I say, speaking very emphatically, trying to bring my own humour to this conversation. "Two of us can better share the impact of her hatred, because it'd be devastating to be the only parent she loathed. And she's so fluently bilingual now she can be scathing in two languages. Three, actually. She's doing brilliantly in Spanish, too, did I tell you she went to Madrid for a week and we didn't know where she was?"

"Juliaaa!" Lennie's voice is raw with exasperation. I've gone off the topic again. But how can I not, when everything is so connected and layered? How can any conversation be linear when life itself is so snarled and twisted, so thick with memory? What is it that she remembers that I said, I wonder. I hadn't thought I ever divulged so much to her about Martin and me. Funny what you tell people about yourself without knowing it.

"Okay," I say, "tell me whether anything I say now is going to make any difference in how you feel. No, first just tell me what you feel."

"How I *feel* is that I want out of my life," Lennie says, always quick with a dramatic phrase. That's how she's got where she is, isn't it? She has a way with words, it's the Celtic tongue that goes with her looks.

"Well then, nothing I said in the past or nothing I say today or tomorrow is going to change that, is it?" I say. As Lucy's grown I've had to keep up with current child-raising techniques, all that stuff about letting them figure out the consequences, and allowing them to explore the world through their own feelings. Works just as well with adults as with kids. "You're the one who has to . . ."

"Be straight with me," she interrupts, and I hear in her voice tension ready to break, tears ready to flood. "Don't practise your psychobabble crap."

"Okay," I say, "but what do you want?" I'm starting to get a little annoyed. "The story of my life has nothing to do with yours, and you've been the first person to tell me that in the past. I don't understand what this is about, Lennie. Has he hurt you?"

(If that's it, if he's being abusive, then I'll know what to say. At least the world has moved along enough so that there are a few solid facts women can pass on to each other. We have one true, across-the-board thing we must say to our friends, to our sisters and our daughters: *Never let him hurt you.*)

"Oh, that's not it, Jule," she says. "There's nothing violent or abusive about Richard. Maybe me, but not him. Christ, he's not even jealous of my success and he's got every right to be. No, it has to do with me, just me. What I'm trying to figure out is how long the lapses between love are. What do you and Martin have that was worth acting your way through, for days and weeks and months of your life? What do you hold on to?"

That's the kind of question I used to ask myself in the

middle of the night, and here's the baby sister asking me at dawn, when I'm barely awake even after nearly an hour of talking about the immorality of war. This is just like Lennie, she has no sense of timing, she thinks she can just phone up at any hour and I'll be on the other end of the line ready to bare my soul. What can I tell her? At my age, you stop asking difficult questions of yourself.

What I am supposing is that Lennie has some great job offer somewhere, it could even be CNN, who knows? And she's kind of hooked on herself right now, even when she's doing the humble bit I can tell that really she's in love with herself, the idea that it's *her* face and *her* name. What man can come between a woman and her self?

Anyway, that's what I'm silently mulling on my side of this conversation when the door to the bedroom opens and Lucy is standing there looking at me. Martin was coming and going during the last hour, and shut the door after kissing my forehead good-bye about ten minutes ago. He spoke a few words to Lennie as he was leaning over me, his usual fond pet names for her, and then said he'd see me at dinner and not to forget to fill the Peugeot and au revoir. It was as soon as she knew he'd gone for the day that Lennie started with her questions, now that I think of it. I told you she was sharp.

But there's Lucy, dressed head-to-toe in black, as is the *mode* among her set. As it is among everyone in Paris, or so it seems—I've never seen so much black. Three years ago, just after we first arrived, Martin's father died in Winnipeg and he went back to the funeral but Lucy and I stayed behind here, she was just getting settled in school. Wanting to connect with Martin's grief in some material way, I discovered enough black in my closet to wear proper mourning for the week of his absence, believing that my dressing this way would elicit some comment from, if no one else, the apartment concierge. I wanted to *tell* someone that my father-in-law had died, I had memorized the phrase. But no one said a thing, and as days passed, I realized that on the streets of Paris, women—of every age and station—wear black. Black can be elegant or angry, but it is always possible.

Lucy is fair, very similar in appearance to Martin, and black doesn't suit her, she looks drab and peaked. But that may well be her intent, it's the done thing to look ill if one is at *lycée*. It may be part of the radical student movement to which she most ardently belongs, or it may simply be a hiccup from the past. I too wore black three decades ago, but I would not be so foolish as to tell Lucy that.

"What do you want, sweetheart?" I say, cupping the receiver with my hand. She is looking at me in stony silence, as if something is really wrong, as if I have let her down in some dreadful way.

"This is the morning you're meant to babble babble babble." Lucy is telling me something I've forgotten at the very moment Lennie is choosing to tell me what her real problem is. My head feels as if someone is wrapping very loud barbed wire around it. Now I know that doesn't make sense, but that's how it feels, as if the wicked little barbs are sharp, harsh noises digging into my scalp.

"Listen, Lennie, we'll have to talk later, there seems to be a problem here with Lucy," I say, feeling that if I have to choose between the two of them, then Lucy, standing there glowering at me, is the immediacy I need to deal with first. "Call me back in half an hour, okay? Or I'll call you, whatever."

"Great, Julia. Thanks a lot," says Lennie, and slams her phone down hard enough that I know her feelings are hurt. But my god, I think, she's an adult, surely she can understand

that if my daughter is in a state about something then she
has to come first? I put my receiver gingerly in its plastic
cradle and focus on Lucy, and what it is she's said.

"Okay, sweetheart," I say, and pull myself up on the
pillows. This last hour with Lennie drained me, even my
elbows ache as I press my palms down onto the mattress and
straighten my shoulders. "What?"

"You really are a mess, Mother," she says. "Brain dead.
Never mind, I'm going. I'll do it myself."

She turns and slams the bedroom door, and I hear the
clatter of her black leather boots on the hallway tile and the
apartment door behind her slam. Slam, slam, slam. Everybody's slamming things and I can't defend myself because I
don't know what I've done. Or not done.

So I sit here in bed for a while, stunned by the noisy anger
circulating in the room, and then I go out to the kitchen
where Martin has, as always, made strong Italian coffee and
put it in a thermos. I pour myself a full cup black in one of
those bowls the French use for café au lait and I finish the
tail of a croissant left on the counter. Martin must have been
listening to the BBC news earlier, for the Sony shortwave is
still on, making strange galactic noises—the reception has
gone wonky and there seems to be an overlay of two or three
other stations and that keening, screeching sound of . . . what?
Colliding wavelengths? After all our years abroad it has become
a familiar sound, this layering of military marches, Strauss
waltzes, Hungarian urgency, and something vaguely oriental,
or Arab. Yes, something coming in from North Africa, that's
what that is. I fiddle with the dial for a moment until the
cultivated tones of the Beeb come again smartly to heel—
there now, that's better.

These Brits with their marvellous accents want to tell me
what to think about everything in the world but I rather liked

the shortwave reception as it was, or as it is at night when there are too many stations struggling for attention; it always irritates Martin, but I am attracted, moth to the flame, by the wild diffusion and that sense I have, listening to the jumble of voices and music and static, that there are millions and millions of us, and none of us understands anything. We are just here, flung out into space, waiting to be fine-tuned ourselves.

I come back into the bedroom and settle down under the covers to try to work through what it is that has just happened. How amusing, I think, my poor busy head is like the little Sony out there, needing a clever and patient hand on the dial. If I can stay calm perhaps I will remember at least two things; what it is I was meant to do for Lucy, and what it is that Lennie wants from me. What it is that I am holding on to.

I need to explain to her how my generation grew up (oh, the years between us are an enormous gulf) believing that you are meant to take the bad with the good. You know, that stuff about how even when things get bleak or tough or rotten or empty, you whistle a happy tune and keep your head erect like Deborah Kerr in the movie or who was it, on stage? That actress with the wonderful voice, who died? You know who I mean, Gertrude somebody.

Our mothers did it, and their mothers before them. They put on a happy face. Maybe what I should do is to sit down this morning and get out our old Broadway LPs and make lists for Lennie, lists of all those lyrics by which women like me were taught to live. Those songs flowed around and through us, shaping our lives the way rivers change landscape. Now that stuff is nothing but Muzak, but how could we have become ourselves without Rodgers and Hammerstein?

Acting your way through. Did I say that? It sounds as if I

were advocating hypocrisy—was that just Lennie's tone of voice? I meant it the way people are meant to square their shoulders and get on with it. I didn't ever hate Martin and pretend that I loved him, nothing like that, and in Lennie's words that's how it sounds, as if I'd been false to him. Or myself.

But nobody's life turns out exactly right, does it? There are always times when you have to hitch up your skirt and wade through. Acting as if everything's going to be okay— doesn't everybody do this?

I knew from the very beginning (I think I knew) that I wouldn't love Martin *all* the time, because I hadn't yet ever loved anybody every minute and couldn't conceive of it. I accepted that. And I imagined there might be occasions when he'd accommodate some small passion or other, that's the kind of man he seemed to be. Of course I was hurt the first time but I didn't make a fuss, or carry on crying and blaming everybody, or acting as if my world had ended. That kind of nonsense I've always considered lower than low. I've always seen myself as the classy dame who's still on stage for the final curtain.

Not to say it was all on his side. If we're going to go into this, I might as well admit my own slips from grace. Not many, not as many as . . . well, it hardly matters now, does it? Lennie is going to say, I can hear her, that if I'd had my own bank account, my own *life* apart from hanging on to Martin's coattails around the world, I would have left him years ago.

No, I don't think so. I could have, he would have let me go. He would have been a perfect gentleman about it, all discretion and tact, those very qualities which have moved him up in the diplomatic corps, posting by posting. We would have had careful separation agreements and custodial privileges allotted equally, and he'd have continued to be gracious, and generous—enough guilt on his side he'd have made sure I was nicely equipped to set out alone.

What kept me? Funny, it's not a song that comes to mind, it's something from real life. It's us, Martin and me, looking in through the gates of the Royal Chelsea Hospital. Oh, this was years and years ago, at the very beginning, really. We were on our honeymoon in London, on our way to the Continent. Our suitcases got stolen in Victoria Station, what a time we had . . . we spent one entire afternoon walking and ended up, where was it, near Sloane Square? And through the grillwork of the iron gate we saw these two ancient men, with wizened little English faces, sitting on a bench set against the brick wall. Dark red brick, that rich colour that is nearly brown.

And there were roses, masses of them, small white climbing roses on a trellis near the bench. It was a hot July day, I remember the sun felt warm on my skin—I was wearing a blue linen sundress and my shoulders were bare. Martin had opened his shirt two or three buttons, an unusual thing for him to do, and the fair hair on his chest glinted gold, I can see it now in my mind's eye.

Those old men were wearing bright red coats with lots and lots of brass buttons, there must have been some formal event earlier that afternoon and they were tired out, resting together after it was all over. What's clear now in my memory is that they were sitting very close together at one end of the long bench, side by side, their bodies so frail they were barely inhabiting their uniforms, and they were holding hands, those two old men. Holding hands, two veterans of who knows what war, the Boer?

It doesn't matter. Martin put his arm around me as we stood there peering through the iron grill, and he said, "That'll be us someday, Julie. We'll make it through the wars and still be holding hands."

Now, that sounds ridiculous, doesn't it? To have that as your reason for staying together? Acting as if your marriage is going to last so that you can be a withered old person sitting on a bench holding hands with another one? I can't tell Lennie this story, she'd never in a million years believe it could be something as small as that. Or she might think she understands, but she'll not really get it, not really. I'm not even sure I get it myself, and yet I'm sure this is the answer to the question. Yes, I'm quite sure.

I don't think I'll phone her back just yet. I'll let her get over her pique and call me. Whenever she does we can deal with everything then. She's going to tell me she's sleeping with that producer who called her a stupid cunt, I'll bet you anything that's what's really going on and that's what she was going to confide when Lucy interrupted. She knows Richard would never in his life do such a thing, and she hates herself for betraying him with this foul-mouthed jerk. She doesn't think it's possible that she still loves Richard, or else why is she doing this? How can she act this way, she's wondering, if indeed she loves him. I can hear the conversation already—it isn't going to be about my life, it's going to be about hers. And it's going to be about ego, not about love. That's okay. I don't think I have any wisdom to pass along anyway.

I have to put my mind to Lucy now, and whatever it is I've forgotten. You know, I could do with a cigarette. I think I'll get dressed and go down to see the concierge, I've seen him smoking American cigarettes. Just one is all I need. For old times' sake, that's all.

KNOWING PEOPLE

Chrissie, when I finally see her again, says she believes with all her heart that Jeremy must be dead. How else can she explain his absence these last twenty years, his unannounced disappearance from her life? I don't tell her what I think, which is that people *do* vanish just like that and you can't depend on them. This is the era of "letting go," we've all learned not to hang on. But Chrissie is well over eighty, and she believes that affection lasts forever. That's the way she is, good-hearted and loyal. I try to suggest, in as light a tone as I can manage, that she ought not to mourn Jeremy. "Oh, Chrissie, for heaven's sake," I say, putting my arms around her, surprised at how insubstantial and diminished she feels. "I'm sure he's perfectly fine. I'll bet he emigrated to Australia and lost his address book in the outback somewhere. He's alive and well, you mustn't feel sad."

She smiles at my outrageous attempts to keep her from feeling grief, for she and I both know Jeremy would never darken the outback in a million years. He would be as likely to go to the moon. She will not be so easily diverted and quickly returns to her plaintive refrain in which Jeremy is pined for and elevated to a place among the saints.

"Ach, Clare, if you'd seen how good he was to me and poor Duncan before the end. I couldn't've done without his help, I tell you. He must've had a special place for us in his heart, mercy, he gave up his whole summer to care for Duncan. He'd carry the poor soul from his bed to the window, or he'd tell him fine stories to cheer him. He was a nurse, Clare, a real nurse. No, something happened to him or he'd have come back to see me. Something terrible and quick it was, an accident on the M1, oh my dear wee laddie, gone, gone."

Tears filling her eyes, Chrissie reaches for my hand and strokes it in rhythm to her rocking in the chair, remembering the slow death of her husband Duncan and moving from that to the imagined and tragic death of Jeremy. Of course when she saw me again she'd think of him, I should have been prepared—he was as much a part of that summer twenty-five years ago as I was, that August when Britain was hit by a heat wave and the sky was so extraordinarily blue.

The day I arrived at Chrissie and Duncan's front gate Jeremy Kerr was already there, earnest participant in the University of Edinburgh's summer Gaelic program. One of several students boarding on crofts around the outer Hebrides, he'd been on North Uist nearly a fortnight absorbing the ancient and intricate language. We disliked each other on sight. He regarded me as an intruder, infringing on territory he had understood would be his alone; and I looked at him, pale-skinned and thin as a rail, with a striped scarf around his neck even in the afternoon heat, and decided he was clearly one of those pretentious young men given to scholarly affectations. Tedious. Not my sort at all.

Angus McNay, Chrissie and Duncan's only son, junior officer on the liner on which I had crossed the Atlantic the summer before—he had been more my type.

Everyone crossed by liner then, in those days when everyone went to Europe before settling down. The fare was the same as flying and for that you got a whole week at sea, enough time to meet others like yourself with whom you might later travel, or share a flat, or fall in love. Fresh from university or after a year or two earning enough to go abroad, young women like me travelled third class, lodged deep in the bowels of those same old liners that now cruise the Caribbean for the generation we have become. And we felt, as we leaned on the rails and blew kisses down to our parents waving handkerchiefs on the dock, that we might never return. We said of course that we'd be back—but none of us believed that we'd ever retrace our steps. We thought we would simply keep going forever, devouring the world.

My father had given me a carnation corsage to wear, and I threw it down to him as the ship began to move, in what I imagined was a symbolic gesture. I wanted no connection with my parents. I was off to Europe to free myself at last from their embrace. He caught it and waved it at me, and then began pinning it on my mother's jacket. She was weeping furiously, as if she knew what was in my mind.

There were four of us going off together, that bright October day. We'd been friends at university and in the year since graduation had saved enough money for this trip. Patricia was going to write a novel, Judith intended to study French in Paris and maybe get a job as an au pair, and Dorrie and I wanted simply to travel as much as we could. We figured we could make enough money in London as substitute teachers or as waitresses; everyone said it was easy as pie, you could always be a salesclerk at Harrods if worse came to worst.

Looking back, I am astounded at our innocence, at our blanket assumption that our lives would turn out well. We knew nothing about the world, nothing. We were four foolish virgins—in every sense. (At least, I was, and since we always told each other everything, I believed the others were too.)

Three days out of Montreal a severe storm sent most passengers to bed, but I discovered I had sea legs and was quite able to walk the rolling decks without nausea or fear. The sharp wind whipping at my face, my wet hair slicing around my head, salt spray stinging my eyes—this was what I had left home for. Only the rails between me and the dark water—this small amount of danger excited me, made me feel passionately alive. All the old demarcations erased themselves as the horizon disappeared in the turbulence of waves. I paced up and down, ecstatic.

Ahead of me a small grey bird fell on the deck, exhausted and unable to move. There were crackers in my pocket from lunchtime—everyone said sucking on Saltines kept seasickness away, and I kept them handy in case my good luck ran out—so I crumpled them into bits to toss at the bird, talking to it, telling it that everything would be just fine.

Several bullying gulls wheeled above me, screeching so loudly it took a while to make out my phrases being repeated behind me, in a male voice, deep and musical. When I finally did turn around, too curious not to look, it was Angus, in his navy-blue uniform, introducing himself as one of the ship's officers. When I asked what that meant he said he helped to steer the boat, and gave a great laugh. He had a paper bag in his hand which must have held a sandwich, for he took out a brown crust and began breaking it up, throwing it across the deck at the bird, who was by then too full to eat any more and lay there looking up at us in mute despair. And then we walked into the face of the wind and I stole looks (he seemed at least thirty, maybe older) and tried to put him together sufficiently in my mind so that I could describe him in detail to Dorrie and Patricia and Judith who were down in our cabin, languishing on their bunks.

He was quite ordinary-looking, dark-haired, not much taller than I was but heavier, with broad shoulders and a nice enough face—a lovely wide smile, the kind of generous smile you automatically trust. He felt me taking these quick, surreptitious glances and took hold of my arm, stopping our progress along the deck. His eyes were dark blue.

"And shall you meet me then for a drink when I come off the bridge at ten?" he said. Hardly a question at all.

I said yes.

"Oh, it's too perfect," moaned Patricia, holding a pillow across her stomach. "Too wonderful. I'm so jealous I could die. Here we are puking our guts out and you're up there having a True Romance."

"You just said yes, that's all you said? Clare, you are so cool. Do you understand what you're saying yes to?" Dorrie mixed scorn and admiration equally.

"Shut up, all of you," I said. "I just said I would meet him, that's all. It's no big deal." I wished, now that it was too late, that I hadn't told them anything at all.

Angus hardly bothered with conversation. He bought me a drink of whisky at the bar and as soon as I finished he said he had some very good malt in his cabin. We would have to be careful, he said, since officers weren't meant to mingle with passengers except on A and B decks, but it would be okay, he would show me the way. The cabin was compact, dimly lit, and had a small record player which took 45s. He put on a scratchy rendition of "There Is a Rose in Spanish Harlem" and set the arm so that it would replay. He poured me a tumbler of pale Scotch whisky, the like of which I had never tasted before. The warm aroma, the feel of it would come to me months later when I was walking in the Highlands, when I would smell the peat smoke from cottage chimneys in the hills. I drank it quickly without a qualm and drank another more slowly, feeling myself become silky and liquid and perfect.

I think there may have been some preliminary kissing, and some murmuring on his part, words of endearment I couldn't quite catch. I like to think it must have been Gaelic but it might just have been that he too was a little drunk and slurring his speech.

He carried me across the room and undressed me, stroked me a little and then, without any of the difficulty or pain I'd been warned would attend this matter, entered me as if we'd been doing this together all our lives. It was the easiest thing in the world and I couldn't think why I hadn't done it before. And then, as we were moving and moving and moving and my spine felt as if it were going to splinter into gorgeous, gorgeous stars, I suddenly remembered. Babies. That's why I hadn't done it before. Babies. Pregnant. Oh God. "Stop," I said. "I mustn't . . . what if I . . . did you . . . oh," I said. "Oh."

"Eh, lass, don't worry. I was out in time," he said. There was a box of tissues beside his bed, and he took them and with great tenderness wiped himself, and then me, and lay beside me, his head on my shoulder. "You're fine," he said. "Never fear. That was great, just great."

"I never did it before," I said. "That's all. And so I wasn't
. . . I don't know if . . ."

The look on his face was one of utter astonishment. "You
don't say?" he said, a kind of rhetorical question, his eyebrows
making a straight line across his forehead as he looked at me,
our faces only inches apart. There'd been no blood, no breaking through—what kind of virgin had I been, after all? I felt
hot with embarrassment, seeing myself in his eyes as some
kind of freak. Never done it before. Perhaps I hadn't even
done the thing the right way, who knew? I'd always stopped
well before this point. But with a sweetness I was later to
know in Chrissie, he put his arms around me and said, "Never
mind then, lass, we'll make up for lost time. Just let me rest
a little and we'll try it again."

The funny thing was, I couldn't share it with the others.
Even though they all swore up and down that I looked different, in a smug sort of way—"You did it, *I know you did,*"
Dorrie said darkly, in a voice meant to sound like my
mother's—I maintained that we'd stayed in the bar all night,
telling each other our life's stories.

"Look," I said, offering proof on a scrap of paper. "He
gave me his parents' address in the Hebrides so if we're
travelling up there we've got a place to go. He's genuinely
nice, not what *you* think at all."

They didn't believe me, but then they probably wouldn't
have believed the truth either, how after a night which left
me aching and quenched we had knelt naked at the porthole
of his cabin watching the sun come up over the calm ocean.
Everything out there rosy and golden, the water ahead of us
still as glass, a few stray gulls swooping over the wake. And
then three nuns, in heavy brown habits, fingering their ro-
saries, gliding by noiselessly out on the deck. The sun glinted
on the silver between the beads one of the nuns was holding

and the moment transfixed itself in my brain. I felt holy, chosen by God for bliss.

Of course I never saw Angus McNay again after the day we disembarked in Southampton, although once he left a message for me at Canada House on Trafalgar Square, to say he'd been in London but didn't know how to find me. The note ended with "Remember, if you do visit the Isles, my parents love company, they'd treat you well."

I hankered after him for a few weeks, feeling as if I ought to be in love with him after what had happened, but the piece of paper with the three-digit telephone number was really enough. I did not get pregnant and in a fit of gratitude to God and the saints found a small Roman Catholic church near our bedsitter where I lit candles of thanksgiving and remembrance.

Dorrie and I set up together in London right away, finding jobs and making weekend forays out into the countryside. In the new year we crossed over to Europe and met up with Judith in Paris, with whom we hitched rides down into Spain and then up along the Riviera. (Patricia had gone to Oslo with a fellow she'd met in a bookstore—we never saw her again, I believe she settled in Norway.)

When we had run through all our money we crossed back over into England where Dorrie and Judith got late-night jobs serving snacks to gamblers in a Soho casino, and I took a temporary position in an Infants' School near Holland Park. Our lives swerved away from each other's and I began to think seriously about going up to Scotland at the close of school in July. Alone.

When I put forth the idea neither Dorrie nor Judith seemed the least offended, they were by now so entranced by the shadowy world in which they dwelled as Sandwich Girls. Dorrie said she wouldn't mind hitching with me as far up as Gretna Green if I wanted, since she had a few days off, but that was as far as she wanted to go.

"It's you who wants to find her Highland roots anyhow," she said. "And you're probably still lusting after that sailor, aren't you, Clare? Would you really have the nerve to call on his folks?"

"I don't see why not," I said, defensive as always with Dorrie. She seemed to know how to get under my skin. "There's no harm in phoning when I'm up there. I want to see all the islands from Mull up to Lewis. I don't think any of my people ever came from Uist, but you never know."

My people. We always called our relatives our "people" in my family, and the word itself took on special meaning. I tried to talk about this with Jeremy later that summer, in the long discussions we'd have far into the night after Chrissie and Duncan had gone to bed. Jeremy. He is included in every memory of that August, too, whether I wish him to be or not.

Jeremy and I would walk down to the edge of the croft where the land met the sea and marvel how the sky wouldn't truly darken even at midnight. We would lie side by side in the grass, never touching nor wanting to, two beings as separate as it was possible to be and yet coupled by mutual experience and chance, the chance that had brought us together with the old McNays. We were as different as fire from water, as earth from air. But we would smoke strong handrolled cigarettes together and drink Guinness from cans and argue about words until one of us would tire of it and get up and stumble back to the small stone house in the semi-darkness. The *way* you said a word, I maintained, gave it a range of meanings a dictionary could not chart. But Jeremy, budding linguist and intellectual purist, would never agree.

I had a vivid childhood memory I used as validation of my position, a memory concerning my father's sister, Auntie Jean. She'd been staying in Portree on Skye, where she'd been looking up our people in cemeteries and registries. She'd met a very old man at a *ceilidh* to whom she'd talked in great detail about her quest. "He knew exactly who I was," she said, relating this event to us on her return. "He *knew* me."

How marvellous, I had thought at the time, that man knew her and he'd never even seen her before. I wondered how Auntie Jean must have felt, having a stranger know her right off the bat like that. It seemed something I would both like and be afraid of, fear and desire at the same time, wanting —I must have been around eleven then—both to keep parts of myself private and to be perfectly understood. Encased in my aunt's tremulous voice, being *known* meant being fathomed entirely, for generations, and took on a mysterious new significance. It was all in how she had said it, I declared. Jeremy was not impressed and declared that proof by anecdote was a fallacious form of argument.

I still feel my temper rising when I think of that English boy and his infuriating self-composure, his uncompromising certainty that he was always right. Four years younger than I was, he was as dogmatic as someone four times older; but far more irritating was his absolute devotion to his own needs and his utter self-centredness. Maybe it was a transient flaw of late adolescence, more likely it was an essential part of his character, that single-minded pursuit of perfection. He was in the Hebrides to study and that he would do: the fact that there were chores to help with around the croft (clearly the reason the McNays had signed up for a student) or that it would have been decent to take up a drying towel as the tea things were being washed, never occurred to Jeremy. And if he were asked—by me, never by Chrissie or Duncan who were awestruck by his arrogance and treated him like a royal visitor—he'd smile a tight, thin smile and say, "But Clare, you enjoy mucking in. I do not. I enjoy my books."

Toward the end of our month together, if I dared to trouble him, he'd mutter something in Gaelic that would set the two old McNays laughing and laughing. Chrissie had a laugh like bells in the wind, like old jokes told in the dark, so rich that even though I would stand there excluded and bitter, not understanding the Gaelic, her laughter would bring me to my senses and I'd flick my tea towel at him in a cheerful, older-sister kind of way, and end by laughing too. He was, after all, very young, very callow, I'd say to myself. And somehow the intensity of his focus was enviable—it was a quality I lacked. Here I was wandering around Britain and Europe, not yet knowing what I was going to be . . . and he, Jeremy, already knew exactly what he wanted to know.

Chrissie would have been nearly sixty then and Duncan older, although I never knew his age for sure. He probably looked nearer to seventy than he was. He'd been a weaver so long, bent over his loom, that his body had taken on a permanent forward stoop, and his hands were enlarged with muscle—not only from the handling of the shuttle but from life on the croft itself. They were the hands of a farmer, a fisherman, a man of the earth and sea. Frail earth on these isles, only a thin covering of it on the rock, just enough to plant potatoes and turnips, get an acre or two of hay for the milk cows. Most of the land around their croft was peat bog thick with heather, roamed over by dimwitted sheep who needed to be brought back in from time to time.

Chrissie and Duncan were not my people (my father's had emigrated to Canada from Skye generations ago, and my

mother's were all from over by Wick), but they might well
have been for the warmth with which they received me. The
day I telephoned her from the mainland Chrissie said, "Ach,
lass, a friend of Angus is welcome, very welcome. Will you
come and stay a day?"

She met me at the gate and embraced me, saying as we
walked up·to the house she could tell I had Highland blood
by my colouring and the set of my head. "Macleod, lassie,
and you carry yourself like a Gunn. Ach, you did well to
come here, you did well."

In front of a smoky peat fire in the sitting room we ate
scones and oatmeal cakes with rhubarb jam, and drank tea
with creamy milk, and I looked around the room hoping to
see a photograph of Angus. I had trouble remembering what
he looked like, although his mother reminded me of him in
ways I couldn't explain.

There was a framed picture of him in the bedroom she
said I would sleep in, sitting on a crocheted doily on a low
dresser. "Aye," she said, picking it up and running her hand
across it to dust it, "this is our Angus. He'll be eight years
older now, but he's still the same lad. Are you close friends
with him, did you say?"

Looking at the broad, bland face of a young man in a
merchant sailor's uniform, I tried to think of him, and felt
my mind go blank even as my body flushed with a memory
of its own. What to say? What was she asking? Had there
been a stream of deflowered young women flowing through
this small room, staying for a few nights in Angus's bed alone?
The walls were papered with a pastel print, flamboyant peonies tied together with ribbon. I couldn't imagine Angus ever
being here. I couldn't imagine how *I* had had the audacity
to come.

"Well no, Mrs. McNay, but he was ever so kind when I

told him I wanted to spend time in the Isles. I do hope you don't mind me phoning and all."

"Ach, no, lass, I think you were sent," she said. "As soon as I saw you striding up the road I knew you were sent. We'll speak to Duncan about it at tea, but I want to ask you to stay for a bit and help out. The old man won't say so but this season is getting too hard for him, and I know myself the haying gives me the aches. If you'll just stay for a bit now, you'll have this room and your meals, and for the rest of it, free as you please. There's another boarder too"—she said "too" in a long birdlike trill—"but he's not got the muscle in his back I see in yours. He's pure Sassenach, the poor laddie. But you could give us a real hand in the fields, dearie. You could help the season finish smooth."

And so I stayed for a month, helping to tie up the hay and toss it on the wagon and load it in the byre. And I dug the potatoes and laid them in rows to dry and then brought them into the small cold cellar at the side of the house. I fed the chickens and collected their eggs, and weeded the small kitchen garden where tomatoes and cucumbers grew as fast as they could in the short span of sunny weather.

The McNay croft was one of twelve grouped together along the shoreline, and during this period of harvest all the crofters helped each other, so that some days I was sent by Chrissie to work over at the McKinnons' in return for their wagon the day before. These old weather-toughened crofters said, as we worked side by side in the sweltering heat, that there'd never been a sky so blue. This was not praise of the heavens—such tropical brilliance hardly conformed to their stern Calvinist standards—but was dour commentary for my benefit: I was to understand this glorious sunshine was not their usual lot. Life was much harder and more bitter here than a stranger could possibly know.

Sometimes I would urge Jeremy to join us not so much because I thought he should help but so that he could hear Gaelic being spoken in the fields, still a living, vital language. Occasionally he would saunter to the edge of wherever we were working and listen, and scribble in a small notebook he carried everywhere with him. Once when four or five of the older women were singing, he asked them to stop now and again so he could transcribe their song. But his interest, it eventually dawned on me, was not in learning Gaelic to *speak* it, but to understand how the grammar worked and how it fitted together with other languages.

Most of the day he spent indoors with his Gaelic worksheets and Celtic histories, or his Greek and Latin texts, working at translations or reading for pleasure. It astounded me that anyone would, or could, choose books over the smell of freshly-cut grass, but it was clear that Jeremy's passions were entirely academic and that he had no interest in the physical world. We'd go round and round arguing in the evenings, dissecting our differences and coming no nearer to understanding each other. He was as bewildered by me as I by him.

"Really, Clare? You don't know what you want to do with your life? I find that pathetic," he'd say, in his most withering tone. "It must have to do with the inferior grade of schooling in the colonies." I would take offence and we'd debate, far into the gently descending darkness, the relative merits of the British and North American education systems.

When he wasn't with his books he was with Duncan, which I thought was silly because Duncan himself barely spoke, there'd be no gain in Gaelic there. They spent most of their time in the weaving shed where the sounds of the whirring shuttle and clacking loom were a constant music, noisy enough to make conversation difficult. When the wind came a certain way from the houses down the line you could hear the other weavers, each with his own rhythm, each with his own particular design and his own stamp to put on bolts of coarse tweed.

Chrissie and I would start at seven, putting on the tea and mixing up the morning scones, the kind cooked on a griddle on top of the stove. She taught me to make crowdie from the soured milk in the pail she kept in the pantry, she taught me to pull the long teats of three old cows from which we got the milk. She talked all day long, in a continuous, melodic flow of words in which all conversation referred to events of that day itself, or possibly the day previous. "Ach, wasn't that a morning!" she'd say at noon. And at tea, "Clare my dearie, did you ever see such a fine day?"

Only at supper, a small meal we all ate together in front of the fire at ten, would she talk about the past and then only in answer to Jeremy's questions in Gaelic. It would begin with a reading from her Gaelic Bible, which she would hold on her lap in an attitude of reverence, reading slowly, her finger tracing each word as she spoke. Duncan would sit stooped over, gazing into the last glowing bits of peat as if he were listening intently, but his eyes held a dreamy look that seemed to have nothing to do with the Word of God. Jeremy would be agitated, anxious to grasp every word and nuance, would make her go back and explain—sometimes in Gaelic, sometimes in English—and then he would have a go himself, with Chrissie's soft voice correcting him, filling in for him, making it all sound right. Then he'd move from questioning the verses they'd been reading to her life, to Duncan's life, to who they were and why they had stayed in this remote place when so many others had left and were living in comfort with kin on the mainland.

Once, Chrissie said, she had stayed over in Dundee with one of their married daughters while she was recuperating from a gall bladder operation. "It near killed me," she said, meaning not the operation itself but being away from the croft. Duncan had travelled more often and widely—he had fought in France during the war although he wouldn't speak of it—"but there's nothing out there I don't have here," he said. One of their sons-in-law was a skipper on a McBrayne's ferry out of Oban and could get them free passage anywhere along McBrayne routes, but they'd only gone twice, "to keep him happy," Chrissie said.

Later, when we were alone, Jeremy and I would chew on such bits of information about lives so different from our own. "Could you stay here forever?" I'd ask. "Can you imagine it?"

"As long as I had a good supply of Catullus," he'd reply. "And the Greeks, of course, I'd need the Greeks. Yes, I think I could. *Pourquoi non?*" His mouth curling in a smile meant to annoy me, he'd state his creed. "An Englishman can survive anywhere as long as he has his books."

"Oh, dry up, Jeremy," I'd say, fed up with his attempts to lord it over me because he was British and therefore the Real Item. He had pushed this advantage in too many arguments and it had lost its bite. He was always trying to paint himself as pure intellect and me as some lumpen clod, but his insults seemed also a boyish show of camaraderie—possibly he thought this banter was how to be friends. "Just piss off. You wouldn't last a minute. You'd shrivel up and die in a couple of days, you still haven't figured out which end of the cow gives milk."

Before he could have the last word I'd go off walking in the rough heather by myself, dreaming of a life here, being married to a sailor—someone like Angus, say—who would come and go and leave me to my own devices in between. I would have several children with wonderfully pink cheeks and a hired girl to help with the chores. I would spend my time . . . and here my mind would go blank. Doing what? What would I do? What was I becoming?

These days on the croft were completely fulfilling, I wanted only to rise in the morning and start again. I loved working side by side with Chrissie, loved how *used* my body felt after hours of physical work. But surely one couldn't go on like this, not forever—you'd go mad, wouldn't you, just *being*? That's what worried me and I wanted to talk about it, but Jeremy's disdain for any options other than a bookish life kept me silent.

Back in my room at night, surrounded by the full-blown peonies, I sometimes opened the wardrobe where Angus's clothes were hung and buried my face in the dark blue serge of his jacket, hoping for some memory of him to come. But I had known only the moist, sharp smell of his skin, and his weight in the dark, and the needle dropping again and again on the rose in Spanish Harlem.

On the last afternoon of the haying, when the men with their wagons had gone and Chrissie and I were lying exhausted on the sweet dry grass in the loft of the byre, she turned and said, "Ach, it'll be low tide now. Fetch towels, lass, we'll go down for a swim."

It had never occurred to me that one might venture into the cold green water of the Atlantic—it was rocky at the end of the croft, and the waves splashed up against the cliffs in a menacing, unfriendly way. But I got the towels and followed her down past the chicken house and the garden, through the small treeless pasture where the McNays' cows stood gazing placidly out at the horizon. I patted my favorite old Holstein on her rump as I passed, and began the careful clamber down the rough and jagged bluffs to the base where the departing tide had left stretches of white sand among the ochre-coloured rocks. There was a path of sorts, which Chrissie seemed to know by foot as much as by eye—she was nimble on her way down, far more agile than I'd ever seen her.

"Look," she said. "There are pools for us. Come now Clare, leave your clothes here and we'll have a good wash." She began to strip off the sweaty mauve housedress she'd been wearing. Beneath she wore long cotton bloomers of the type I'd worn as a child, baggy with elastic at the knee, and a white brassiere which, when it came off, let her large breasts fall loose in a tumble of flesh. Her skin where it had been exposed to the sun during these past days of work in the fields was burnt and freckled, but the rest of her was a lovely pale ivory colour, soft and satiny. After a second's hesitation—where was Duncan? where was Jeremy? would anybody see us down here?—I took off my shirt and jeans and underpants, feeling oddly brazen.

Chrissie hadn't waited for me, she'd gone right ahead, wading through the shallow water out to a place where the receding tide had been caught among the rocks. She'd found a pool the size of a large bathtub and had immersed herself already, making little cheeping sounds at the surprising chill of it. "Ooooh! Tch! Eh, Clare lass, get yourself in! Oooch!"

I stood ankle-deep, unable to go further. The rocks, all of them, were covered over with seaweed, slippery seal-brown kelp and bladderwrack, tangled with a rubbery dark-green substance that could only feel disgusting against one's bare skin. And there were creatures in amongst those slimy fronds, I felt sure, little sharp and biting things, with nasty claws and tiny teeth. I couldn't stop myself from shuddering with loathing at the thought of my body next to these slubbery rocks and I hugged myself in apprehension.

"Eh lass, is it this?" asked Chrissie, watching me and reading me exactly. "Ach, come in, it'll not hurt you at all. Look now, it's lovely stuff."

She raised herself out of the water and sat on the edge of a great rounded rock, pulling the bladderwrack off and winding it round her body, all her gestures exuding vitality and good humour. Her iron-grey hair which had always been tight back in a knot at her neck had come undone, and hung now in spiraling strands down the sides of her face and her shoulders. With her blue eyes and sun-reddened cheeks and the seaweed around her, she was amazingly beautiful, like a mermaid, teasing away my foolish fears. "See now, Clare, what a laugh, eh? Come, come, come along in."

The water felt alive, thick with salt and rich with its memory of knocking against this island forever. I dunked myself down in it, opened my mouth and drank it, squirmed around in it, feeling my bones go cold inside my body, feeling my body slide against the strangely smooth and friendly rocks. I came up for air laughing, and draped myself as she had, feeling the sudden sea-wind on my face burn. I had been pulled into the water by Chrissie as surely as if she had taken my arms and yanked me in, or as if she had put a spell on me. I wrapped a final rope of seagrass around my shoulders.

"Hey, Chrissie, we're like mermaids, what do you think? Some sailor out there would go wild for us!" I waved my arms at that place on the skyline where one blue became another as if to signal a whole crew of sex-crazed sailors. No lover had replaced Angus in all these long months of travelling, and there were times I felt beset with my own sexuality; nights alone in bed I felt I would do almost anything to quiet my body's insistent demands. Sometimes I wished I'd never found out what was possible; it really had been easier before I knew.

Chrissie seemed to sense this, and often in the evenings would cut short her readings with Jeremy so that "the young folk can go out and have a time together." She'd wink, and push Jeremy with her hand, as if to encourage him, and he'd wince and look uncomfortable. I tried to tell her one day over the turnips we were weeding that Jeremy wasn't my type, he was too young and bookish and besides, I thought it likely he didn't care for girls. I wasn't sure of that, but somehow it didn't seem *normal* to me, this preoccupation with learning.

"Ach," she said, "even the booky ones have the same goods as the rest of us, Clare. Give the wee lad a chance."

But I was adamant, and eventually Chrissie gave up her good-natured attempts at matchmaking. Nothing changed between Jeremy and me; our verbal sparring and scrapping never let up and he did nothing to indicate he felt physical need in general or desire for me in particular. Our natures were such that we couldn't get along.

Chrissie had coiled more seaweed around her body, and she'd made a kind of turban for her head. With cupped hands she kept splashing water over her legs and her breasts. She'd begun to hum something and I joined in as she started singing the words. It was a Gaelic lament she'd sung at the close of supper the night before about death and separation and longing, so sweet that if it hadn't been translated by Jeremy I would have believed it to be about wandering through hills and forests with the faeries.

"Now you," said Chrissie. "Now you sing, lass." I sang, very self-consciously, the first song that came to me: "My

Bonnie Lies Over the Ocean." And then I sang "You Are My Sunshine," and then we sang together "Loch Lomond" and "The Road to the Isles" and finished off with a rousing version of the "Skye Boat Song." I kept time with my kelp-bedangled arms, water droplets flashing in the sunlight as I swung them to and fro. Chrissie rocked back and forth in enjoyment, her head tossed back on the high notes, all abandon and rapture. When we finished, we rinsed ourselves off in the shallows, and dried ourselves with the towels, and put on our clothes and walked back up the cliff through the pasture to the house.

"There now," said Chrissie.

Seeing her again now, elderly and frail, somehow less herself without Duncan in the room, I am wondering whether to remind her of that day, whether it's the kind of memory she wants discussed in front of my husband and children who have come with me here to see her. As if she knows my mind, Chrissie leans forward in her chair and whispers quite loudly, "D'you ever recall the day we went for a dip, Clare? D'you ever? Ach, I get such a good laugh when I think of it. Oh lassie, wasn't that a time."

And then she wants to talk of Jeremy again, and how he came summer after summer through the rest of university and afterwards too. By then Duncan had his cancer and had stopped weaving, just sat in the chair by the fire or lay on his bed, not wanting to eat or drink or talk, she said. And that's when Jeremy came and stayed, "came that May and didn't go till we buried poor Duncan the end of September. Clare, Clare, I couldn't have done't without him. None of my own could take the time, they'd come visit their old Dad but they always had to leave again, they all had their *lives.* But Jeremy stayed the whole summer through. The whole time."

I feel unaccountably annoyed at Jeremy for worrying Chrissie by disappearing the way he seems to have done. Surely over these many years he could have written, sent a postcard, phoned. . . . Typically thoughtless, I think, just like Jeremy. But then, hadn't it also been Jeremy who spent his summers here with these two old people, Jeremy whose tender devotion to Duncan had so touched Chrissie's heart? It hardly seemed like the boy I'd known, with his scarf and his books and his superior attitudes, who didn't seem to care for anybody but himself.

I feel myself wanting to dwell on his neglect of Chrissie rather than on his caring for Duncan, and I recognize a sharp stirring of what in my children I would call sibling rivalry. He's the one she loves. I was once her "dearie" but he's the one she longs for. Maybe she's right, maybe he *has* died. Maybe I hadn't known the stuff Jeremy was made of, hadn't really known him at all. Which of us was it, in the end, who had the loyal and giving heart?

On the mantel over the fireplace there are framed photos, the most recent of Chrissie's eightieth birthday with her children and grandchildren gathered around her. I look to see if I can tell which is Angus, and guess it must be the heavy-set man in his fifties standing in the back row. He works in the shipping offices in London now, Chrissie told me earlier. He has a bad back and no longer comes up to help her dig peat for the winter. But that's all right, she says, for all the others along the line have also changed over to coal and they chip in together and get a good price from the supplier.

I miss the smell of the peat fire, I miss Duncan sitting in

the chair, stooped and silent, his large hands hanging over his knees. I miss myself as I was then.

"Chrissie," I say, "is there anything we can do for you while we visit? Anything at all? Maybe some chores the children could do, just tell us." My children, all three now in their teens, are maddened with boredom, unable to conceive why their mother has brought them to this old lady's house on a flat ugly island it took hours to get to across rough water. These are city children, they have no notion of what to do here, no desire to go out and chase sheep through the heather or gather eggs from the wandering hens. The old cows are gone now, and there's no garden to speak of; the house and the yard look not so much shabby as worn out. Even my husband, who knows a little of the story of why we have come to visit old Chrissie McNay, is unusually subdued. He is perfectly polite but uneasy, perhaps a little worried about what buried parts of myself we are digging up on this family trip around Scotland.

She laughs, dismisses the offer with a shake of her head, and says, "Eh, just go show the bairns where we had our great time, Clare. Give them a laugh, now, away you go!"

All these years I have never been back—somehow, settling down in Toronto, teaching school and raising our three children, there was never time or money until now. I always sent Christmas cards, I sent condolences when she wrote that Duncan had died, I remembered her from year to year. I just never came back the way I promised I would the day I left.

Dorrie had written to me from London saying they were moving from the flat where we'd been and I had better come down and see to my things. The heather had come into bloom by then, and honeybees were humming in the air along the road. I looked back and saw Duncan's large hands waving above Chrissie's head as they stood by the gate where we said our last farewells. Chrissie's hands were hidden in the apron she was using to wipe at her tears, but she gathered herself and called out across the fields in Gaelic, telling me to hasten back soon. Jeremy had not come out, but the night before he'd given me several poems by Catullus he'd translated during the past weeks, written out in his spidery script. He told me not to read them until I had gone, and I didn't. I folded the pages into a neat little packet and kept them to look at later.

I looked back at the little stone house and the great expanse of blue ocean and sky behind it and thought about how life worked, how some things did seem destined to happen, how that small bird falling from the storm had brought everything to pass. I walked down the road and hitched a ride to the ferry, believing in predestination and believing I would return.

I saw Jeremy once in London, right before I flew back to Canada in the winter of that same year—my father was ill and I'd been called to come home. We made arrangements by mail to meet at a pub in Earls Court not far from where I was living then; he was coming down from Edinburgh to visit his uncle in Richmond and agreed to meet for a drink.

I waited for him at a small table by the door, expecting him to appear just as he did, with his long striped scarf tied carefully and casually around his neck, and his hair falling forward across his face. He was very thin and his skin was like parchment, that white, pinched look the British get in wintertime; and in spite of his scholarly airs—he was carrying a large pile of books—there was something fragile in the way he looked, something vulnerable that I'd never noticed on North Uist. But that was only his appearance, for his tongue was more caustic than ever.

"Just the sort of pub I'd expect you to pick, Clare," he said, looking around with a little laugh. "Full of rugby players. Not exactly a refined establishment, is it?"

"Oh, Jeremy, cut it out. Be pleasant. Have a Guinness and tell me how you are. And the McNays, when you left, how were they? Have you heard from Chrissie?"

"You had a thing with that son, didn't you?" he said, ignoring the question about Chrissie and Duncan. "He came up to see his folks the same day I was leaving, and I could tell from the shifty way he looked when he heard you'd been sleeping in his bed. It certainly throws a new light on your reason for being there, Clare."

"My life is none of your business, Jeremy," I said, taken aback and as defensive as I might have been with Dorrie.

"Eh, Clare lass," he said, mimicking Chrissie's musical accent exactly, "of course it's my business. I know you now, dearie. I know who you are."

"How could you know anybody but yourself, Jeremy Kerr? You kept your head in your books the entire time and never did a lick of work and never paid attention to anything. You never listened to a thing I said, all those talks we had were just for you to listen to yourself being witty and wonderful. You couldn't know another soul!"

A wild rush of self-righteous anger blazed up violently as I considered how fate had paired me with this faggotty bookish boy when what I had *needed* was Angus. Or someone very like Angus.

"Oh, I knew a lot more than you think I did," said Jeremy, in his own voice now, flicking his scarf and smiling in that way he knew made my temper flare. "And I heard the mermaids singing down by the sea. How humiliating to have such a limited repertoire that all you can come up with is 'My Bonnie Lies Over the Ocean'!"

"That's a wretched thing to say!" I cried. "Why are you being so mean when all I want to do is say a nice good-bye?" Tears were springing to my eyes even as I spoke. "That was a beautiful time I had with Chrissie, and don't you try to spoil it. You had no right to look at us, no right at all!"

"I only heard," he said. "Your voices carried on the wind. I didn't spy on you." But he had high spots of colour in his pale cheeks and his eyes glittered. Of course he had. He must have seen us, naked and wrapped round with seaweed, or why else would he have said we were mermaids? His words, perfectly aimed, pierced and stung.

"Okay, Jeremy," I said. "So you know me. So you're right, I have corny taste in music. So what do you want me to do about it, apologize? I am who I am." I stopped, astounded at both the vigour and simplicity of my defence. I suddenly sensed we were engaged in a struggle far larger and more complex than Chrissie and me singing, and it seemed to do with things I didn't understand. "Look, I'm leaving the end of the week, let's not be horrible to each other. Talk to me about Chrissie and Duncan, or tell me what you're working on these days. What have you been translating?"

"You never read the Catullus, did you," he said—a statement, not a question.

"Well you told me not to read it then," I said, caught out. I'd put his present in my knapsack and quite forgotten about it, and back in London I'd stuck the papers in with others, meaning to have a look later. But his writing was so difficult, and what point could there be in reading some old Roman? "But I still have them, the poems. I'll read them tonight before I finish packing."

"It doesn't matter now," he said. "Never mind."

We left the pub together after a pint of stout, having soon

given up the pretence of conversation. Jeremy kept sitting with his head bent over the table, pushing his glass mug back and forth in a miserable, childish way. Our splendid old quarrels about language and standards of education all dwindled into commonplaces out of context—we needed the croft, we needed the slow August night and the sound of waves slapping the rocks. We needed to be lying in the grass together, not touching and not wanting to.

I walked him to the tube stop a block or two away, and leaned over to kiss him before he went through the metal gates. It was meant as a gesture of conciliation, a way of bringing things to a satisfactory end. I hated the way his bad spirits were ruining things, obliterating what I wanted as a happy memory—the summer, the croft, Jeremy himself an interesting but essentially inconsequential component. His nasty temper had the potential to ruin it all.

"Oh, stop it," he said, as my face neared his. "I know I'm not your sort. I saw the kind of big lug you go for. You'll be sorry one day, Clare." He didn't turn again, but headed away quickly, giving his scarf one last toss as he got his books up under his arm, his head held high in contempt at my clumsy hypocrisy.

"Well, I give up, Jeremy Kerr!" I shouted at his skinny shoulders disappearing down the escalator. "Sorry for what? I'm only sorry I ever met you! And I'll never forgive you for spying, never." I turned and ran from the tube station, enraged and indignant. I had only tried to be nice, and this was the thanks I got. What a little snip he was! And how dare he say he knew me! How dare he!

As I said I would, that night I read the poems he'd copied out for me, the Latin verses followed by English. There were several, but one poem in particular surprised me—I hadn't known Catullus had written so passionately.

I hate you and I love you. Why do I do so, you wonder.
I do not know but I feel what I feel and I am in torment.

I never made any attempt to contact Jeremy again after
that night and, until this moment in Chrissie's warm and
cluttered front room by the fire, had seldom thought of him
except as an incidental aspect of the story whenever I told
about the summer I spent in the Hebrides. But now, seeing
her old face suffused with love and longing, I have to think
about him and I do not really want to think about him—he
was quite right, he was not my type. But that never made
me feel sorry. Why I feel sorry now is that I don't understand
what he wanted from me and I don't know what meaning
he attached to those poems. Did he think that because we
were such opposites we made up a whole? Did he think that?

I feel, suddenly, terribly sad. Not because he might be
dead, although of course that would be reason enough for
grief—what saddens me is that knowing people is such a
delicate affair, and people so seldom get it right.

My children aren't the least bit interested in seeing the
spot where their mother swam naked a quarter-century ago,
but they are good-natured enough to accompany me. It is a
cool, cloudy afternoon and the colours of the landscape seem
much less sharply defined than I'd remembered. We walk
slowly through the long grass on our way to the end of the
croft, where the land suddenly breaks away and falls down
to the sea which is rolling in now at full tide. Chrissie and
my husband have stayed behind by the fire, and I wonder
what she is telling him, and what questions he will ask tonight
about the weeks I spent on this remote and desolate island.
At the moment, I am feeling the salt wind sharp on my face,
and the heat of that long-ago August is only a memory.

Beneath that, I sense another surge of questions coming

up against the life I have made. Like the cold black water crashing against the rock and smashing upwards in white plumes of foam, the questions are endless. Why we enter each other's lives and how we are meant to fit together is more than is given us to know. And yet that's what we want, isn't it? That's what we want to understand.